The
FIRST
BLOOD

S. EVEREST

THE VEIL
SERIES

THE FIRST BLOOD

THE VEIL SERIES • BOOK TWO

PLAYLIST

Into the Fire
Asking Alexandria

The Summoning
Sleep Token

Like A Villain
Bad Omens

Bad Things
I Prevail

Hunting Season
Ice Nine Kills

You and I
PVRIS

All The Things She Said (Cover)
The Weight of Atlas

Blood // Water
grandson

Rush Over Me (Acoustic)
Seven Lions, HALIENE

Take Me Back to Eden
Sleep Token

Wish You Were Here
Incubus

Kneel Before Me
SLANDER, Crankdat, Asking Alexandria

This book does *not* have a Happily Ever After.

This book contains sensitive subjects, such as drug and tobacco use, mentions of suicide, adult language, religious characters and views, and graphic violence.

There are also explicit sexual scenes, some containing acts of aquaphilia (arousal from water) and hematolagnia (blood play).

This book is only intended for those 18 and older.

To E, for breathing life into my dreams.

AUTHOR'S NOTE

Growing up as a Christian, there are many things that I have learned about religion, the most important being that I will never fully know the answers to life's questions. It's a peace I've come to accept.
In this book, there are characters I've taken from folklore and religion, and in using them, I want to make one thing clear. I do not claim their existence as fact, but I also do not deny it. I am simply taking the essence of their being and mixing it with my own creativity.
The story you are about to read is fiction, even though some characters may not be fictional.
I do not claim any plot lines, locations, or scenarios as truth.

Enjoy.

THOMAS

A sweep of dust filled my lungs as I stepped into the building. I did my best to cough it up before slipping on my N95 mask, creating a seal around my nose and mouth. Here I was, back at Stoney's. It's been two years since I've been inside, the last time being a memory scared deep into my core, playing in my head over and over.

Kissing Laila.

Stabbing Laila.

Realizing she's actually Lilith.

Not in that particular order.

Getting my neck sliced open by Laila—I mean Lilith. Fuck.

I walked onto the main floor, past the bar and stage, eyeing the tables. What once was a place full of life, traditions, money, and drinks was now covered in dirt, dust, grime, and cobwebs. The place wasn't completely derailed, since the closing only happened about two years ago, but anyone could tell this building wasn't going to last much longer. I stepped over to a booth that was pressed against the wall, kicking an empty beer bottle in the process, sending it rolling. It was known that teenagers would come in here as a hideout- to drink, smoke, fuck, whatever. There was evidence of it, with spray paint along all the walls, covering the tables, and even painted on the catwalk. I swiped a finger along the booth's tabletop, my print brushing against the red symbol sprayed on, lifting a heavy layer of dust. Even the spray paint was covered in neglect.

A dark figure stepped into the doorway, blocking all sources of light coming in from outside. I turned to see Darrell slipping on his mask and looking at me.

"Some good memories here."

I chuckled. If he only knew.

As he made his way in, the daylight reappeared, illuminating the inside and allowing me to see again. The bar was empty, save a few broken drinking glasses, the chairs and stools that weren't stacked were knocked over onto their sides, and the walls were chipping paint, a dark brown color that I had never noticed since the place was always under red lighting.

And yet, I still found myself looking for traces of *her*.

Laila.

I turned and walked back to the catwalk, remembering the first time I ever saw her. My eighteenth birthday. She was dancing, on this stage, as I approached her and gave her money. It was such a harmless act, but it was the start of something that would change my life forever.

Darrell slipped down the hallway, toward the private rooms. I could hear him opening each door in search of anyone or anything. Sometimes people hide out and take shelter in abandoned buildings, especially during the winter when temperatures drop. Within a few minutes, I heard his heavy footsteps coming back, his hands brushing the dust off his palms.

"All clear," he said, his voice muffled through the mask. "Good in here?"

I did a quick scan across the room, my eyes moving from floor to ceiling in search of anything out of the ordinary. Thankfully, there was no one here. After I gave him a single nod in confirmation, he walked out the entrance, gravel rolling under his shoes as he made his way to the other side of the building.

As I took a deep breath, as deep as I could with the mask on, I began to walk back to the doors. Broken glass crunched under my boots with each step. After today, this place will no longer exist. There were talks about transforming the building into a dollar store, a veterinary clinic, or even just another restaurant, but all plans fell through, and Diesel Construction Co. was hired to demolish the building. What the plan was after that, I wasn't sure, and I didn't care. All I knew was that there would be no more Stoney's.

Right before I reached the doors, I looked to my left, down the hallway of private rooms.

And there she was.

Anna.

Standing there, watching me, her shirt to her mid-thighs and her strawberry hair blowing in a breeze that I couldn't feel.

My heart jumped. Seeing her never gets easier.

It was strange having her in here, in a place where I never brought her. I never brought it up, never mentioned coming here, never told her about my past, even though I should have.

Maybe things would be different if I had.

But her eyes, piercing through me like a sword, told me she knew. I didn't have to explain anything because she already had the whole story.

It took everything to tear my eyes from the sight of her, but once I did, I stepped through the doors and into the bright sun. I tore the mask off my face, taking a deep inhale of the fresh air around me.

"Any stragglers in there?" a voice asked. I didn't know who it was, and I didn't bother to turn and look. All I could do was close my eyes and feel the heat from the sun on my face.

I thought of Anna, standing in the hall, and shook my head. "No. No one's there."

"Go ahead, Jim," Darrell shouted, standing in front of the excavator, moving his arm in a circular motion. I stood off to the side, my hard hat tucked under my elbow, watching. The guys seemed to have everything under control, as always. I wasn't needed, and my lack of motivation to do anything wasn't helping. But I was required to be here, so here I am.

Darrell stepped to the side as the arm of the excavator raised itself high. Once it hit a certain height, Darrell gave a thumbs up, and the claw of the excavator came crashing down into the brick building.

My hand rested on my side as I watched, my eyes squinting in the brightness. I could feel the corner of my mouth curled up in a subtle smirk.

It was good to see that place crumble to pieces.

The guys started at the back, demolishing the storage rooms first. Once that was turned to rubble, they moved up to the dancers' dressing rooms. I took a deep breath, bracing myself, remembering everything that happened in that room. The blood, the kissing, the promise of everlasting torment. "The Fallout" was what Laila called it. There was no doubt that she followed through on her word since Anna was standing behind the excavator, watching me. I tried to brush off the heat of her stare, but it wasn't working. And, if we're being honest, it never worked in the two years that I've been trying.

My eyes stayed still on the building, focusing on the fall of the structure. Dust kicked up in clouds, filling the air with deep brown ashes as the sound of bricks crumbling rattled my ears. The outside wall came down first, allowing me to see the inside of the dressing room. It was the same as the night I was in there, except now, it was empty. I could picture myself standing in the middle of the room, across from Laila, both of us covered in blood.

Then, Jim knocked down the far wall, and the memory was gone.

There was a silent hope in me that demolishing this building would also clear my head of any lingering memories. It was part of the reason why I didn't put up a fight in working here today. I could've easily switched jobs with someone else, since there's always room for progress on our framework at our subdivisions. Or, I could've sucked it up and spent the day at the warehouse, finishing some office work. But there was a voice inside me, telling me I needed to see this with my own eyes.

Jim finished knocking down the dressing room walls, the bricks and wood forming a heaping pile of debris. Just then, as the rubble began to settle, I saw a flash of bright white *something* sandwiched between the bricks inside. The brightness stuck out to me since everything else in the demolition was covered in dust and dirt. No one around seemed to notice, so I kept a close eye on it as I yelled to Jim, trying to get his attention before he continued.

"Hey! Jim! Wait!" I did my best to project my voice through the cab of the excavator, yelling over the sound of the loud motor. Darrell noticed me and began waving his arms to Jim, also trying to get him to pause.

"What the hell, TD?" Darrell asked from the other side of the excavator, but I ignored him, running up to the destruction. Jim stopped the claw as I climbed the mountain of bricks, my hard hat dropping to the ground, tumbling down onto the pavement. Even though I was out of my damn mind for going into the rubble without safety gear, I didn't have time for it. I needed to keep my eyes locked on this object, whatever it was, because I was afraid that if I blinked, it would disappear.

Making it up the side of the rubble, I reached up and pulled it out.

It was an envelope pressed between two bricks.

I flipped it over. It was sealed. I pressed it between my fingers, trying to get a feel for what was enclosed.

It felt like a folded paper.

And on the front of the envelope was a T.

Holy shit.

This was for me.

"TD, what are you doin', man?" Darrell yelled up to me, his hand covering his eyes from the sun. "Get outta there!"

Shaking my head, I tried to remain calm, even though my stomach felt twisted. I quickly shoved the envelope into my back pocket. "Sorry.

I thought I saw something." After easing my way back down the rubble, I walked through the parking lot, past Darrell.

"Don't pull that shit again, TD," he said through my stride, only trying to cover his own ass. He trusted me, and he knew I was able to take care of myself, but one slip in a situation like that could've ended a lot differently. I gave him a nod, then slid off to the side, away from everyone as they resumed the demolition. My palms suddenly felt sweaty as I pulled out the envelope, the weight of it becoming increasingly heavy.

I flipped it over to the back, my fingers gliding along the seam. If I opened this, there was no going back. I was about to open a door that was never fully closed but never open enough for me to walk through.

I glanced up, and there was Anna.

She was standing across the street, watching me hold the envelope.

My stare locked with hers.

I took a deep breath and slid my thumb into the fold, ripping the paper open.

The thing I'll always hold onto is this— your darkness is my light. You fill my entire soul like a lightning bolt in a cloud, like a flash from a camera. Your spirit guides me and leads me as a star unbroken. The humming I feel from you, from your highs and your lows, is like a drunken buzz. It's a warmth that keeps me ahead of the mania. Feel me, taste me, and break away from the chain. Remember me as you look to the walls that collapse, and as you run your fingertips over the fresh graffiti. I will be there, flowing through your veins, breathing through your lungs, feeding off your aura.

THOMAS

What the fuck?

What in the actual *fuck* is this?

The last time I saw Laila, she wanted me dead and gone. And now she's here, writing me love letters? With stupid fucking inspirational quotes? Was she just finding a bunch of fortune cookies, writing down all the messages inside, and hiding it for me to find?

I looked at the envelope, then to the letter, and back to the envelope. The corner of the paper was slightly worn, with the whiteness fading into a hint of brown, but it didn't look like it was sitting in a wall of an abandoned building for years. If I had to guess, it looked like it was placed here within the last six months or so, which means she didn't plant this before Stoney's shut down.

She's been here.

Whether she was here for a minute or a month, I wasn't sure. All I knew was that she wanted to send me a message, and she accomplished it.

And now that the door was open, I was stepping through it, although I wasn't sure what was waiting for me on the other side.

But after these past two years, I was desperate to go after anything. With Anna always on my heels, reminding me of the shit I've done and been through, I've felt like giving up the fight more often than not. In the beginning, I could barely sleep, I could barely eat, I could barely breathe. People at work began to notice and ask questions, and all I had to do was tell them that Anna left me and moved back to Pittsburgh. But that was the farthest from the truth, because she watched me as I told them the same lie, over and over, while trying to keep the ache in my chest to a minimum.

With a small pang of humiliation, I forced myself to get tested for any sexually transmitted diseases. It wasn't the testing itself that was embarrassing, but the fact that I had to leave any reasoning for my desire to get tested off the questionnaire when asked. I knew it was the right thing to do after, you know, fucking a dead body. I did it not only for others, but also for my own peace of mind. And by some miracle, I was in the clear, even though I felt like I deserved *something* as punishment.

I couldn't even bring myself to get my hair cut by someone else. Every two months or so, the moment I realized it was growing too long for my liking, I would grab my buzzer and shave my head, cutting it close to the scalp, until it would grow back and I'd start over again.

Something as simple as a fucking haircut set me back into my darkest misery.

After some time passed, and things didn't feel to be getting any easier, my mind only became worse.

A lot worse.

The pain was like a giant boulder on my chest that I couldn't move away from. Her stare was like a knife to the eyes, blinding me in my own hatred. It got to the point where things were so bad, and I was so *fucking* miserable that I grew numb. I couldn't find happiness, even in the smallest of things. And in that numbness, I didn't care about anything. I didn't care about work, I didn't care about myself or anyone around me, and I didn't care about being alive. There was no point. If dying meant that I could be with Anna, even if for just another *minute*, then I wouldn't hesitate.

But when I tried sticking a gun in my mouth, the second I pulled the trigger, it jammed.

Whenever I got close to driving off the road or the town bridge, my tire would go flat, or my truck battery would die.

So I would get out of my truck and try to jump off the bridge, only to have a stranger grab me before I could get there.

Laila wouldn't let me die.

As it turns out, I was being punished in more ways than one.

And now, she's reappearing to me in the form of a letter.

And that's something I can't ignore.

I folded the paper and tucked it away into my back pocket. Darrell was still supervising the demolition as I jogged over to him, picking up my hard hat along the way. As soon as I reached him, I engulfed him in a bear hug. I could feel his body go stiff, confused as to what was happening, but he hugged me back anyway.

"Everything ok, TD?" he asked, his hand clapping my shoulder as he pulled away.

"Yeah. All good." Taking a step back, I exhaled and handed him my helmet. "I quit."

With his eyes widening in shock, he narrowed his eyebrows. "What the fuck?"

There were no words I could use to explain myself right now, so instead, I let my expression do the talking. I've been stuck in this hell of a company since my dad came back on as owner. The job itself wasn't bad, and the guys I worked with were more than great. But the looming dark cloud that hung above me, day in and day out, was something I couldn't live with any longer. I was done answering my dad's commands, especially when he wasn't around half the time to even see if I followed through on them.

This was a decision that has been in the making for a while. I've always considered leaving, and the letter from Laila was the push I needed to go.

Darrell looked at me, really *looked*, before sighing. From the time Anna "left" me, to the years that followed, to now, there was a noticeable shift in me. I could feel it, and he could see it.

I needed this. I needed to go.

There was a relief written all over me, signaling that it was time. I was done.

A silence passed between us before he nodded, taking the hard hat from my hand. "Good. Get out of here."

I gave Darrell a nod, gave Jim a salute, and jogged over to my truck. There was a part of me that was weighing heavy on my shoulders, knowing that Darrell was going to be the one to pick up my dad's slack every day. I knew he could do it, he was more than capable, but I felt bad letting him take the fall without me around.

But this was something I needed to finish. There was no doubt in my head that I was making the right choice.

Once I climbed into my truck and shut the door, I pulled my phone out of my back pocket, along with the letter. I pressed on my dad's contact and held the phone to my ear, sitting through two rings before he answered.

"Yeah?"

I smirked, eyeing the envelope. "I quit."

Before he could respond, before I could hear another word come out of his mouth, I hung up the phone, blocked his number, and tossed it on the seat next to me. It fumbled over onto the passenger seat cushion, stopping right next to the door, and I looked up to see Anna standing right outside my truck.

She was already staring at me through the open window. We locked eyes, just as we always do.

My mind went back to the first time she sat in this truck, right in the seat next to me. I picked her up at her apartment and took her to one of my construction sites, one that had an incredible view of both the sky and the river. It was a night I will never forget.

We even had our first *real* kiss in this truck. She climbed over to me and kissed me without any hesitation or fear. It was something I was aching to do every time I looked at her but didn't have the courage to follow through with. Then again, she was always braver than I ever was.

Looking at the ghost of Anna, I wanted to tell her that it was happening, that I was going to find Laila to make her pay for what she's done. I wanted to tell her that everything was going to get better and that I loved her.

But I couldn't.

The words were stuck inside me, nailed to the inside of my ribcage, growing roots and wrapping around my bones. I already let her down once. I couldn't protect her. I couldn't let her down again.

As I stuck the key into the ignition, I felt a trickle of liquid run down onto my upper lip. I brought my fingers to my face and looked, only to see blood.

Fuck, when was the last time I had a bloody nose?

I quickly brought the hem of my shirt up to my nose, wiping away what I could. Thankfully, it wasn't a heavy bleed, leaving just a small streak on the fabric. I bushed it off, figuring it must have been from all the dust inside Stoney's.

I glanced up one last time at the building. More than half of it was already demolished. The guys were making their way over to the other half.

Finally releasing a heavy exhale, I turned the key in the ignition, the truck roaring to life.

"Ready?" I asked Anna through the window, without looking over at her. She wasn't going to answer me anyway.

THOMAS

The door to apartment six was painted a light grey, with both the knob and number shining silver. I turned the deadbolt and pushed open the door, kicking off my work boots without untying them. I took a deep breath as I immediately walked to the living room and sat on the couch. Normally, I would take my time, take a shower and crack open a beer, but there was too much on my mind to settle. Starting now, there was no time to relax. This was the time when I needed to figure out a plan, even though I'd spent the last two years trying to conjure up some sort of way out of this. The night I burned Anna's body, I made a promise to her and myself that I would find a way to get to Laila.

But I had no starting point.

There were no leads, no clues as to where to begin in my path. And if I did find her, I needed to know how to take her down, to kill her for good, since simply stabbing her a bunch of times didn't work then and won't work now.

I ran my hands down my face, sighing, knowing this was only the beginning.

In front of me was a coffee table, and on that coffee table was a manilla folder. The folder held a stack of papers about an inch thick.

Just because I didn't know where to start doesn't mean I wasn't preparing for it.

I opened the folder, my eyes scanning numerous research papers, historical documents, articles, book excerpts, you name it, all on the subject of demons.

How to find, how to trap, how to manipulate. How to talk to, how to entertain, how to kill.

Now, if there's one thing I know for sure, it's that nothing is clear-cut. There isn't one single surefire way to do all these things. Lore changes by culture, by time period, and by religion. There are some consistencies, although very few, and those are the things I pocket. I memorize everything, keeping facts stored away like a filing cabinet in my brain. But after combing through the internet on all things demon, all things *Lilith*, I know I have a good chance at accomplishing what I need to do.

I just need to find her first.

In addition to researching, I've been in a consistent rotation of news stations on the internet. Every day after work, after I shower and eat, I turn to my laptop and begin my cycle. I go state by state, county by county, refreshing the local news stations to find any obscure story about someone saving a life. I've even tried to search internationally, but that sent my mind into a fucking tailspin. There was so much ground to cover outside of the United States, and there was always the possibility that she may have left the country, but if I wanted to keep my head on straight, I needed to focus on the areas where I could physically go. Of course, I could fly to another country if I found something that led me there, but so far, nothing has. There have been a few stories that broke through to me, but after looking deeper into them, it turned out to be a dead end. Either Laila wasn't handing out The Gift anymore, she didn't want to be found, or the revivals were happening under the radar.

Now that I think about it, Anna's accident was never written about. There was no news story, no article. I pinched my eyebrows at the thought. Was that part of Laila's doing? Or was it a simple accident with no significant details to form into a story?

Considering the officer on the scene was her best customer at Stoney's, I think I know the answer to that.

I shook off the thought. That didn't matter anymore. I needed to focus.

There was no sign of Laila anywhere in the country up until last night.

About halfway through my news cycle search, with my eyelids growing heavier by the minute, I found a story in Ohio, only about four hours west of Kittanning. A twenty-one-year-old woman was in a bad ATV accident. Paramedics were called to the scene, with the caller claiming the woman had severely broken her neck and spine. But once they arrived, she was up and fine. According to her boyfriend, she went from having a broken neck to having absolutely no injuries. I tried to dive deeper into the story, looking up postings on social media and the comments that followed. Apparently, according to hearsay, she wasn't the slightest bit sore, nor did she have even a minor case of whiplash. No one could explain it, not her, not her boyfriend.

The story sent chills all through my body that I couldn't shake, and after reading it, there was no doubt in my mind. It was The Gift.

I printed out the story at the warehouse this morning, keeping it in my truck until I could add it to the folder. I placed the paper on top of the others.

It was the first breakthrough I've had. I couldn't get the story out of my head last night, and I was itching to leave right then and there. I wanted to get up and drive to Ohio, to find this guy and ask him what he knows. And maybe even break the news to him about what's going to happen to his girlfriend less than a year from now.

It was like a timer looming over her that just began its countdown.

Going through each station's website every single night for the past two years was draining. It took hours upon hours. It would take me well past midnight, especially if a story needed looked into. I would end up stumbling into bed with bloodshot eyes, saying a gravelly goodnight to Anna before landing face-first into my pillow.

It was like a second job to me. One that would only pay off in the outcome I desired.

Then, I would wake at dawn, the day starting whether I was ready for it or not. I would force myself out of bed to get ready for my real job.

At least I didn't have the burden of all extra tasks as owner. When my dad took back the company, he took all the responsibility, too. Well, most of it. Some things he still let slide, but of course, I was expected to be there to help him keep things afloat.

But not anymore.

Now that I have this letter, this news story from Ohio, and now that I quit, nothing is stopping me from getting what I want.

And I *always* get what I want.

I pulled the envelope out of my pocket, the "T" staring at me in two dark, bold lines, and set it on top of the papers, closing the folder over it.

Bringing my fist up to my chin, I needed to think. Now, I know Laila isn't stupid. That letter was there for a reason, and she knew I was going to find it. She has those supernatural senses that I don't. She'll be able to feel me coming, to know that I'm looking for her.

Her voice from that night echoed through my head.

I have your blood, Thomas.

I closed my eyes at the memory.

There's no doubt that she'll be able to see me from a mile away, which is why I need to be calculated. I can't go into anything blind, and I definitely can't go into anything with guns blazing. That will only send me deeper into the shit I'm already in. I need to think everything through, to be three steps ahead of everyone around me. I'm not going to let anything slip between my fingers.

Not this time.

After taking a shower and eating a quick dinner, I went through a checklist of things I might need. I packed a bag with a few changes of clothes, soap, shampoo, conditioner, my toothbrush, deodorant, whatever. After looking through the medicine cabinet, I closed the mirror to see Anna standing behind me.

Fuck, sometimes she really scares the shit out of me.

I leaned down on the sink, my hand gripping a tube of toothpaste while trying to settle my racing pulse.

"Anna, dammit."

I could feel my heartbeat pounding in the scar on my neck. I reached up, running my hand down the raised vertical line. It was a constant reminder that what Laila did was real and that I needed to fix this.

After that point, I ended up throwing a bunch of things into my duffel bag without looking. If I needed something, I'll just stop somewhere and buy it.

I cleared out my fridge, throwing out anything that could spoil. I have no idea how long I'll be gone, and I don't need the apartment smelling again. It took me long enough to get the smell of Anna's corpse out of the walls. I can't go through that again.

I turned off the lights and made my way to the front door. I did one last visual sweep of the apartment, the duffel bag strap crossed over my chest, only to find Anna standing at the balcony doors. With one hand on the doorknob, I held the box of her ashes in the other hand, my thumb brushing along the smooth, polished wood.

With me, I had two versions of Anna, and neither one was a version I could marry. Or kiss. Or have kids with.

I shut the door, locked it behind me, and made my way down the building's steps.

"Thomas?" A quiet voice squeaked behind me as I rounded the stairs on the second floor. I stopped and turned to see Rose, the woman who lived directly underneath me in apartment four. She was older, probably in her late thirties, and was a single mom to a nine-year-old who hardly ever made a peep. Those were the kind of neighbors I liked. She poked her head out of the doorway, her body still inside. I raised my eyebrows, waiting for her to continue.

"Sorry if I'm holding you up." Her eyes flickered down to my duffel bag. "The faucet in the bathroom is leaking."

I exhaled and rubbed the stubble along my jaw. I really didn't have time for this. I wanted to leave.

"I tried texting you a bit ago, but…" her voice trailed off as she watched me hover in the stairwell. I haven't checked my phone in hours, since I called and blocked my dad.

With a nod, I dropped my duffel bag in the doorway and made my way inside her apartment. A leaky faucet is such an easy fix and should only take me a few minutes as long as there wasn't a larger problem at hand.

I made the decision to rent out the apartments shortly after Anna's second death. I had a good number of inquiries, and within a few months, apartments one through five were occupied. At first, I was hesitant, but everything is going surprisingly well. The tenants are all respectful, and there are no complaints from anyone. Of course, there are some hiccups here and there, with things such as a leaky faucet, but there's nothing I can't handle.

It made me realize that I should've done this sooner.

And I think a big piece of me knew, deep down, that I was always going to quit my job at some point. And with that feeling, I needed to have a safety net, another source of income, so that I would never have to worry about money at any point in my life. I still have the leftover profit from selling my childhood home tucked away into savings, in addition to all the rent money that is deposited into my account every month. Having a steady flow of revenue is never a bad thing.

All the faucet needed was a little tightening and it was fixed. I made my way back out, said goodbye to Rose, and headed down to my truck. I could tell she wanted to ask what I was doing and where I was heading, but thankfully she didn't. All she did was stare at my bag and wave me off, closing her door behind me.

I made a mental note to text Darrell the next time a tenant needed me, with an offer that doubles, even triples his normal pay with my dad. I used to do payroll, so I know how much he makes, and I know how much it would take to convince him to help out. All the fixes around here are so easy, I'm sure he wouldn't have a problem with it.

But who knows, maybe I won't be gone for long.

Maybe I'll find Laila tomorrow and end things for good.

I hopped in my truck, placing the box of Anna's ashes on the passenger seat. I unzipped the duffel bag, pulled out the manilla folder, then placed the bag on the floor.

I opened the folder, eyeing the top news story from Ohio.

Here we go. This is it. I'm finally following a trail that I wasn't even sure led anywhere.

But it was a start.

And every trail that leads somewhere has to have a beginning.

THOMAS

After mindlessly driving across an empty stretch of highway for four hours, with Anna standing on the side of the road at every single mile marker, I made it to the town I was looking for.

Kenton, Ohio.

It was a small town, reminding me a lot of Kittanning. There was one main road slicing through the middle, small shops on both sides of the street, and a mixture of nice and rundown houses on the outskirts. I searched for a hotel on my phone, and thankfully there was one only a few blocks away. My eyes were growing heavy, and my grip was starting to loosen on the steering wheel. As much as I want to find this guy and talk to him about his girlfriend right now, I want a bed and a pillow even more.

And I didn't want to raise any suspicions.

I needed to be calm. Calculated.

I arrived at the hotel, paid for a room, and didn't make it two minutes before saying goodnight to Anna, collapsing on the bed, and falling asleep.

The next morning, after showering and gathering all my stuff, I grabbed a plain bagel from the complimentary breakfast bar and made my way to the front desk. There was a woman working, with sleek, dark brown hair and pale skin, wearing a black blazer that reminded me of Laila.

I pushed *that* thought away. I can't think of her every time I see a woman wearing a fucking suit jacket.

"Hi. Checking out." I handed her my room key just as her eyes darted down to the scar on my neck. I brushed it off, grabbing the strap of my bag that was hanging over my shoulder, my other hand still gripping the bagel.

She began typing something into her keyboard as my mind drifted elsewhere. I honestly had no idea what today would be like. I wasn't sure if I would be able to find the person I was looking for, or *anything* I was looking for, really. And if nothing came up today, I would have no problem coming back here for another night and continuing the search tomorrow.

It's a marathon, not a race.

Although every bone in my body wanted it to be a race, to find Laila *now* and do things to her that she would never recover from. Visions flashed in my head of me, cutting a slit across her lower back and reaching my hand inside, yanking her spinal cord out. I gripped it like a chain in tug-of-war, cracking and breaking all her ribs in the process. I could hear her pretty little voice screaming out of fear, out of pain, out of submission to me.

"You're all set." The woman beamed a smile at me from across the counter, her voice snapping me out of my fantasies.

I smiled back, enjoying the fact that she had no idea what I was just thinking about, then inhaled sharply. "Do you know if there are any strip clubs nearby?"

Even though I had searched online for strip clubs within the vicinity, rendering no results, I figured it was a fluke and thought I'd ask.

The woman glanced at me sideways, her smile faltering only half an inch. Suddenly, I was aware of how this looked. I was in a hotel, asking for a strip club at 8:30 in the morning. Great.

"There are no Gentleman's Clubs nearby, but there are two bars down the road."

Her wording gave me another punch to the gut. Gentleman's Club. If I didn't already feel like a piece of shit, I definitely do now.

"They are both on your left as you head south. The first one is about a half-mile from here. It's called 'Walkers In.' The other is another half-mile after that one, and it's called 'Indigos.' I don't believe they are open right now, but I can check their hours for you if you'd like."

I could hear a tiny hint of judgment in her voice, but I ignored it. Her answer was not what I was hoping for, but nevertheless, it was a place to start. "It's alright. Thank you." I nodded and walked to the entry doors, feeling her stare as I left.

Once in my truck, I opened the local news website on my phone, taking bites of my bagel. When the initial article about the man saving his girlfriend was published, it didn't release any names. Today, I was hoping there would be an update.

And there was.

John Mitchell, twenty-three years old, saved his girlfriend, twenty-one-year-old Lacey Sinclair, in an afternoon ATV accident a few days ago. Of course, those weren't the exact words written in the article, but I knew enough to read between the lines. If it turned out to be nothing, then I'd keep on looking.

But I know it's not nothing.

My seventh sense is telling me it's something.

And that's a feeling I don't ignore.

I started up the truck and drove out of the parking lot, down the road. Within a matter of minutes, I found the giant sign for Walkers In. It was a brown circle with the words in neon lights, which were unlit, and a darker brown cowboy boot kicking the 'W' to the side. The hours were plastered on a sign right out front.

NOON TO 2 AM.

Well, I had time to kill. I drove down to the other bar, Indigos. The sign was a bluish purple, with the "gos" of the name falling into a liquid drip. The building was also painted the same color, with flecks of silver along the siding. I squinted at the sign.

This… looked like a strip club.

If I were driving by and didn't know any better, I definitely would've assumed it was.

I looked for the hours and found them on the door.

And inside the glass door was Anna, right behind the sign that held the hours, staring at me. I squeezed my eyes shut as hard as I could. She shouldn't be here. She shouldn't be getting dragged around from place to place with me, looking for answers. Answers for questions that I shouldn't have to be fucking asking.

I looked away from her and to the sign.

2 PM to 2 AM.

Well, looks like I had even more time to kill. Fuck.

This is going to test my patience more than I was expecting.

Calm. Calculated.

I decided to drive around, getting a small feel for the town, making sure I could place where things were if anyone mentioned it. I didn't mind looking like an outsider, or someone new in town, but I also didn't want to get caught off guard for *anything*. Always one step ahead. I drove by the hospital, where I'm sure Lacey Sinclair was taken for evaluation, and the cemetery, where Lacey will be buried if I don't get this fucking thing moving. I passed the grocery store, the movie theater, the library, everything.

After that, I pulled into the parking lot of Walkers In and waited. I still had another hour before opening, so I pulled out my phone and began my rotation of news websites, still searching for any headlines that could lead me in a certain direction. Site after site, there was nothing.

That must've killed enough time because once my eyes started burning, I looked up to see a man unlocking the front door. He stepped in, the glass door falling closed behind him, and then I saw the inside lights turn on. He switched his sign to "Open," even though there were still ten more minutes before noon. I turned back to my phone, continued my news cycle search, and waited until a few people strolled inside before me. It was ten after twelve before I jumped out of my truck, the scent of grease and fried food going right to the pit of my stomach, forcing a deep rumble.

I was starving.

Once inside, I sat at a table close to the bar, in case anyone wanted to sit and drink and *talk*. I wanted to be able to hear everything, no matter how irrelevant their topics may be. There were only two other people in the place, sitting one table over, and their conversation carried easily over to me.

It was a shame that I didn't care to hear more about their bulldog's pancreatitis.

As I tuned them out, a waitress approached me. "Hi, sweetie. What can I getcha to drink?" she asked, passing me a menu.

"Just a Coke, please."

She nodded and walked away.

Inside the building wasn't anything special. There were tables and chairs, only a handful of booths, and a long bar that stretched across the far wall. It was small, way smaller than Stoney's. The walls held some local memorabilia, and the bar had a good amount of alcohol on its shelves, but other than that, the place was plain and simple. Tan walls, brown floors, warm, hanging lights. Boring, if I'm being honest. But as I've come to find out, the most insignificant places usually had the best food.

I was wrong.

About halfway through my subpar burger and fries, I watched as the guy from earlier, the one who unlocked the doors, stepped behind the bar and began organizing the glass bottles. He was big, with meat on top of muscle, his stomach was round, and his brown beard hung down to his chest.

"You own this place?" I asked, chewing on a fry.

He briefly looked over his shoulder at me, then continued on with the bottles. "Yeah."

I breathed a sigh of relief. Being the owner meant that he was here all the time and most likely knew everyone in town, including John and Lacey. But as he kept his back to me, I got the sense that he wasn't much of a talker. Good thing I wasn't either, so I knew exactly how to play this in my favor.

"Seems pretty empty. Is it always like this?"

I could hear his exhale over the bar top. "No."

"Oh," I said simply. "When does it pick up, usually?"

I could see his shoulders drop. I was annoying him with these questions. Good. Pulling any emotion out of him, even if it was irritation, would bring his attention to me. And his attention was what I needed if I wanted any information out of him.

"Around six," he said, taking a moment to scratch the back of his head, then turned around to get a better look at me.

I took another bite of the burger, forcing myself to chew through it with a smile.

"Where you from?" he asked, his beard jutting in my direction.

This is where my incredible ability to lie comes into play.

"Columbus," I said, wiping the grease from my mouth with a napkin. "Just passing through on my way back from a conference."

"Oh, yeah? What for?" he asked with no enthusiasm, whatsoever.

"Physical therapy. I specialize in injuries to the neck and spine, but I went to learn more about knee injuries."

"No shit," he chuckled slightly, grabbing a drinking glass and wiping it down with a clean rag. "You should hear about my buddy's nephew and his girlfriend. She just got into an accident and really fucked up her neck."

Thank God I was in a small town. Everyone knows everyone. Just like Kittanning.

I furrowed my eyebrows. "What kind of accident?"

He shrugged, still wiping down glasses. "I dunno, man. All I know is it was bad, but they say she'll be okay."

I nodded. "That's good to hear." I took a sip of my Coke before continuing. "You know, that's how I got started in physical therapy.

Busted my neck up pretty good in a dirt bike accident." I pointed to the scar on my neck, and he looked. "Ever since then, I've wanted to help people heal their neck injuries, since I know how shitty it can feel."

The rag on the glass stopped moving. It was exactly the pause I was waiting for. I could see the wheels spinning in his head, the idea popping into place as if I didn't plant it there myself. I took another drink of my Coke, eyeing him over the rim of the glass, waiting for him to step exactly where I wanted him.

"You know, I'm sure she's probably already got someone set up, but maybe I could see if my friend's nephew could stop over real quick and meet you? Maybe get some advice from ya? Your food would be on the house." He pressed his palms on the bar top. "I owe my buddy a solid anyway."

"Oh, absolutely," I said, pushing the plate away. "Not a problem at all. I could show him some stretches that would really help."

The guy straightened, a small smirk forming under the shadows of his mustache and beard, then walked around the bar to me. "I'm Jet." He stuck his hand out, and I shook it.

"Thomas," I said in return. I watched as he pulled a cell phone out of his pocket and stepped aside to make a phone call. He moved far enough away that I couldn't hear what he was saying, but at this point, it didn't matter. If John wanted to come, he would. If he didn't, well, then it was out of my hands.

Thankfully, that wasn't the issue.

John walked into the bar about twenty minutes later, with brown, shaggy hair and his jeans ripped at both knees. "Hey, Jet." He nodded to Jet, who was still organizing the back of the bar.

Jet stepped out and clapped John on the shoulder, his voice booming. "Hey, Johnny."

I introduced myself with a shake of John's hand. Even though he tried his best to appear lively, his face looked tired, and there was an ounce of hesitancy in his eyes that I knew all too well. Too bad. Once I was done with him, the look will only get worse.

"Sorry to hear about your girlfriend," I said sincerely. I meant it. No one should have to go through this shit like I did. Like I still am. Even now, I was reminded of it as Anna stood in the corner of the room, watching me over John's shoulder.

"Thanks," he said, and with the new crease between his eyebrows, I could tell he was beginning to wonder why he came.

"Why don't you tell me exactly what happened so I could get a good idea of her injuries? I also have some pamphlets out in my truck for you to keep."

John nodded as we both walked out of the bar. I waved and said thank you to Jet, who resumed his work.

"So, this happened three days ago, on Tuesday. We were on our four-wheelers out at my friend's house, and she turned a little too hard, and it flipped her." I could see him swallow hard, as if he was reimagining it all. "The thing crushed her, but it was more in the way she landed..." he trailed off, his emotions becoming uneasy as he moved his hand to the back of his head. At this point, we were at my truck, both of us leaning against the hood. The sun was blazing and the heat was scorching, all without a single cloud in sight.

"How did she land?" I asked, squinting one eye from the sun.

John winced. "Her shoulder slid right out of place. That was the first thing she landed on. Then, the four-wheeler kind of twisted her legs up to her head."

I could hear the quiver in his voice. This was all so fresh, it was understandable that he was still shaken. I know I was after seeing what happened to Anna.

My mind reeled back to her spine bending over the hood of the car and then her face smacking on the pavement below. I swallowed the memory down like a dry pill.

"I thought I saw—heard her neck break." He leaned in slightly, his voice dropping low. "Is that normal for a neck injury?"

His eyes were searching mine for an easy answer, but I had nothing to give. "No."

He immediately straightened, trying to cover his brief panic. "Well, after I got the thing off her, I did CPR until the ambulance came."

His statement made alarm bells ring in my head, as if I had just won the jackpot at a casino.

I tilted my head to the side, pausing for a moment. "Why would you do CPR for a broken neck, John?"

He glanced to the side, unsure how to take my question. "I just thought—"

"Did she have a pulse?"

No answer.

"Was she dead?"

"I think I should—"

Before he could turn to go, I stopped him. I had enough information and unspoken clues to make my assumption. "Did your kiss bring her back to life?"

Instantly, his face went pale as his eyes widened. I swear I saw goosebumps line his arms even though we were standing in the hot sun. He quickly scanned the parking lot for a sign of anyone else listening, but there was no one around. He opened his mouth to speak but couldn't seem to find the right words to say.

"It happened to me, too," I said, shoving my hands in my front pockets, leaning back on the truck.

His voice was so low, I could barely hear him. "And?"

I sighed. This was the part that wasn't going to be easy. "And…you shouldn't have done that."

His eyebrows cinched, forming another small crease on his forehead. "What do you mean? She's my girlfriend. Of course I'm going to save her."

I could feel my jaw tense. I understand everything, every emotion he's going through, every battle he's been fighting. The only thing I don't understand is why Laila does the things she does. But my lack of understanding will never stop her, and I needed to get in front of this.

"This ability, this 'Gift' you had. Who'd you get it from?"

John's eyes looked to the ground, a flash of guilt running across his face.

"From a woman with red hair, crystal blue eyes, and legs for days?"

He blinked up at me, his eyes wide once again. That was a yes. Hopefully now he knows I'm not fucking around.

"How long have you had it?"

"Almost a year."

"Did you get it here, in Kenton?"

He shook his head, looking around once more. I could see his face start to glisten from a nervous sweat. "My buddies and I went to one of the World Series games in Kansas City. Game five. She was sitting in the row behind me, and we got to talking…" Suddenly, his face turned sad, with his eyebrows turning upward. "Please don't tell Lacey. It was a mistake. I didn't mean to—"

I cut him off. "I don't give a shit about you cheating on your girlfriend. I just need to know more about this other woman. What did she tell you her name was?"

"Eve."

Of course. Old habits die fucking hard.

Well, at least I know she's still out there, giving this shit out like candy.

I shut my eyes, inhaled deeply, and took one step toward John. I stared at him, unblinking, my eyes burning into his as I dipped my chin and gritted my teeth. "Listen to me. Really *fucking* listen to me. This isn't a joke. Do you think it's okay for your girlfriend to break her neck in half one minute, then get up, snap it back, and walk the next? This whole kiss-and-revive thing isn't what it's painted to be, John. You didn't save your girlfriend. You think you did, but all you did was prolong her death and fail Eve's test."

John looked at me like he was about to shit himself.

I could tell him who Eve really was, but what benefit would that have? It would just unnecessarily complicate things. He didn't need to know she was actually a demon, and even if I told him, I'm not sure he would believe me. And I had a feeling he cared about his girlfriend more than anything. More than Eve—Laila. As it should be.

"You need to go be with your girlfriend. Spend as much time with her as you can. I'm going to try to fix this. I promise you, John, if I succeed in what I'm trying to do, your girlfriend will be fine."

He stared at me, unmoving. "And if you don't?"

I paused. He didn't want the real answer, and I didn't want to give it to him. Not yet.

"Just…whatever you do, do *not* let Eve anywhere near her."

EMMA

The single, tinted glass door swung open, forcing a beam of sunlight through the gap. Glancing over my shoulder, I watched as a couple walked in, the man letting the woman step ahead of him in an act of chivalry. I silently sighed. What a gentleman.

"Welcome to Indigos," I said, brightening my smile as I grabbed a round serving tray. "Go ahead and find a table and I'll be right with you."

The couple nodded and walked past me, away from the door. That's when I noticed, right there in the almost deserted parking lot, an old grey truck sitting with a silhouette of a man in the driver's seat. The sun's reflection kept me from seeing his face, but I knew that hair, those shoulders, those arms. I've been *waiting* for him.

It's about fucking time.

Without saying a word to the manager, I threw the tray onto the bar top, pulled the apron off my hips, and walked out the door. Now that he was here, I was done with this place.

Apparently, he didn't hear me approach his truck, because my two slaps on the hood startled him out of his thoughts.

"Well, well, well. If it isn't the famous Thomas Diesel."

I leaned against the driver's door and propped my arm onto the open window frame. He straightened his spine and looked at me through his aviators. His light brown hair was tousled, his dark grey shirt stretched nicely across his shoulders, and even through the lenses, I could see his blue eyes dilate, a swirl of confusion spiraling through them.

I chuckled. "God, don't look so happy to see me."

His eyebrows pinched. He tried to be discreet, but I didn't miss the way his eyes scanned me from head to toe. I glanced at the vertical scar on the right side of his neck. That definitely wasn't there the last time I saw him.

With a slight tilt of his head, he spoke. "I'm sorry, where do I know you from?"

The corners of my lips turned up into a grin. I extended my hand to him, and he placed his warm palm in mine. "I don't think we've been properly introduced. I'm Emma."

At the mention of my name, my hand still in his, I could see the flashbacks go through his head.

Stoney's.

The bar.

The free drink I gave him the night he met Lilith.

The way he tried to slide into the dressing room, grabbing the door behind me.

Me, sending him playful winks both times.

I was there then, and I'm here now.

He instantly dropped my hand and searched the parking lot, avoiding my eye contact. "How do you know my name?"

There was a hint of something in his voice. It wasn't fear, since he didn't seem like the kind of person to be scared easily. Maybe it was nerves, or perhaps it was suspense in the fact that he was trying to be cautious.

"Everyone who worked at Stoney's knows Thomas Diesel," I said as a matter of fact.

He cleared his throat and swallowed, my eyes watching the movement. "What are you doing here?" he asked, his low voice falling even lower.

"Relax," I said through a soft laugh. I pushed off his truck, walked around the hood, opened the passenger door and climbed in, feeling his hardened eyes on me the whole way. With my brown cowboy boots, I shoved his duffel bag to the side, then pushed a folder along with a wooden box into the space between us. I could see his eyes squeeze shut behind his sunglasses, trying to keep something either out of his vision or out of his mind. Maybe both.

"You're looking for her, aren't you?" I asked, crossing my legs at the knee and craning my neck to get a better look at his face. He took off his aviators just so his eyes could burn into mine.

"Who?"

Raising my eyebrows, I smiled. He was playing dumb, just to test me. I could appreciate the attempt, but it missed the mark. I sat there, wallowing in the silence that was stirring between us, waiting for him to realize that I wasn't here to waste his time.

"Where is she?" he finally asked, his jaw tight and his teeth locked.

"Fuck if I know."

He rolled his eyes and turned his face away from me, back to the building ahead.

I quickly shook my head. "I'm not playing games with you. I really don't know where she is. Last time I saw her was the night you were at Stoney's."

Just the simple mention of that night had his ears perking back up.

"Did she say anything to you about what happened?"

I shook my head again. She didn't say anything to the rest of us, but I can put two and two together. I'm not stupid. She was in a good mood, then Thomas showed up, then she was in a bad mood. No, not a bad mood, a *horrific* mood. I was used to her having a stick up her ass sometimes, but that night she was on a totally different level. She was biting off heads with a single breath without any apology.

"What about you?" he asked. "How did you end up here?"

"Well, after Stoney's closed, I worked up in Cleveland for a while. Then one job led to another, and now I'm here. I've been crashing on my friend's couch for a few weeks until I can find something more permanent."

He nodded, a pause settling between us, then inhaled. "Well, I wish you the best of luck, Emma. But if you don't have any more information, I need to get going."

By moving his hand down to the key that was dangling in his ignition, he tried to signal that he wanted me out. But I wasn't ready to end things just yet.

I lowered my eyebrows, taking my turn to ask a question. "Was it the four-wheeling accident that led you here?"

As soon as the words left my lips, he froze, his body still, his breathing stopped.

"You're looking for Lilith. Something had to have brought you here, to Kenton." I waited, no response. "Was it that?"

He angled his shoulders to me. Clearly, he wasn't expecting this.

"What do you know about that?"

I shrugged. "Nothing really, but people are talking, and that story has her name written all over it."

Not only was he caught off guard, but he was confused, and he didn't hide it well.

"What do you me—"

"Thomas," I began, cutting him off. "Those girls, the ones who worked at Stoney's…"

He blinked, waiting for me to continue.

"…we are all the same."

Still no response. I guess that didn't register with him.

"Think about it. We are all like her."

Silence.

"Like *Lilith*."

Finally, the lightbulb turned on. His eyebrows tilted back up, his eyelids looked to be glued open, and his breathing quickened, only slightly, but it was enough for me to notice.

"Get out," he said, his voice stern and his chest hardening.

"Thomas, I—"

"I said get *the fuck* out!" he shouted, and I flinched at the volume. Thank God there was no one around, since his windows were still rolled down and his voice was deep and loud enough to carry.

"No," I said firmly. "I'm going with you."

That got a small huff out of him. "The fuck you are," he replied, then turned his key in the ignition, bringing the truck to life. He leaned over and reached across my legs, his arm grazing my thighs as he grabbed the door handle and pushed it open. "Get out."

I stared at him. His eyes flared with anger as heat was swimming through his veins. I could feel it radiating from across the truck.

I can't say I hated it.

A minute passed, his anger unrelenting. "I want to find her, too," I said softly.

"Then find her yourself."

God, he was starting to piss me off. He wouldn't even take a second to hear me out. He put up all his walls the moment he found out who I was. Who we *all* were.

He wasn't listening.

"Being with you is the best shot I have to take her down."

His ocean-blue eyes locked on mine as I raised my eyebrows.

"Let me go with you."

THOMAS

A demon. Emma was a demon. All the women who worked at Stoney's were all *fucking demons*.

It made sense now that I look back. The women there were flawless. Perfect hair, perfect skin, perfect teeth, everything. And it explains why, after living in a small town my whole life, I couldn't recognize a single one of them.

It was a good plan on Laila's part. If a customer comes in and sees someone they know or recognize, it might prevent them from coming back again. But if the customer doesn't know anyone, which is hard to accomplish in such a small town, then they will come back for more. Especially when the women look, dress, and dance the way they do.

Why didn't I see it earlier?

By the time Emma and I were done arguing, it was close to six. I hadn't planned on spending—no, *wasting*—my time with her when I could've been driving to Kansas City. Or at least looking into it more. I was angry with myself for blowing through almost a whole day while getting absolutely nothing accomplished.

I walked into the hotel lobby, the same one I checked out of earlier, to see the same employee from this morning behind the desk.

She turned to me as I approached, a subtle, puzzled look washing through her face.

"Can I get another night, please?" I asked, placing my forearms on the countertop, my duffel bag slung over my shoulder.

"Of course," she nodded, then began typing.

I watched as she studied her screen. "You're still working?" I asked, trying to make small talk. She's been here since I checked out this morning.

"Double shift," she answered without looking up at me. "One king bed?"

My hand brushed the back of my head. "Two beds, if available."

"Okay," she continued typing.

To my right, coming through the entrance doors, I heard the tap of cowboy boots walking toward me. I looked over to see Emma, with her chin held high and a smirk on her full lips. Her straight, light blonde hair fell past her shoulders, and her light blue tank top and cut-off denim shorts complimented her smooth, tan skin. I inwardly groaned. I should've known she wouldn't listen to my directions to stay in the truck.

"Did you get a room?" Emma asked as she approached my side, her voice light and sultry as she wrapped her arms around my bicep. I tried to pull away, but she kept her grip tight on me, and I wasn't in the mood to cause a scene. The desk clerk looked up to Emma, then to me, then dropped her eyes back down to the computer. Between our conversation this morning, and now seeing Emma latched onto my arm, I'm sure she had the wrong idea in her mind.

"Two queen beds. Room 412." The clerk slid two room keys across the countertop. Emma grabbed them before I could.

"Oh, we won't be needing two beds. But thank you!" She flashed a playful smile and trotted away, pulling me along with her. I followed, but only after taking my arm back in annoyance and stepping away from her. What the hell did she think she was doing?

We walked to the elevator and Emma pressed the up button, calling it to the lobby.

"I thought I told you to wait in the truck," I spoke quietly through my teeth.

I could see her shrug out of the corner of my eye right as the elevator bell chimed. The doors opened, and we both stepped through. Emma pressed the number four, and the doors closed as we turned to face them. And of course, there was Anna, in the elevator with her back to the doors, facing us.

"I'm just having fun with you, Diesel."

Immediately, without a second thought, I thrust Emma against the wall of the elevator, pinning her with one of my arms across her chest. My other hand grabbed her jaw, pushing her head up, forcing her to look at me.

"I will say this one time. One *fucking* time, and I won't explain it. You will *never* call me 'Diesel' again. Got it?"

Her breathing increased as she cast a slow blink through her heavy eyelids. By the way she was staring at me, I could tell she knew it was a threat, and that I wasn't taking any of it lightly.

I could feel Anna's eyes searing into my back.

"Yes," Emma finally choked out, and I let her go. I stepped back to my side of the elevator, making brief eye contact with Anna before the doors opened to the fourth floor.

No one calls me Diesel. No one but Anna.

I slid out past Anna's ghost and began making my way down the hall. Emma's footsteps were slow, but I could hear her trailing behind me. If she was upset with me, good. If her pride was wounded, fucking good. I don't need her, and the sooner she leaves, the better.

Once I approached Room 412, I slid the key card in and pushed the door open. Emma quickly entered behind me, and I threw my bag onto the first bed, only a few feet from where Anna was standing. Emma plopped down on the other bed after grabbing a standing folder from the nightstand.

"I'm starving. Wanna get room service?" She flipped through the small booklet. At least she wasn't the type of girl to dwell on arguments, thank God.

I sighed and rubbed a spot under my eyebrow.

"What are you doing, Emma?" I asked, stretching my arms open. "What is your goal here?"

"I mean, I was thinking pizza, but…"

I walked to the small space between the beds and sat down on the edge of the mattress across from her. "Emma…"

She exhaled and laid on her side, propping herself up on an elbow. "I want to find her."

"Why?"

"Because, Thomas, I don't know how much you know about demons and Hell, but there's a hierarchy down there. And guess who's Lucifer's right-hand woman? Lilith. She holds all the power, right next to Lucifer himself. It's an extremely important position for numerous reasons. And right below her, is me. I've been dealing with her pretentious shit for *centuries*, Thomas, and I'm sick of it. She belittles me and treats me like absolute garbage, in Hell *and* here on Earth. So, that's why I'm going with you."

Letting her words run through my head, I tried to think back to all the research I've done. Never did I come across any hierarchy, or order of sorts. There was no talk of power rankings besides Lucifer being the king of Hell, and that was obvious to anyone. Everything Emma said was news to me.

But then I shook my head. Back in my truck, I never agreed to let her travel with me. We argued about it, and in the end, I gave in and told her she could come with me while I did more research at the hotel. To be honest, I was hoping she might be able to give me some insight that I wouldn't be able to find on my own. And already, she has proven to, but I never said yes to taking a road trip with her. I'll be damned if I let a demon become my sidekick.

"You want to kill her?" I asked.

"Yes."

"Then why haven't you already?"

She let out a giggle, her hair cascading down her arm as she tilted her head. "You think demons can kill demons?" She leaned forward and licked her lips. My eyes couldn't stop from flicking down to her mouth. "We love that shit. Torture, blood, violence. If we could kill each other, that's all we'd be doing. It would be an endless blood bath. No one would be able to stop any of us."

I locked eyes with her.

"Humans can kill humans. Demons can kill humans. But humans are the only ones that can kill demons."

I get it now. She needs me. She wants Laila gone, but she can't do it herself.

"And in all my life, out of everything I've ever seen, you, Thomas, are the only one to make Lilith vulnerable."

THOMAS

I sat on the edge of the bed, my laptop on my legs, browser tabs opened to all Kansas City news stations. I filtered through every story from the past year, even going back farther to when John was there, and the World Series was held. I clicked on every headline and read through every article, unable to find a single lead. My eyes were beginning to burn, and I could feel the redness fill the whites of my eyes.

"You know, I never really took her as a city girl," Emma spoke over my shoulder as she took a bite of her pizza. Earlier, I filled her in on what John told me, and she agreed it was a good place to start. But of course, there was hesitancy on her end since she thought she knew Laila better than I did. She might be right, but something deep in me told me to keep looking. So, I did.

"Fuck it. I'm just going to drive there tomorrow."

Emma paused. "You sure that's a good idea?" she asked, setting down her paper plate with an uneaten pizza crust. I shook my head. Of course, she didn't like the crust.

"You got anything better?" I asked, looking over my shoulder. She rolled her eyes and stepped away. Exactly. That's what I thought.

"First thing tomorrow?" she asked, slipping off her cowboy boots and tossing them to the side, then made her way to the door of the bathroom. Before I could answer, before I could rekindle our endless fight about her coming with me, she grabbed the hem of her tank top and pulled it over her head, revealing a white lace bra. I rubbed my eyes, pinching the bridge of my nose in the process.

"Emma, what are you doing?"

She slid off her shorts, adding to the heap of clothes on the floor, revealing matching underwear. I looked back up, and my eyes drifted down her body, from her chest to her tight stomach, to her toned, bronzed thighs.

No. Fuck, no.

I looked at Anna, who was on the other side of the room, standing in the corner.

"What, a girl can't take a shower?"

Right as I looked back at her, she turned away from me. She reached up behind her back, unclasped her bra, and let it fall to the floor, not a tan line in sight. "I'll be quick," she said without looking back to me, then shut the door.

I exhaled. No. I can't do this. I can't have someone distracting me from what I need to do. I have one goal, and it's to find Laila. I can't be preoccupied with this.

I heard the shower water turn on, and my cock instantly hardened. *No.*

Trying to keep my mind off the demon in the shower, I moved to the top of the bed, resting my back against the headboard.

"Hey, why don't you check the obituaries?" Emma shouted through the door, sounds of heavy water slapping the ground.

It wasn't a bad idea. It was a long shot, but it was worth trying. There might be something I missed in the news that I could find in the obituaries, or there might be someone who already ran through their extra year of life. I pulled up the website with Kansas City deaths and began to search. I skimmed through them pretty quickly, weeding out the ones I knew weren't from Laila.

But then I clicked on a name, a young male, and skimmed over the obituary.

Brock Porter

March 16, 2000- April 12, 2024

Brock Porter, age 24, was called to his heavenly home on April 12, 2024, in Lawson, Missouri, following his one-year remission from cancer. He lived a life full of joy, happiness, and peace. He was always smiling while surrounded by his loved ones, his family, his friends, and his dog, Skipper.

He was a loving son to his parents, Lincoln and Jeanie, his stepmother, Christine, and a caring brother to his stepsister, Soren.

In lieu of flowers, donations may be made to the local children's hospital.

One year. He was in remission for one year, and then he died. Coincidence? Maybe, but things were beginning to add up. Lawson, Missouri was right outside of Kansas City, where Laila was known to be. Brock Porter died one year after being cancer free. It was too suspicious for me to ignore.

I didn't even glance up when I heard the bathroom door click open, hot steam flooding the room.

"Find anything?"

"I think so," I muttered, my eyes glued to the laptop screen. I wanted this to be something. I *needed* this to be a lead.

Emma stepped out and padded to the other bed, a white towel wrapped around her body. I glanced up, watching her wet hair drip between her shoulder blades and down her bare back.

No.

My gaze found Anna once again, who was still in her corner, watching me.

"Let's go," I said confidently while shutting my laptop, unable to take my eyes off my ghost.

My chest tightened as I could feel Emma turn to look at me, confused. "I'm glad you're finally letting me tag along, but don't you think you should sleep first?"

"No."

"Come on, Thomas, you need to sleep. We can head out early. Driving now won't get you very far."

"No," I said again, this time sharper.

Then, as I went to stand up from the bed, I felt a hand press on my chest.

"Stop."

I looked up to see Emma, still wrapped in a towel, pushing me back down on the bed. Her eyes burned a shade of red, her irises glowing in color. She was serious.

"You're no good to me if you're tired. And if you're tired, you're weak."

Her hand remained firm on my chest, and I may have been imagining it, but I swore the heat of her palm was intensifying.

I eyed her, my mouth growing dry at her gaze. She may act sweet and charming, but there was no doubt she was a demon.

"If I'm so good for you, then what's in it for me?" I asked as her fingers moved up my shirt and fisted the collar.

She cocked her head to the side and her eyes slowly tamed, turning from red back to blue. Her breathing was slow as she lifted one leg and pressed her knee into the mattress beside me, then did the same with her other leg, straddling me. Her towel gently hiked up her thighs, and her wet hair dangled in the space between us.

"I'll give you whatever you want," she whispered, and my dick pulsed at her voice, deceiving me. I didn't want this, I didn't want to betray Anna, and I didn't want the distraction. A surge of anger rolled through me.

But, fuck, I had needs, too. And they were needs that Anna could no longer fulfill.

And that pissed me off even more.

Before I could think too hard about it, I grabbed Emma's hips and pushed her off me, forcing her legs back onto the floor. "Emma," I grunted, "that's not what we're here for."

Although the pressure in my jeans said otherwise.

She gripped the top of her towel and took a step back. "Fine," she paused, staring at me. I could see her mind at work, like she was trying to devise a plan to keep me on board. The hotel room was deafeningly quiet, and my ears began to ring from the silence.

"I'll give you immunity." She spoke with a forced confidence, like she was unsure of herself.

I arched my eyebrow. "Immunity?"

"From Hell," she added with a nod. "You're going to do a lot of shit, Thomas, on top of the shit you've already done. Your front-row seat in Hell's theater is already reserved for the rest of eternity."

I inhaled, my jaw and chest firm.

"If—when—I take Lilith's place, I'll make sure you never step foot down there. Ever."

There was a stifling inability to tear my eyes away from hers. I was trying to read her, to figure out if she was bluffing or not. Her face was soft, her shoulders were back, and her hand still gripped the top of the towel. She was exposed, she was hesitant, but she was being honest. She wanted this, and she needed me.

My vision caught a drop of water falling down her collarbone, sliding along the skin of her chest.

Everything was telling me to *not* put my trust in a demon. To tell her to fuck off and find her own ride. But she was right. For some reason, I made Laila vulnerable.

"You have my word, Thomas," she added, clearing the air, and my eyes moved back to hers.

Fuck it.

I nodded. "Deal."

Tilting her chin up, she smirked. "Good." With an exhale, she glanced around the room. "Now, do you have a shirt I can wear? I don't have any clothes with me."

I narrowed my eyes.

"Unless you want me to stay naked."

I stood up and moved to the end of the bed, unzipping my bag and fishing out a grey t-shirt. I tossed it to her, then she thanked me and made her way back to the bathroom. Right before she was about to shut herself in, I stopped her.

"Emma?"

Her eyes questioned mine as her hand rested on the door handle.

"Do you guys…sleep?" I asked. With all the research I've done, the thought had never occurred to me.

Emma shrugged. "Not like humans, no. But we do need some sort of refueling or healing so we don't become weak. We need rest, not sleep."

I nodded, watching her close the door. After stripping down to my boxer briefs, I pulled back the sheets and climbed into bed. Emma walked out, looking annoyingly good in my shirt, then climbed into the other bed.

"Goodnight, Thomas," she whispered as she reached up and turned off her lamp.

This was too fucking weird for me. I forced out a "'night," then rolled over and turned my back to her, facing the wall. And against that wall stood Anna.

A deep ache formed in my chest, one that I haven't been able to shake for two years.

I could picture her walking toward me, lifting her side of the covers and slipping under them, sliding close to me. Our skin warm on one another, our legs wrapped in each other like twisted ivy. Her head on my shoulder, my nose in her hair, inhaling my favorite scent in the world. If I thought hard enough, if I forced my memory into overdrive, I could smell her in the room with me. Right now. The scent of jasmine wafting around me as if she had just showered and washed her hair. I shut my eyes, succumbing to the torture of my memories.

God, what I would do to have her climb into this fucking bed with me right now.

THOMAS

"Rise and shine, sleepyhead."

Emma ripped open the curtains, allowing a barely orange sunrise to pour into the room. I peeked one eye open, my vision adjusting to the light, and lifted my head to face the clock. It was barely five-thirty AM, and my body felt like it *maybe* got thirty minutes of sleep. Between Anna staring at me and a resting demon to my back, I couldn't get my brain to turn off.

I lifted the sheets away from my body, sat up and rested my elbows on my knees, rubbing my eyes. I could feel Emma's gaze on me as she walked past our beds and headed for the door. Her steps were brisk and full of life, which means she's probably been up for a while.

"I'll grab us something from the breakfast bar. You better be ready by the time I get back."

I looked at her over my shoulder and squinted my eyes. It took me a moment, but I finally noticed. "Your clothes. They're different."

She wore the same cowboy boots from yesterday, but today she was in white denim cut-off shorts and a loose grey v-neck shirt. Her blonde hair was a bit messier as it hung loosely over one of her shoulders.

She nodded and opened the door. "I took your truck during the night and got some of my clothes from my friend's house." Slipping out of the room, she added, "hope you don't mind," then closed the door behind her.

Guess I got more than just thirty minutes of sleep.

After brushing my teeth and getting all my things together, I was ready to go. Emma wasn't back, so I left and met her down in the lobby, where she was gathering food for us in a paper bag. The aroma of coffee surrounded me as she handed me my own paper cup, the heat instantly warming my palm.

We checked out, thankfully with a different desk clerk this time, and headed out to the truck. She had an overnight bag filled with her clothes and essentials, and once both of our bags were inside, space was tight. There wasn't room for anything else.

She began to climb into the passenger side before I stopped her, grabbing her elbow at the door.

"Listen," I began, "I don't know what you're expecting out of this, but I'm not here to fuck around. You help me, I help you. One strike, and you're gone. Got it?"

Her wide blue eyes stared up at me, the sunrise giving them a glimmer of promise. She didn't look afraid or worried, she seemed indifferent. With a simple nod, she pulled her arm out of my grasp and climbed into her side of the truck. No fighting back, no bickering, just agreement.

I got in behind the wheel and drove off toward Missouri.

The highway was a long stretch of empty land with a few bursts of corn fields in between. A couple of barns, a handful of billboards, and sporadic rest stops guided us along. Emma was nose deep in her phone, typing and scrolling away as my hand gripped the top of the steering wheel. The only noise around us was the roar of the engine and the roll of the tires on the pavement, giving me the freedom to mindlessly drive and sit inside my own head for a few hours.

I wanted Laila's games to end. For me, for John, for everybody. The things she was doing weren't fair. She was taking lives away from innocent people and playing mind games in the process, all because she could, because she was bored, and because she liked to test peoples' limits.

My limit was tested, pushed, driven to the extreme, and I failed. I broke. I couldn't protect the one person I needed to. On my balcony, I promised her I would be the only person to ever save her.

But I didn't. I lost her.

I searched for her, my eyes needing to find hers in a desperate attempt to connect. I knew she was here, somewhere.

My mind went back to Laila.

She will always be with you.

My eyes flicked to the rear-view mirror, my gaze suddenly meeting Anna's. The swirl of my blood began to heat. I needed vengeance.

Once we hit the halfway point, Emma looked up and pointed to a road sign, Rest stop, three miles.

"Can we stop here? I need to pee."

I glanced over at her and cocked a brow. "Demons pee?"

She rolled her eyes so hard I thought she was going to have a seizure. "Fuck off, Thomas."

I couldn't help but chuckle to myself as I kept an eye out for the exit. It was a legitimate question, but I kind of enjoyed the way she got annoyed with me.

I pulled onto the ramp and into the parking lot of the rest area. As soon as the truck was in park, Emma hopped out of the truck and went inside. I followed, then met her back at the truck when we were both finished.

"I have some information for you," Emma said to me, her voice light as she leaned against the bed of the truck. I walked up next to her, facing her as I raised my arms in a stretch.

"Okay," I said hesitantly. I wasn't sure if she was about to give me good or bad news.

"So, get this. I searched your lead, Brock Porter, and tried to deep dive into it. I looked up everything I could for every person who was close to him. Turns out, his stepsister, Soren, was the closest."

I narrowed my eyes, waiting for something useful.

"All her shit is set to private. I couldn't see anything without finagling my way through," she paused, expecting me to give some sort of reaction. When I didn't, she sighed. "Anyway, I did. I made my way in, and look what I found."

She turned her phone screen to me as I dropped my arms. There was a picture of three girls, their arms all wrapped around each other, laughing. All three wore really nice, short black dresses. They looked to be outside, on a sidewalk, with cars parked in a line along the curb. The picture was taken at nighttime, so it was hard to see, but it looked like they were leaving a bar. Or restaurant. Maybe a nightclub. I looked away from the screen and up to Emma.

"And?"

She smirked. "Look closer."

I looked back at the picture. A few streetlights, the three girls looking at each other instead of the camera, giant smiles plastered to their faces. Looking past them, I tried to see what Emma was pointing out. And that's when I saw, right over one girl's shoulder, the top of someone's head. It was a woman with red hair. You could barely see a sliver of her face since the flash was on and illuminating the girls in front. My pulse began to accelerate. Without a doubt, I knew.

It was her.

"Holy shit," I muttered, leaning in closer to the phone to get a better look. I could only see the side of her eye and forehead, but I knew that piece of profile anywhere. I've seen it in my dreams, I've seen it in my nightmares. I've seen it in my fantasies, and I've seen it in my plans for revenge.

Laila.

This is the first *actual* sighting I've had of her since the last time I saw her at Stoney's.

She was still out there.

"When was that taken?" I asked.

"About a year and a half ago."

Fuck. That was before John met her. She's probably long gone by now.

Emma continued. "And that's the only picture she's in. I checked them all."

"Which one is Soren?"

Emma pointed to the girl in the middle. She had dark brown hair falling to the middle of her back, golden skin, and a tight, strapless black dress that stopped at the middle of her thighs.

"May I?" I asked with my hand out, and Emma gave me her phone with a nod.

I scrolled through her pictures, studying her, trying to get a read on her. There were a lot of pictures of her with her friends, more with her family, and even more with her stepbrother, Brock. She looked happy in every single one, with a bright smile, rosy cheeks, and glistening hazel eyes. I wondered if she was exactly the kind of girl Laila would prey on.

I handed Emma back her phone and ran my hands through my hair, slightly pulling at the roots.

"We're heading in the right direction, Thomas." She leaned in, speaking through a whisper. "We're going to find her."

By the time we reached Missouri, most of the day was gone. The sun was still high but beginning to dip, the heat wasn't as harsh as it was a few hours ago, and my legs were aching to get out of the truck. Since the only thing Emma and I were running off of was gas station food, our bodies were begging for a good meal and rest.

"For the love of God, Thomas, pull off here and let's get some food."

"No," I said sternly as we passed an exit with a large selection of restaurants. "We're close."

Emma groaned, her head hitting the back of the seat as her body slid down. I was just as hungry as she was, but I was eager to get to our hotel more, and there were only thirty minutes left until we got there. I already felt like I wasted two years. I wasn't about to waste two more hours.

Emma took a deep inhale, and I could see her roll her head to face me out of the corner of my eye. I kept my vision locked on the road ahead of me.

"Can I ask you something?"

I nodded. Most of the road trip was silent on both of our ends. She wanted music, but all the radio stations I could find on my truck radio were static. I'd rather listen to the wind in my windows anyway.

"What happened?"

My eyebrows cinched. "What do you mean?"

"I mean," she began, the tips of her fingers rubbing her upper arms, almost hesitant to ask. "Why are you looking for her?"

I paused, gripping the top of the steering wheel tight. I knew it was only a matter of time before she would ask, if she didn't already know.

"What did she do to you?"

I could hear the sympathy in Emma's voice, and it pissed me off. I didn't need her sympathy. I didn't *deserve* it.

I glanced to her. "She didn't tell you?"

Emma shook her head, a piece of her blonde hair falling over her eyes.

I thought back to that night at Stoney's, and how Laila was covered in blood.

Her blood, my blood.

And then she wasn't.

"She took something from me."

It was an unfair statement, but it was all I could muster out. Yes, Laila took Anna from me, but more importantly, Laila took Anna's life completely the night she died outside of my apartment. And she did it for absolutely no fucking reason.

There was a long stretch of silence, with Emma's gaze never leaving me.

"I figured as much," she said, her voice trailing off as if she wasn't done with her sentence. "But what happened that night?"

Memories came flooding back.

Smashing her head in the mirror.

Seeing her silver car.

Stabbing her everywhere.

Kissing her, our tongues coated in blood and my hands caressing her wounded body, mere seconds away from ripping off my clothes and fucking her right then and there.

Then came my rejection, her fury, and the cut that is now a fleshy scar on my neck.

I took a deep breath, trying to figure out a way to explain it all without having to relive it any more than I just did. I still don't even know if I can trust Emma, so I did my best to keep it simple.

"I chose the person she took from me over her."

Emma raised her eyebrows. "Oh, shit."

My jaw tensed as my foot mindlessly pressed harder on the gas, eyes still on the road as Emma added, "she doesn't take rejection well."

I cocked my head in her direction, a small smirk forming on my lips. "I know."

She returned the smirk, her fingers still brushing her arm, her chest rising and falling with each breath. Inside me, there was a surge of anticipation swirling with the memory of anger, leaving me in a fog of uncertainty.

"Is that why you have…" she pointed to the vertical scar on my neck, leaving her question unfinished.

With a sigh, I answered. "Yeah." My eyes moved to the side of the road where Anna was standing, watching me drive past. "And that." I quickly pointed to her ghost, the sight of her never less heavy.

Emma's face grew puzzled as she sat up straighter. "What?"

I waited a moment before Anna reappeared, still staring as we approached. I pointed again. "Her."

Emma scanned the road, her vision shifting from left to right, unsure as to what I was referring to. "I don't…who?"

Anna's ghost stayed motionless as the truck sped past. I shifted uncomfortably in my seat, trying to keep some focus on the highway. Was she fucking with me? I was used to the guys at work not being able to see her. I understood that. But Emma was a demon, after all. Couldn't they see the dead? Couldn't she see Anna in the hotel room with us back in Ohio? Then again, she never mentioned it or said anything. She even came onto me, not fazed in the slightest as she pulled herself onto my lap while Anna stood and watched.

I scratched the back of my head. "You don't see her?"

Emma looked at me like I was crazy. And right now, I kind of felt like it. "See who?"

I pointed out the front windshield at Anna as a last-ditch effort before driving past. "Her!"

Emma looked, gave me a supportive side eye, then shook her head. "I don't see anyone, Thomas."

Well, fuck. I knew I was alone, but I didn't know I was *this* alone. Not even demons from Hell can see someone in the afterlife.

"It's my punishment," I said, my voice dipping low after a moment of quiet.

Emma nodded, her eyes dropping to her shorts, her hands playing with the frayed hem. "Yeah, that's not surprising."

I stole a glance in her direction.

"It's her thing."

"Her thing?" I asked.

"Punishment. It's Lilith's gift. Taking lives because of a wrong choice. Forcing people to suffer because they didn't make the right decision."

I internally winced at the word "gift." It hit way too close to home.

But God, all these words were ringing true. Taking Anna away because I saved her. Making me see Anna everywhere because I wouldn't give in to temptation.

It's what Laila was known for, apparently.

"Was she your girlfriend?" Emma asked gently.

I nodded, keeping my stare straight and my grip tight.

"And you see her—"

"Everywhere," I answered her before she could finish. Everywhere. All the *fucking* time.

"Well, damn," Emma said, her tone becoming more lighthearted. "No wonder why you're so moody."

ANNA

VIZWQP

EMMA

"Take the next left here," I said to Thomas, glancing down at the dot slowly moving on my phone. According to the map, we were almost to the restaurant, and my stomach was practically eating itself from how hungry I was. Despite his constant grumpy outbursts and mood swings, Thomas and I were finally beginning to get along better. I felt a shift, a small softening toward me after we talked about the ghost of his girlfriend that he constantly saw.

The ghost that I claimed I couldn't see.

But I can.

She's everywhere; he wasn't exaggerating. I didn't notice her until he and I were in the elevator together, when he made it very clear that he didn't want me to call him by his last name. Which was fine, but he didn't have to be such an asshole about it.

I told him I couldn't see her for a number of reasons. I didn't want him to focus on her. I didn't want him trying to get me to do something about her, to try to make her talk or come back or go away. Even if I was willing to help, she was Lilith's ghost, so I couldn't do anything no matter how hard I tried.

The only person who could change the circumstance was Lilith herself.

Also, I wanted to gain some emotional ties to Thomas. He let his guard down with me for a second, exposing the ghost to me and pointing her out. I took that and ran. Lying to him wasn't anything personal. I have a goal, and conveniently, he has the same goal, which means we can both use each other to our advantage. I needed him to trust me, even if it was just barely. It was Thomas opening a door to me, and I gladly stepped inside.

Having her there was a good reminder for him. It kept his motive in eyesight.

But I need him with *me*, not with his ghost.

Plus, I kind of liked having her watch as I crawled onto his lap last night.

The thought made me smile. I'm twisted as fuck.

"What are you grinning at over there?" Thomas asked, side-eyeing me as he tried to focus on the road ahead.

I shook my head innocently. "Just thinking about the burger I'm about to demolish."

Thomas let out a chuckle as he pulled into the parking lot of a restaurant called Bradford Tavern, which, according to her social media, is also where Soren works. It was a place that you could tell was extremely nice and new, but decorated in a way that made it look worn. Cracked paint on the window frames, fake rustic wood siding, and double front doors meant to look like they came from a barn. All the looks with no charm. I shrugged it off. I had nothing against it as long as it had good food.

Thomas pulled into a parking spot and shut off the engine. Before he could say *anything*, I hopped out of the truck and shut the door behind me. It was bad enough that he made us check into our hotel before coming here, but then he wanted to shower. I almost gave up and got room service. Thank God he takes fast showers.

And glancing back at him, watching him follow me inside, I can see why Lilith loses her shit over him. I almost did the same when I saw the way his skin glistened when he walked out of the bathroom in just a towel. The way his wet, brown hair dripped over his forehead, the way his vertical scar led my eyes down his neck, over his chest, and to the muscles in his stomach.

I blinked hard, forcing myself back to the scene in front of me. Thomas stepped ahead and opened the door for me, letting me inside first. My eyes raked over his body, from his dark jeans to his grey t-shirt, to his light blue eyes and his tousled hair. A wave of need pulsed down between my legs.

Maybe *I* was the one that needed to stay focused.

The lighting was dim, the large wooden tables were neatly arranged in a wide rectangle, and the bar fit snugly in the middle of the room. There was a second floor, with tables and a wooden balcony, and I could immediately tell this was a building that doubled as an event venue. It was too nice and trendy not to be.

"Do you see her?" Thomas asked, leaning in close to me and whispering.

I shook my head, inhaling him before he moved away.

We made our way to a table off to the side and sat down across from each other. The place wasn't very busy, and there didn't seem to be many people working. Maybe we came at the wrong time. But as my stomach released a deep grumble, I suddenly didn't care about technicalities, only food. While we waited for a server, Thomas eyed me, then the phone in my hand.

"Did you search for any strip clubs around here?"

Placing my elbows on the table, I leaned forward. "What makes you think you'll find what you're looking for at a strip club?"

Thomas stared at me, those piercing blue eyes sending signals to every part of my hellbent nervous system.

"Strip clubs make for easy targets," I continued. "People come in filled with lust, greed, even gluttony. The sins come in by the bucketful every single night. It's like level one, stereotypical, beginner stuff. We're past that."

I waved a hand. Thomas sat motionless.

"Take Abby, for example. She worked at Stoney's with me, and now she's a fucking *dentist* in Phoenix. She does root canals on people who don't need them." A small smirk formed at the thought. "Pain is her gift."

I paused with Thomas still staring at me, his expression blank. Holy shit, he can be a hard egg to crack.

"Now that you pushed Lilith past her limit, and she pushed you past yours, you think she's waiting around in another strip club? Recreating the same exact scenario so you can find her with your little mouse brain at the drop of a dime? Get your head out of your ass, Thomas, and think outside the box. She met John at a fucking baseball game. A family event, of all places."

I could see his throat swallow.

"So, no, I didn't look up any strip clubs, and I'm not going to. Remember, *punishment* is her gift."

I grabbed a menu that was propped up in the middle of the table and opened it. Even with my head down, my eyes on the laminated paper, I could feel his stare burning into my skin.

"What's yours?" he asked, leaning forward.

I responded without looking up. "What?"

"Your gift."

I sighed. Dammit, we were doing so well. Now, if I tell him, he will return to seeing me as untrustworthy. But then again, if I tell him the truth, maybe that will gain his trust just a little bit more.

My gaze met his, blue eyes on blue eyes, a moment of edge passing between us.

"Deception."

His bottom lip jutted out in a frown, and then he nodded, shaking it off. "Good to know."

Good to know?

Great. Fantastic.

Right now, I wish demons had the ability to read minds. But unfortunately, we can't. We can read people, read body language, read their aura, but we can't read their thoughts. I always thought it was bullshit.

He leaned back in his chair and looked around the room, either waiting for a server or avoiding eye contact with me. With his hands resting on his thighs, I couldn't help but look over my menu to sneak a peek at his arms. They were strong and tan, with corded muscles and veins running down the length of them. Fuck, the way he could take me and shove me—

"Hi! My name is Stacey…"

With a slight jump, I looked up. I didn't even see her come up to the table.

"…and I'll be your server today. Have you had a chance to look at your menu?"

"Cheeseburger and fries. No tomato. And a sprite."

I handed the menu to her, noticing a subtle scoff on her lips.

"Uh, I'll have the same," Thomas added, his eyes back to me. "*Please.*"

I rolled my eyes.

Before the waitress could leave, Thomas spoke up. "Do you know, by chance, if Soren is working?"

Stacey hesitated. "She's not currently, no, but her shift starts in…"

She checked her watch.

"…thirty minutes."

"Perfect," I said, leaning back. Just enough time to tame the beast in my stomach and get back on track. Stacey turned on her heel to leave, and Thomas narrowed his eyes on me.

"It doesn't hurt to be nice to people, you know."

I let out a quiet laugh. "Do you know who you're talking to? You want me, a demon from the depths of Hell, to say please? I make people get on their knees and beg for all eternity. They're the ones that say please. Not me."

Thomas dropped the subject. A few minutes later, Stacey brought our drinks, and about fifteen minutes after that, out came the food. We ate our dinner in complete silence.

Fuck, I felt like I was taking steps backward. Maybe I should ease up on the demonic act. I needed to get—and keep—Thomas on my side. I needed his trust. He was the one that had to take down Lilith.

I needed him.

Even if that meant throwing in a "please" every once in a while.

As I put my last bite of burger in my mouth, I saw a woman walk through the entrance. Her brown hair was pulled back into a bun, her black tank top accentuated the deep glow of her tan skin, and her jeans hugged every curve in her body. She held a small bag over her shoulder and a sweatshirt in her arms. She looked like she was ready for her shift at Bradford Tavern.

It was Soren.

I nudged Thomas' hand, forcing him to look up from his plate. He looked over to her just as she was rounding the corner, slipping into an employees-only room.

"That's her?" he asked with a french fry in his mouth.

"That's her."

After a few minutes, she stepped out wearing a new black t-shirt and a small apron around her waist.

"Soren!" I cheerfully yelled to get her attention. Her head snapped over to me, and she glanced around the room to see if any other employees knew what was going on. She didn't recognize Thomas or me, obviously, but she put on her best customer service face and came over to us anyway.

"Hi, can I help—"

"I'm Emma." I stuck out my hand, and Soren gently shook it. "This is Thomas Diesel." He smiled reluctantly and shook her hand as well. Her cheer instantly faded, her hand falling limp in her shake.

"I'm sorry," she spoke, her eyebrows furrowing. "Your name?" she said to Thomas. He stole a glance at me, then looked back to Soren.

"Thomas Diesel."

At the sound of his voice, her face went pale. She faltered, taking half a step back, bringing her arms up to her chest.

"Thomas Diesel," she repeated, more to herself than to us.

"Is everything okay?" Thomas asked, ready to stand and catch her if she were to pass out. By the increase in her breathing, it looked like she was about to.

Soren took a moment, then nodded. "Yeah, I… Let me… Stay right here."

She stumbled, walking away from our table and back into the employees-only room. Thomas and I looked at each other, a moment passing with both of us unsure as to what was going on.

"The fuck?" Thomas mouthed.

"Do you know her?" I asked in a whisper.

"No," he whispered back, sounding as surprised as I was.

The employee door shut, the sound forcing us to turn and look. Soren trotted back to our table with a white envelope in her hand. Standing before us, she took one last look at the paper before turning it to us.

"Thomas Diesel."

There it was. His name, written on the front of the envelope.

I know that handwriting.

That's a letter from Lilith.

THOMAS

In my hand was a white envelope with my name scribbled on the front. My full name, not just a "T" like last time. I gripped the paper, feeling its shape and weight in my palm.

It was another one.

Another letter from Laila.

But this one was actually hand-delivered to me.

No searching, no digging. She knew I would be here.

Holy shit.

I looked up at Soren, who looked as surprised and confused and astounded as I felt. She shrugged her shoulders, giving me her answer before I could even ask a question.

"What the fuck?" Emma asked, grabbing the envelope from my hand. "How did you get this?" she asked Soren, who was slowly regaining the color in her face.

"I… um… it's a long story."

"Well, start talking." Heat coursed through Emma's tone, causing me to narrow my eyes at her. There was no reason for the sudden anger since this was clearly a step in the right direction. If anything, she should be happy that we had another lead.

Soren looked over her shoulder, a split second of uncertainty flashing over her face, and glanced back to the employees-only room. "Listen, I can explain everything later, but right now, I can't just stand around or else my boss will be pissed."

Emma groaned, and I shot her a look, telling her to chill the fuck out.

"I get off at eleven. I can meet you guys out back by my car, okay?"

Before we could answer, she left the table and went to the computer screen behind the bar.

I turned back to Emma, who had steam coming out of her nose and ears.

"Emma," I began, my teeth clenched and my voice gritty. "You need to take it down a fucking notch, yeah?"

And I thought *I* was being impatient, but Emma was taking things to a whole new level, with her expectations at an all-time high. She must be used to getting everything she wants *when* she wants them, but that's not how things work, especially when you're trying to follow through with something that will alter the world.

And the world after it.

She sat back in her chair, tossing her blonde hair over her shoulder and crossing her arms. Her demeanor screamed entitlement, and entitlement doesn't get you very far with strangers.

"You can't take your frustration out on her. We don't know *anything* about her yet. For all we know, she could lead us straight to Laila. So, let's not ruin this before it even starts."

Emma inhaled deeply and her chest expanded, my mind forcing my eyes to stay on her face. Her only response was a slow blink, and then her attention was back on the envelope.

"Are you going to open it?" she asked, her arms still crossed.

I didn't even think twice. Opening the first letter was like opening a door that was already cracked open, a small stream of light filtering through, with no way to close it. So, why wouldn't I open this door, too? I've already come this far. My thumb slipped into the seam, tearing it open from corner to corner. I pulled the paper out and unfolded it, holding my breath.

With you, there is no plan. We run, and then we keep going. We go, and go, and go. But will there be a time when you end the war? Because, with you, I'll go. With you, I'll run. I'll give you everything. Whatever you ask of me, I'll do. I will stay with you, near or far. I'll go.

Fuck.

I read it.

I read it again.

Fuck. *Fuckfuckfuckfuck.*

"Thomas?" Emma uncrossed her arms and leaned forward. "What does it say?"

Her words began to sound muffled as my thoughts overpowered everything around me. I tried my best to remain calm, but pieces of my delirium were breaking through the cracks of my stability. I silently ran my fingertips over her handwriting, feeling the indents of the words, the letters scribbled in faint black ink.

"Thomas?"

I looked up to Emma, whose face was contorted in worry.

"I don't... I'm not sure."

Emma snatched the paper from my hands and read it herself. My eyes were glued to the back of the letter, the white paper bright in a dim surrounding.

Why was she talking to me like this? Why was she talking to me *at all?* What was her goal, besides sending me to the darkest corners of insanity? What did she want from me? Did she know what my plan was? Or where I was going, who I was with, why I was doing this?

"What in the actual fuck?" Emma whispered, her eyes still on the paper.

My brain was running one hundred miles an hour, trying to think of any explanation. Her words rang in my head like an echo, bouncing around with nowhere to go.

"I thought she hated you?" Emma asked after finally looking back up, placing the paper on the table in front of me.

"I thought she did, too."

With a soft nod, Emma tilted her head. "Maybe she's only acting this way to get under your skin."

It definitely was possible. Laila was endearing when she had a motive.

"Yeah," I looked at the letter once more, then folded it and tucked it back into the envelope. "Maybe."

I sighed, then pushed the envelope into my back pocket, the paper crinkling under my weight. Emma's eyebrows creased together, a look of confusion crossing her face.

"Thomas…" She pointed to my face, and that's when I felt a small drip under my nose. My hand brushed my upper lip, only to find blood on my fingertips.

A nosebleed.

But this time, the blood continued to flow down past my lips and onto my chin.

"Shit," I muttered under my breath. I pressed the heel of my hand against the bottom of my nose, keeping the blood inside as I got up and made my way to the bathroom. Once there, I grabbed a few paper towels and leaned over the sink, letting the blood fall in drips before cleaning myself up.

I could already see the reoccurring theme.

My first nosebleed after Laila's first letter.

The second nosebleed after Laila's second letter.

It doesn't take a genius to figure this one out.

I have your blood, Thomas.

She was punishing me.

Punishment is her gift.

But the fact that she knew the exact moment when I read her letters was something I couldn't wrap my head around. Then again, there are a lot of things I'm not understanding.

After the bleeding slowed to a stop, I washed up and stepped back out to the main area. Emma stood by the bar, her elbows leaning against the wooden top, waiting.

And up on the second floor was Anna, standing against the balcony railing. My eyes flashed quickly to her, then to Emma.

"All good?" she asked. Judging by the sleek smile on her face, she must've seen me glance up at Anna's ghost. She didn't make another comment before walking ahead of me.

I paused. "What about our food?"

"What about it? I paid for it. Let's go."

With my lips forming a small grin, I couldn't help asking. "Demons pay for things?"

Emma turned around, planted a palm on my chest, and shoved me hard. "Thomas, will you shut the fuck up?"

I laughed, stumbling backward. I couldn't resist, and I really did get a kick out of pushing her buttons.

"Only if you say 'please.'"

EMMA

Thomas and I waited for hours in the parking lot of the Bradford Tavern. We were both in the bed of his truck, with him lying diagonally inside, his head resting on the arch that covered the tire. I sat up on the side, the metal edge digging into the backs of my thighs. The sun was long gone and the temperatures were dropping, forcing Thomas to pull on a plain black hoodie, with the hood up and covering his hair. God, he looked so unnecessarily broody. I changed my shorts out for jeans and pulled on a maroon Harvard University sweatshirt. Thomas smiled, clearly getting a kick out of it.

"Harvard? Really? You went there?"

"Fuck no. I found it."

Thomas kicked his head back and laughed, and fuck me, his laugh sounded so good.

I wanted to wait inside the truck where the seats were more comfortable, but Thomas wanted to wait outside, making our presence known to Soren the second she stepped outside after her shift. I tried making small talk about his favorite food, favorite movie, and even the weather. He was *not* interested. I tried talking about deeper things, like his life before Lilith, his life before all this shit went down, but every answer was short and clipped. He didn't want to engage with me. The remark about my sweatshirt was the only crack in the brick wall that is his personality. His mental and emotional walls were still very much up around me.

So, to kill time, I decided to play a game.

"I spy with my little eye, something…"

Thomas rolled his head to my direction, clearly unamused. I looked around briefly.

"…green."

"No." Thomas looked away, with no desire to feed into my entertainment needs.

"Come on, Thomas. She still has forty minutes before her shift is over. This is boring."

His deep blue eyes flickered over to me, a hint of mischief in them. I instantly knew what he wanted, and in turn, it made me think about what *I* wanted. My thighs squeezed together as the corner of his lips curled up in a smirk.

I put on my biggest fake smile, showing all my teeth, even if they were clenched together. "Please."

That made him flash a grin, making my plea worth it.

"Green?" He made no moves to sit up, he simply exhaled and looked around the building in search of the color. "Hmm. The grass?"

"No."

"The trees?"

"Thomas. Don't be an asshole." I kicked his legs, which were crossed at the ankle.

"Fine." Now, he made more of an effort, this time lifting his head slightly to peek out of the truck. He turned and looked into the cab. "Your bag?"

It was a dark, forest-green bag, but he was wrong. "Nope."

He sighed, already tired of this. He looked at the building, his eyes scanning the siding. "That plant?" He pointed to a small potted plant inside a window, sitting on the windowsill.

I smiled. "Yep. Your turn."

Thomas rested a hand over his hood, his other hand draped over his chest, debating on giving in to me and playing the game. He looked at me, his stare locked onto mine, and at that moment, I would give anything to know what he was thinking. Part of me did not want him to be so guarded around me, but since I was a demon, I knew that if he were to *ever* let go with me, it wouldn't be for a very long time.

So, for now, I'll take the little things. Like playing a game of I Spy.

And admiring how fucking good he looks in that sweatshirt.

He tore his stare away from me, his features softening for a split second. He was enjoying this, even if he would never admit it. I was chipping away at his hatred toward me, piece by piece. Little by little. Minute by minute.

He searched for something for the game, his eyes moving high and dipping low, sweeping left and right, until his eyes landed on his ghost.

My gaze followed his, my eyes landing on her as well as she stood in the far corner of the parking lot. He didn't know that I was looking at her, too, and I wanted to keep it that way.

"Thomas? Are you okay?"

And just like that, his softness was gone. He rested his head back down and closed his eyes. "I don't want to play anymore."

"You didn't want to play to begin with." I playfully nudged him with my foot, but he ignored it. I let a quiet moment pass before speaking. "Did you see her again?"

Once again, he ignored me, his one hand still resting on his chest. I found myself studying his fingers. They were long, tan, and nimble, as if he knew how to use them. And knew how to *use them*.

I quickly shook my head and slid off the edge of the truck bed, kneeling down next to Thomas. He gave no reaction to me moving closer, which was better than a negative reaction, honestly.

I tried my best to be soft, caring, and nurturing. The opposite of everything I know.

"Thomas, I'm sorry. I didn't mean for you to see—"

"It's fine, Emma." He raised his palm, his eyes still closed, probably trying to wish away both me and his ghost.

I let him calm down for a minute before continuing.

"It has to be hard for you."

His eyes peeked open in my direction, his eyelids formed into narrow slits. He was suspicious of me, rightfully so. I took a deep breath, needing to keep up my act. I need him on my side.

"It's a wicked punishment. And all because you rejected her? Sounds like bullshit to me."

His eyes stayed glued onto me, taking a moment to drop down my body before landing on my face again. I could feel the breath catch in my throat. This wasn't nerves, no. I don't get nervous. This was anticipation. This was promise. This was the calm before the storm.

He licked his bottom lip, his teeth gently grazing on his skin. My eyes moved to his mouth.

"I tried to kill her." His voice was a dark, gravelly whisper.

My lips formed a wide smile. "And?" I whispered back, leaning closer. "So what? Do you know how many people have tried to kill her in the past? How many *demons* have tried to do the same?"

He blinked, studying my words.

"And yet, none of us have gotten a punishment in return. At least, not for that."

My statement hung in the balance between us. It was true. She may punish people for making the wrong choice, tempting fate and messing with destiny and all that shit, but she never "punished" anyone for trying to take her down, all because she knew no one could. No one really knew how, and if they did, they couldn't catch her off guard long enough to pierce through her awareness. She was always one step ahead of everyone.

That is, until Thomas Diesel came along.

That's when everything changed. She didn't get what she wanted, so for the first time in her existence, she abandoned everything and fled.

I kept the same whisper in my voice. "You don't deserve this."

Thomas' eyes never left me as he sat up, his face level with mine. He pulled his legs up, his arm hanging over his bent knee. "Maybe I do."

The ice in his eyes sent chills through my entire body. And being from the pits of Hell, that says a lot.

There's nothing better than a man who thinks he has nothing to lose, simply because he already lost everything.

I swallowed, tilting my chin up slightly, breaking the tension. "One more round?"

He gave no reaction, his stare still fixed on me.

"I spy with my little eye… something…"

My eyelids dropped, creating a sultry, hooded look I've perfected. I leaned in, only by an inch, flirting with our boundaries.

"…long…"

I moved in another inch while Thomas remained motionless.

"…hard…"

My eyes dropped to his full lips as my fingertips slowly made their way to his leg. It was subtle, and if he noticed, he didn't stop me.

"…and thick."

I watched his broad chest rising and falling with each breath, slowly increasing in pace. I was getting through to him, even if I had to use his dick to do it.

A click of the entry doors made us both turn and look, our focus torn away from each other. There was Soren, leaving the building with her messy, brown hair in a bun and wearing the grey sweatshirt she was carrying earlier.

Of course. Perfect fucking timing.

"Soren?" Thomas called out as he pulled his hood down, and her head snapped to our direction. Her polite smile wavered as she walked over to the truck. Thomas hopped out and pulled the tailgate down, allowing her better access to climb in and join us.

"You're out early," I said, trying my best not to sound so bitter.

But I was failing.

"Slow night," she stated, sitting cross-legged between myself and Thomas, the three of us forming a triangle. She pulled her bag off her shoulder and placed it down next to her. "Boss let me go home early."

Thomas leaned back against the inside of the bed, his arms resting along the edge. "Thank you for coming to talk to us."

Soren nodded. "Of course. This whole thing has my head spinning."

"Yeah, me too." Thomas gave a half smile, the empathy in his eyes matching hers.

How fucking cute.

"So, Soren," I interjected. "Tell us how you got that letter."

She sat up straighter, recalling her memory. "Well, there was a woman who came into the tavern. She sat at one of my tables and ordered a drink. Nothing else. Then, she pulled out the envelope, with your name already written on it, and handed it to me. She said you'd be in to get it," she motioned to Thomas, "but she never said when. It sat in my locker in the back room for a while. Honestly, I forgot about it until you introduced yourself."

"Let me guess," I began, squinting. "Was she tall, had red hair, probably the most beautiful woman you've ever seen?"

Soren hesitated.

"Besides me, of course."

Thomas cleared his throat, his attention never slipping away from Soren. She slowly nodded, confirming what we already knew.

"Did she tell you her name?"

Soren looked down at her hands as she fidgeted with the skin along her fingertips. "Her name was Eve."

I let out a snort. "She's sick."

Thomas grinned. At least that's one thing we can agree on.

I continued. "And she definitely knows how to hold a grudge, that's for sure."

"When did this happen?" Thomas asked.

There was a pause as Soren thought back. "About a year and a half ago," she stated, never looking up from her hands. Besides her initial greeting, she had yet to break a smile with us, not even a fake one. Thomas looked to me, and I to Thomas, both of us thinking the same thing.

"Soren," he said, rubbing the stubble along his jaw. "Is there something you're not telling us?"

She looked up to Thomas, then to me, her eyes wide with worry. "No."

The way she said it so quickly ensured she was lying.

"Are you sure?" I asked, pulling my phone out of my back pocket and unlocking it. I opened the picture of her and her friends, their arms around each other, laughing, with Lilith in the background. "Because it seems like there's more to the story here."

Soren looked at the picture, her eyes growing even wider, her body turning frantic. She cycled through looking at the phone, then to me, then to Thomas, then repeated it all again.

"I—Who are you guys?"

She grabbed her bag and began to shift backward, slowly easing her way out of the truck. I let out a small chuckle. Humans get so nervous so easily. They cry about their anxiety and their feelings, as if wallowing in their problems will help anything. One little shift in the conversation and it's over, with the girl running to the hills and not looking back. She would never survive Hell.

Then again, no one does, do they?

Down there, there's no escape.

Soren looked at me, taking my laugh as some threat, and hopped out of the truck. She pulled her bag over her shoulder, and Thomas went out after her.

"Soren, wait."

She ignored him and kept walking, making my heart flutter with a small amount of satisfaction.

"Ignore Emma. Please. She's not… It's complicated."

Soren let out a fake laugh over her shoulder. "Complicated. Right."

I watched from the truck as she walked to her car, unlocked it, and pulled open the driver's door.

"I don't know what kind of stupid games you guys are playing, finding my private pictures and leaving letters to each other and shit, but leave me out of it."

She climbed in the seat and slammed the door, wasting no time speeding out of the parking lot. Thomas was left standing where her car once was, his hands placed on his hips, his stare fixed on the pavement.

"That went well," I said. Thomas quickly made his way back to the truck, his long legs bringing him back in seconds. He slammed the tailgate closed and opened his door.

"Get in," he growled, pointing to my door, then getting in and closing his own.

I rolled my eyes, hopped out of the bed, then climbed inside. As soon as I shut my door, his hands were on my neck, pinning me back to the seat.

"I swear to *fucking* God, Emma, you will not screw this up for me."

He leaned in close to my ear, his breath hot on my skin. I gripped the door handle, not even having time to let it go. Little does he know that I absolutely love when his hands are on me like this. I smirked, silently begging him to squeeze my throat harder.

Come on, Thomas. Leave little marks. Claim me.

"You're a demon, remember? I have the ability to kill you. And if you even *look* at Soren the wrong way again, I will."

Oh, fuck. I love a good threat. I can feel my pussy tightening, growing more wet by the second.

I closed my eyes, feeling the light brush of Thomas' lips on my ear, sending shockwaves down to my toes. He lingered there for a beat too long, and I knew that if I reached my hand over to his lap, I'd be greeted with a throbbing cock.

But before I could think about it anymore, he moved his face away from me but kept his grip on my neck. My skin grew cold without him near.

"Tomorrow, I'm going to talk to her, and you're going to stay at the hotel."

I grabbed his wrist and flung his arm away. "Fuck that. I deserve answers just as much as you do."

"I can't have you intimidating her."

"It's not my fault she doesn't have a spine!"

Thomas' eyes flared, heat rolling in the space between us.

"You will stay in the truck."

I opened my mouth, but Thomas stopped me.

"You will stay in the *fucking* truck."

My mouth closed. Fine. I'll stay in the truck.

My head gently nodded in agreement.

Trust. I needed his trust.

THOMAS

The parking lot of the Bradford Tavern had only a handful of cars by the time eleven PM rolled around. One of the cars, the one a few spots to the left of me, belonged to Soren Porter. Emma and I have been waiting here since around seven, not daring to go inside after what happened last night. I feel bad about ambushing her after her shift, but there are so many things we need to talk about, and we don't need anyone else around to listen.

Not even Emma.

Her devilish attitude last night pissed me off to no end. The fact that Soren took time out of her night, willing to talk to two complete strangers, was more than I could've hoped for. We had Soren right where we wanted her, but then Emma had to make her uncomfortable, sending Soren running.

I should've hauled Emma's ass to the curb right then and there. But there was something telling me to keep her. She might prove herself to be useful, since she has once already by finding that picture of Laila.

So tonight, even though Emma is sitting here with me, she will be staying in the truck. There will be no contact between Soren and Emma, and if there is, it won't end well. For any of us.

Thankfully, the whole time we've been sitting here, Emma hasn't tried to say one word to me. Maybe I scared her last night, at least enough to take me seriously.

My truck faced away from the doors, and at exactly 11:03 PM, I could see Soren in my side mirror, walking out of the building. Her brown, straight hair was pulled back into a loose braid, and she wore the same grey sweatshirt and jeans from last night. I opened my door and stepped out quietly, trying not to scare her.

"Soren?" I asked, and she looked in my direction. She gripped the strap of her bag as she took a single step away from me. I pulled my hands up in surrender.

"Soren, it's just me. Thomas. Please, I need to talk to you."

She shook her head. "No. Whatever you and your girlfriend have going on, I don't want to be involved."

More steps were taken to her car. I followed.

"God, fuck no. Emma's not my girlfriend. She's not even my friend. And I'm not involving you in anything. I just want to know more about Eve."

"I already told you everything. She came in and gave me the letter, which I gave to you." She unlocked her car and threw her bag onto the passenger seat. "Sorry I can't be of any more help to you."

I grabbed her door before she could get in. She looked at me, her eyes fearful. The last thing I wanted to do was scare her, but sometimes that was the only thing that got someone's attention.

"Soren, it happened to me, too."

Her eyebrows furrowed. "What are you talking about?"

"Your brother, Brock."

"Ah," she raised her eyebrows. "You lost someone to cancer, too?"

Well, yes, but... "No. I lost someone to Eve."

Once again, her face was puzzled. "I'm not understanding."

"Soren," I dropped my voice low, taking a step toward her, locking her between her open door and the frame of the car. Now was my chance. I could be wrong about this whole thing, but my gut was telling me I wasn't. "I know about the kiss. The Gift."

She blinked, her breathing suddenly gaining speed. I could see the wheels turning in her mind, if she should trust me or not, if I was like Laila or not, and if she should admit to it all or not.

"Soren, you good?" A male voice piped up behind me. I didn't bother to look over my shoulder. I knew it was one of the employees leaving his shift, looking out for his co-worker.

"Yeah, Joey. All good," she called back to him, and I could hear his footsteps walking away. Her honey-colored eyes never left mine. My gaze trailed her cheekbones and moved down to her neck where I watched her swallow, her throat gliding up and then down. My one hand rested on her door, the other on the hood of the car. I looked back up to her eyes, sending a plea between us.

"Soren," I whispered. "Talk to me."

Her eyes turned glossy, the moonlight reflecting a shimmer over her irises. "You won't believe me," she whispered back, her voice cracking in pain.

"I promise you, I will."

Her eyes darted out to the trees around us, debating on telling me what I needed to know. My heart began to pick up its pace, anxious to hear her story. I needed to put these pieces together. She doesn't know it, but the future hangs in the balance of this conversation.

"I went to my friend's bachelorette party about a year and a half ago. We went bar hopping in downtown Kansas City. God, we were so wasted, but I remember it all. We went to one place, it had red and orange doors and loud music, I think. I don't know, all of the bars kind of blended together after a certain point. Eve was there, at the bar."

"Working?"

"No, she was drinking. She asked what we were celebrating, and we told her Val was getting married, so she bought us a round of shots."

Soren paused, looking down at her hands before speaking again.

"She was so nice, Thomas. She was fun and outgoing. She actually ended up joining us for a while. We loved having her with us. My friends can get pretty wild, and so can I, if I'm being honest. And you know how those kinds of parties go. Everyone is just trying to let loose and enjoy their freedom."

I remained silent, listening as she continued. She rubbed the side of her neck.

"We were going back and forth from dancing, to sitting in a corner booth, drinking. I was in the booth, and one thing led to another. Next thing I know, Eve is straddling me, dancing on me. I didn't care, it was fun. We were all having a good time. And then she kissed me. She grabbed my face and sent something into my body that I just couldn't explain. I thought it was the alcohol making crazy things happen. I saw these bizarre pictures in my head, and I couldn't escape it."

"Fuck," I muttered under my breath.

"I brushed it off because it was Val's party, you know? I didn't want to be the one to ruin it. But then we left, and Eve didn't come with us."

"That's when you guys took that picture?"

Soren nodded. "I thought that would be the last time I saw Eve, but as you know, it wasn't. She came into my work the next day. I was still so hungover, I thought it was just someone who looked like her. But then she started talking about the night before, and I knew something was off. There was something not right about it all."

She leaned against her car, pulling her arms to her chest. "She told me everything about the kiss. About the chance to save one person by kissing them. I thought it was a joke, but Eve was dead serious. It was kind of scary. Having a hangover that day was a blessing in disguise, because who knows how I would've acted with her if I didn't feel like I was about to throw up at a moment's notice."

I cracked a smile.

"Then she gave me the envelope, told me you would come to pick it up, and left. And I haven't seen her since."

I nodded. There was a pause as I expected her to continue, but she didn't.

"And?"

"And…?" She looked at me, confused.

"Your brother?"

"Right. Brock." She looked down for a moment before looking back to me. "I told you, you won't believe me."

"Try me."

If she already told me this much, she might as well tell me everything.

She took a deep breath. "Brock was my stepbrother. My mom married his dad when we were both two years old, and because we were the same age, we were basically inseparable. He was my best friend. We went to school together, played sports together, even had the same friends and would hang out together. He was diagnosed with Leukemia when he was sixteen, and it was fucking *awful*. Thankfully, he beat it and was in remission up until about two years ago, but God, his downfall was so fast. He was in the hospital, dying right before my eyes. It was so unfair."

Her voice cracked as her eyes began to well up. I remembered being with my mom in the hospital, in that same exact situation. It doesn't hurt any less now than it did then.

"And then, about two months later, it was just me and him in the room. My mom and stepdad had gone home to get some stuff since they knew things were nearing the end, and they would be spending the majority of their time at the hospital. Clothes and blankets and stuff like that. He was barely alive, barely breathing, and all I could do was keep him company. I was sitting by his bed, holding his hand when he flatlined."

One tear slipped out, rolling down her cheek. She wiped it away with her sleeve.

"The machines began beeping loudly, and I could hear the nurses scrambling right outside the door. I got to my feet, leaned up, and kissed him before anyone came in. I didn't even think twice. I know it should be weird because he's my brother, but it wasn't like that at all. I would've done anything for him. And if I could save his life, I was going to."

Fuck. I could feel my stomach twist. I know how this story ends.

"And it worked." She lifted her shoulders in a shrug, giving me a half smile. "He woke up. The doctors and nurses didn't even have to do anything. He opened his eyes before they laid a finger on him. It was weird, knowing that he died for a minute, then woke up like nothing had happened. And even after that, it was like he wasn't sick at all. He went into remission. Doctors had no fucking clue what was going on, but there he was, living, breathing, up and walking around like a whole new person. And there *I* was, so confused and so conflicted. I was so happy he was alive, but I couldn't help but feel a small pang of guilt, knowing that I had saved him with some weird voodoo magic.

"The following year, though, that was the most incredible year, Thomas. He did everything he ever wanted to do. He drove to the west coast and took lessons on how to surf. He flew to Hong Kong and Australia. He got back together with his girlfriend. It was like that small brush with death scared him into living his best life."

I nodded in understanding, thinking back to Anna. Her brush with death made *me* live my best life.

"And now, he's gone. He had another year, thanks to that kiss, and then fell back into Leukemia and passed away. But let me tell you something, Thomas. Even though I know it wasn't natural and it was some kind of sick magic spell, I'd do it all again. I'd do it all over if that meant he could live that year again. And I don't know if that's unfair, but there's not much I wouldn't do to see him smile like that."

By this time, her tears were coming down more freely, and she gave up trying to wipe them away. This was probably the first time she's told anyone about The Gift. Maybe this was the first time she was even admitting to herself that it was real and that it all actually happened.

And the fact that she hasn't seen Laila since she got the letter meant that she didn't know that Brock didn't actually die from cancer. He died because Laila killed him.

Fuck.

"I loved him so much."

It took everything in me to resist the urge to wipe away her tears. I pulled my thumb into my fist, squeezing it into my palm. I know the pain she's felt. I know every feeling she's gone through. We have a shared experience that hardly anyone else in the world has.

For Soren, she's lost someone she's had almost her entire life. Laila may have taken Brock a year after his revival, but he didn't die the first time because of her. He died from his cancer, with no one by his side except for his sister. And the fact that he had a second chance at life, thanks to both Laila *and* Soren, is something I don't think Soren will ever understand as wrong, no matter how Laila would twist it.

I don't think *anyone* would think it's wrong.

I took a deep breath. "I also had someone I loved. I saved her with that same kiss. Unfortunately, she passed away, too."

Soren pulled her sleeve over her hand, wiping the tears from her nose. "I'm sorry, Thomas."

I nodded, rubbing the spot under my eyebrow. If she only knew.

"Can I ask… what does any of this have to do with the letter? And how did you find me?"

I could tell her more. I could tell her everything. I could tell her who Eve is. Who *Laila* is. I could tell her my story, and maybe I will someday. But right now, right in the middle of her vulnerability, I don't want anything ruining that last year with her brother.

"I found your brother's obituary. The timeline matched up, since I already knew Laila was in this area, and I figured I'd come and talk to you."

She looked up at me, her expression confused. "Laila?"

I squeezed my eyes shut. "Yeah. That's Eve's real name."

She didn't say anything.

"It's a long story. I wasn't lying when I said it's complicated."

Soren dropped her shoulders and tilted her head, her focus locked on me, breathing in this moment. I knew there was no going back. She and I were connected, whether we wanted to be or not. There was an automatic, unspoken bond between us since we'd both gone through the same thing. Losing someone, getting them back, then losing them again.

At least she doesn't have a ghost that reminds her of it every day.

"Well, whatever it is you're trying to accomplish, I hope you do."

I could see her breathing at the bottom of my vision, her chest expanding and her throat restricting, and I could feel the muscle in my jaw tense. I only met her twenty-four hours ago, but I already knew that she was the kind of person that deserved to be happy. To not have to worry about changing the life and death of the people she loves. To not let the weight of Laila and her games sit on her shoulders.

She was transparent, honest, and sincere, and I found myself oddly protective of her.

Meeting Soren only confirmed that I was on the right path, doing the right thing.

"I hope I do, too."

My reply was low in the quiet parking lot around us. Her car and my truck were the only ones left. Soren stuck one foot inside, turning to get in before she faced me again.

"Would it be okay if I got your number?"

She paused. I could hear the nerves in her soft voice.

"It's nice having someone to talk to about this."

"Of course."

She pulled out her phone, and I entered my number as she got in her car. I handed it back to her, our fingers brushing against one another, and she shut her door.

"Good luck, Thomas," she said after rolling her window down.

I watched her car back out and drive away.

Once her taillights were out of my vision, my attention turned back to my truck. I forgot Emma was even here, and I'm surprised she didn't make any special appearances. Although, upon walking back to the truck, I noticed the driver's window was rolled down. She was listening to us the whole time, and the thought made me smile. Leave it to a demon to find her way through some loopholes.

"You didn't say anything about eavesdropping," Emma said from the driver's seat. She opened the door for me but didn't make any effort to move back to her side.

"You're right. I didn't. Thanks for staying in the truck."

She gave me a smirk, then looked over to the spot where Soren and I were talking. She took a deep breath. "Keep that conversation at the front of your mind. It will keep you on track."

I ignored her and planted my foot inside the truck, but Emma didn't move.

"Thomas," she began, and I looked into her gaze. Pieces of her blonde hair fell over her eyes, framing her cheekbones softly. My eyes trailed her face, then her neck, and then to the collarbones that were peeking out of her v-neck t-shirt. She shifted her legs over, spreading them, brushing against my body as she turned to face me. Grabbing the collar of my sweatshirt, she pulled me close, my waist fitting between her knees and my torso against her cutoff shorts. In a whisper, she said, "We're getting closer."

"I know," I returned, my voice dark.

"And I saw the way you looked at her."

My teeth clenched at the thought of Soren and the way the moonlight hit her skin so perfectly. There was a silver outline to her, her features so delicate, almost giving the appearance of a halo. It made her appear so innocent, so pure. She had The Gift, yes, but she wasn't screwed over by Laila like I was. She didn't know about everything evil in this world and the world after. There's no way I would ever begin to fuck that up for her.

"You guys definitely have something. But it's a shame, because I know how much of a gentleman you are, Thomas. You wouldn't dare fuck on a first date."

I blinked as Emma squinted her eyes, her words breathy.

"Would you?"

I moved to pull Emma's hands off my sweatshirt, but her grip remained strong. "Emma," I said, my voice barely coming out in a rasp.

"Oh, Thomas, I can practically smell your hunger for that physical connection. It's oozing out of you."

I could feel the rising pressure in my jeans, and I knew she was right. It's been so long since I've had anything, and I knew there was a small drop of pre-cum on the tip of my dick right now.

"Having that build-up with no release isn't healthy. I want you to know that if you ever want to let go and get off, I'm your girl. No strings attached. No feelings."

She moved her face in closer, the tip of her nose touching mine.

"Just fucking."

My fingertips grazed the length of her smooth shin, then rested on her knee.

She tilted her head to me, surprised. This was the first time I was giving into any intimate touch with her, and to be honest, I was surprised with myself. My cock pulsed in my jeans, wanting more of her.

I haven't been with anyone since the last time I was with Anna. A time that I blacked out in my memory for my own sanity.

But now, the desire that coursed through my veins was looking for a way out.

Fuck, I *craved* that release.

But for more reasons than one, I needed to focus.

"If you think I'd fuck a demon, you're wrong."

This time, I grabbed Emma's wrists forcefully and tore them off my sweatshirt as she sent me a glare. I can't think about this shit. Not now. We're moving at too good of a pace.

I climbed up into the truck, using my legs to push Emma back over to her side. She slid over, trying her best to hide a pout from her failed attempt. I turned the truck on and began to drive out of the parking lot.

"Oh, and Thomas?"

I looked over at her.

"I heard what you said to Soren about me. Don't act like we're not friends."

I let out a small chuckle, my hand tight on the steering wheel. "We're not."

THOMAS

Back at the hotel, I sat on the edge of my bed, with Laila's letter staring me in the face. I read it over a hundred times, committing it to every part of my memory. Her words didn't sit right with me, and I couldn't place why.

Emma stepped out of the bathroom in a tight, black tank top and black underwear. I glanced up from the paper as she walked past me, my eyes stealing a quick look at her tight, rounded ass.

No. Focus.

She climbed into her bed, settling herself under the blankets.

"You're still looking at that thing?" she asked, her head resting on the pillow. "It's not going to change."

I ignored her. I knew staring at the words wouldn't change anything, but I didn't want to let a single letter on the paper go unnoticed.

I grabbed the envelope I found at Stoney's and pulled out the letter. I looked at both papers side by side, hoping for more clarity. To my left, I could hear Emma sit up in bed, propping herself up on her hands.

"What is that?" she asked.

I shook my head. I didn't want to show her all my cards just yet. "Just get some rest, Emma."

"What the *fuck*, Thomas?" She tossed her pillow to the side and climbed out of her bed, making her way to mine. She pulled the first letter out of my hands and read it.

"When did you get this?"

I rubbed the back of my head, hesitancy filling my lungs. "Right before I found you."

"Fuck, Thomas. Fuck! Why didn't you tell me?"

"Why do you think, Emma?"

Her eyes flared red as a wave of deep anger overpowered every muscle in her body. She lowered the paper to her side, then moved her face in close to mine. "You cannot keep things from me. If you want to find her, you are going to tell me *everything*. I have been with her since the beginning, Thomas. I know her better than you ever will."

There was a dramatic shift in Emma. This wasn't the playful, lively demon I'd been with for the past two days. This was a different side of her, one I haven't seen before. She was commanding and dominant. She was assertive and firm. This wasn't an act. This is who she really was. This was infernal.

"Keep something from me again, and our deal is void. You *will* burn in the darkest pits of Hell, unable to escape the everlasting torture. I promise you."

My blue eyes locked onto her red ones. My posture straightened as I stood to my feet, my height towering over her. She tilted her chin up to me, not backing down.

"Well, looks like we're at a crossroads here," I began, my teeth gritted, soaking in the shot of adrenaline that was pumping through my veins. "Because, you know what, Emma? You may have a say in my afterlife, but here, on Earth, right now, I'm in control. She's writing these letters to *me*. Not you. I'm the one she's trying to contact. You need me, not the other way around. I've said it before, and I'll say it again. I can do this without you. So don't threaten me. It's not a good look for you."

Grabbing the letter out of her hands, I moved away from her and sat back down on my bed. She watched me, unmoving, processing what I just said. Judging by her suppressed surprise, she's probably never been talked to like that. At least not by a human.

But she doesn't intimidate me. She never has.

I stripped down to my boxer briefs and climbed into my bed as Emma got back in hers. I moved to turn off the bedside lamp before pausing.

"Get your rest, Emma. And don't even think about taking my truck anywhere during the night."

She shot me a glare, then rolled over so her back was to me.

I clicked off the light right as my phone buzzed. My screen lit up with a text message.

Soren: Thank you for listening to me tonight. And thank you for believing me.

Soren: If there's anything else I can help you with, let me know.

As much as I would like to see her again, to keep talking about the things we've been through, I didn't want to involve her any more than I already have. I didn't want her to become collateral damage. I typed back quickly and then placed my phone on the nightstand.

Me: Goodnight, Soren.

I woke up to a pillow slammed on my face, and the blankets ripped off my body.

"Wake up, Thomas."

What the fuck? A gentle approach to waking me would've been just fine. The cold hotel air was brisk on my skin, raising goosebumps all over. I moved to grab the blankets, but Emma ripped them completely off the bed.

"It's time to get up." She turned and flicked on the lights, my eyelids squeezing at the harsh change in brightness. "And nice morning wood."

My hands made no moves to cover myself because I really didn't care, and Emma didn't seem to be in any sort of friendly mood, even with the offer she gave me last night. The offer to fuck her with no repercussions. In theory, it sounded like a good idea.

But that's all it was. A theory.

Although I couldn't help but picture the way our warm bodies would fit together, creating the perfect friction of good and evil. The way her legs could wrap around me, her hands roaming over my chest, our lips connecting with the heated taste of each other. The feel of her breath on my skin, and the dig of her nails in my back.

My cock grew even harder at the thought. Thankfully, Emma had her back to me, her attention on her bag. I searched around the room to find Anna standing over by the door. I exhaled, feeling my dick immediately begin to deflate.

There's no better mood killer than a dead girlfriend.

I stood up, pulled on my jeans, then made my way to the bathroom. As I was brushing my teeth, I heard Emma shout through the door.

"We're going to Colorado."

Okay, what the fuck? We barely discussed plans last night after my talk with Soren in the parking lot. There were no more leads and no more clues as to where Laila could be. We tried to brainstorm our next step but didn't come up with anything, so this talk of Colorado was new to me.

"What's in Colorado?" I asked, opening the bathroom door, my toothbrush still in my mouth. Emma looked over at me, her eyes landing on my bare chest. I watched as her eyes trailed down my front, her words tangled in her tongue.

"Astrid," she managed to squeeze out. The name rang a bell, but I can't remember from where. "She and Lilith were close. She might be able to lead us somewhere."

I paused to rinse my mouth out, then walked out of the bathroom. "You can't just call her? Seems a lot easier than driving all that way."

Emma shook her head, crossing the strap of her bag over her chest. "She wouldn't answer my call even if I tried. I said she and Lilith were close. Not her and I."

I nodded, receiving the hidden meaning of her words. "She doesn't like you?"

Emma scoffed. "Not really. She thinks she should be next in line after Lilith to be the ruler of Hell."

"And that's whose decision to make?"

"Lucifer's."

I raised my eyebrows. Of all the demons we've talked about, Lucifer has never come into the picture, besides the fact that Laila rules alongside him. "Oh, right," I replied. I didn't want to push further into the subject, since that would probably open a whole new hallway of doors that I wasn't sure I wanted to go down.

I looked at the clock to see it was only four minutes past six.

"We should get going," Emma said to me.

I pulled on a shirt and gave her a nod, accepting her new plan. What could it hurt? We could gain insight from someone else who knows Laila. Maybe she knows where she's been, and maybe she knows where she is now. Plus, we had nothing else planned.

I went to gather my belongings, only to see that some things were missing. Or moved. I began looking around, knowing there were important things I had in this room, like the folder of research and Anna's ashes.

Emma made her way to the door and swung it open, holding it and waiting for me. When I didn't follow her, she piped up. "I took down some of your things to the truck already."

I stood still, my legs frozen. It might have been a harmless gesture from her, but for me, it sent my blood pressure up a few points. "Emma, don't fucking touch my stuff."

"I was just trying to save you some time." Her tone became aggressive, and she seemed upset that I wasn't fucking bowing to her for saving us thirty seconds. "God, lighten the fuck up."

Grabbing my bag, I walked past her and down the hall, bypassing the elevators and taking the stairwell. I made my way down and out into the parking lot, where I noticed someone by my truck. A man. He had the passenger door open as he leaned inside. I threw my bag down and ran to him, my legs taking me faster than I'd ever gone, and reached him in record time. I grabbed his shirt right as he was about to straighten up and slammed him into the side of the truck.

"What the *fuck* do you think you're doing?" My voice boomed, and I didn't care who heard.

"Hey man," he held his palms up, a smug ass grin plastered across his face.

I didn't give him a chance to say another word. I didn't give a single fuck. My fist went soaring into the side of his face, deeply cracking his nose. He's lucky I let him say anything at all.

His eyes watered slightly as a small drip of blood pooled at the bottom of his nostril. He blinked a few times before my fist hit the same spot again, a loud crack resounding in the air.

I had no time for this. I had no tolerance for this.

My other hand gripped his shirt at the collar, pulling so hard that I heard the seam rip. I punched him a third time, this one landing right over his jaw, causing him to groan.

"Thomas!" I could barely hear Emma shouting at me over the boiling rage in my ears. Her footsteps ran to me, and right as I reeled back for another punch, Emma stepped between us and blocked my fist.

"Thomas, you're going to hurt yourself."

The man and I were both breathing heavily. His face and my knuckles were both bloody and already beginning to bruise. The space between his nose and eye was starting to swell, the skin turning deep red in color, but he didn't seem fazed.

"Emma," he said warmly while panting, that smug grin reappearing on his face.

I dropped my hand and looked at her. "You know him?"

She paid me no mind as she turned to the man still pinned against my truck. "What the fuck are you doing here?"

"I came to see you." He smiled with blood filling the cracks of his teeth.

I tightened my grip on his shirt, thrusting him back harder. "No. Absolutely not. We don't have time for these stupid fucking games. You want to talk to her? You call her. We have hours of driving ahead of us. She can talk to you then."

I swung him off the truck and launched him onto the ground. He fell, his clothes scuffing on the pavement.

It took him a moment to regain his composure before speaking. "You're into this guy now?" he asked, looking up at Emma, spitting out a wad of blood. He had dark features, black hair, black eyebrows, and black stubble that ran down his neck. Even his eyes looked dark. He wasn't big, he wasn't intimidating by any means, but he had a look in his eye that showed a hint of insanity.

Ignoring his question, Emma walked to him and kneeled down. She held out her hand, palm up. "Give it to me."

"I don't know what you're talking about," he replied.

She wiggled her fingers, waiting. Finally, after a minute, he rolled his eyes and reached into his pocket. He placed something small in her hand, but I was too far away to see what it was. She stood up and walked past me, climbing into her side of the truck. "Let's go."

She didn't have to tell me twice. I grabbed my bag, walked around the tail of the truck, and climbed inside. I backed out, avoiding the man still on the ground, and drove off.

Other than the sounds of my tires on the road, the cab was quiet. Once we made it to the highway, I broke the silence.

"Want to tell me what that was all about?"

Emma watched out the window, her elbow propped up on the frame, her head resting in her hand. "Not really."

I nodded, my grip tightening on the steering wheel, the pain in my knuckles beginning to rear its head. A small, humorless laugh escaped me. "So, let's see if I have this straight. I have to tell you every little thing, down to every time I sneeze, but you're allowed to keep your secrets?"

She ignored me, her stare still lingering out the window.

"That fucker was inside my truck, and you knew him, but since you don't want to talk about it, it's fine, right?"

A pause.

"What did he take from us?"

Emma's eyes darted to me before she reached into her front jean pocket. I watched as she pulled out something shiny, handing it to me.

It was my mother's ring.

The ring that was hidden in the box that held Anna's ashes.

It took all of my control to not slam on the brakes right in the middle of the highway and turn around to find this piece of shit. Instead, I gripped the ring, the metal creasing in my palm, and took a deep inhale.

"Explain." My voice was harsh, my anger cutting the inside of my throat. "Now."

Emma folded at my sternness. "He's my ex."

I waited for her to continue, and when she didn't, I raised my eyebrows. "And?"

"And… he likes to show up where I'm at sometimes. I don't know why. Maybe he misses me." She smirked. There's that playful side of her back in action.

"How did he know you were here?"

She shrugged. "He and I have a connection. We can check in on each other occasionally."

My eyebrows pinched together in thought. My mind went back to the parking lot when Emma broke up the fight. She stopped me because she didn't want *me* to get hurt, not because she didn't want me to hurt him. I'm assuming that could only mean one thing.

He can't get hurt.

"Is he a demon?"

"Yes."

Great. Another one to add to the mix.

"What's his name?" I asked, eyes on the road ahead.

"Levi."

"And why would he want this ring?" I pushed the ring into my front pocket, keeping it safe until we could stop and I could put it back where it belonged. With Anna.

Emma pulled her bottom lip between her teeth, taking a moment to answer. "It's his thing."

I glanced, arching an eyebrow.

"Theft. It's his thing. His gift."

Punishment. Deception. Pain. Theft. Good to know all these demons had identifiable characteristics, as if they were stupid fucking yearbook superlatives, or as if I was trying to rub elbows and make friends with them all.

"Don't take it personally. He steals from everyone. Anything he can get his hands on, he will."

Easy for her to say. She probably has never had anything taken from her.

"Were you ever human?" I asked, letting my thoughts run out in the open.

She shook her head immediately. "No. Demons can't become humans and humans can't become demons. They can be possessed by one, but they can't *be* one."

I ignored her long ass explanation and instead focused on her one-word answer. "Then don't fucking tell me to not take something personally."

Emma rolled her eyes, her head moving to look in my direction. For the first time since I met her, she looked worn down. "Don't you ever get tired of hating me, Thomas? Isn't it draining?"

"I barely know you."

"You've been with me for the last three days, and you spent most of that time either ignoring me or yelling at me."

She wasn't wrong. Ever since we met, with her insisting she tag along with me and me insisting she didn't, we never really got off on the right foot together. She might call it unnecessary anger, but I call it self-preservation.

"Can you blame me? It's in your nature to destroy me."

"No," she corrected. "It's in my nature to use you for my own advantage. Not everything I do will have a negative effect on you. Sometimes I do things to solely pull myself ahead."

I closed my mouth and let her words hang between us. So, she was selfish. Not surprising, since she's a demon. And at least she's honest about it, which is more than a lot of humans can say.

"Thomas," she reached over and touched my shoulder, and for some reason, I didn't have any desire to pull away. "If this is going to work, if you and I are going to take Lilith down together, we have to be on the same page. And for that to happen, you have to trust me."

Trust. Fucking *trust*. The thought of trusting a demon was beyond insane, and everything in me was screaming at myself for even considering it. But she was right. If we were going to do this, we had to be a team.

I rubbed the spot under my eyebrow, then looked over, my sight scanning her. Her blonde hair was resting on her shoulders as her loose, black tank top draped over her breasts. Her tanned legs were bare, with her denim shorts hiked up high on her smooth thighs.

My mind thought one way, while my dick thought the other.

One of them is more easily persuaded than the other.

"You're right," I muttered, barely audible, my eyes back on the road.

Emma's lips turned up into a soft smirk, her hand gently rubbing my shoulder, making my words catch in my throat.

"I can try."

ANNA

V I Z W Q P V I Z W Q P V I Z W Q P V I Z W Q P V I Z W Q P
V I Z W Q P V I Z W Q P V I Z W Q P V I Z W Q P V I Z W Q P
V I Z W Q P V I Z W Q P V I Z W Q P V I Z W Q P V I Z W Q P
V I Z W Q P V I Z W Q P V I Z W Q P V I Z W Q P V I Z W Q P
V I Z W Q P V I Z W Q P V I Z W Q P V I Z W Q P V I Z W Q P
V I Z W Q P V I Z W Q P V I Z W Q P V I Z W Q P V I Z W Q P
V I Z W Q P V I Z W Q P V I Z W Q P V I Z W Q P V I Z W Q P
V I Z W Q P V I Z W Q P V I Z W Q P V I Z W Q P V I Z W Q P
V I Z W Q P V I Z W Q P V I Z W Q P V I Z W Q P V I Z W Q P
V I Z W Q P V I Z W Q P V I Z W Q P V I Z W Q P V I Z W Q P
V I Z W Q P V I Z W Q P V I Z W Q P V I Z W Q P V I Z W Q P
V I Z W Q P V I Z W Q P V I Z W Q P V I Z W Q P V I Z W Q P
V I Z W Q P V I Z W Q P V I Z W Q P V I Z W Q P V I Z W Q P
V I Z W Q P V I Z W Q P V I Z W Q P V I Z W Q P V I Z W Q P
V I Z W Q P V I Z W Q P V I Z W Q P V I Z W Q P V I Z W Q P
V I Z W Q P V I Z W Q P V I Z W Q P V I Z W Q P V I Z W Q P
V I Z W Q P V I Z W Q P V I Z W Q P V I Z W Q P V I Z W Q P
V I Z W Q P V I Z W Q P V I Z W Q P V I Z W Q P V I Z W Q P

```
V I Z W Q P V I Z W Q P V I Z W Q P V I Z W Q P V I Z W Q P
V I Z W Q P V I Z W Q P V I Z W Q P V I Z W Q P V I Z W Q P
V I Z W Q P V I Z W Q P V I Z W Q P V I Z W Q P V I Z W Q P
V I Z W Q P V I Z W Q P V I Z W Q P V I Z W Q P V I Z W Q P
V I Z W Q P V I Z W Q P V I Z W Q P V I Z W Q P V I Z W Q P
V I Z W Q P V I Z W Q P V I Z W Q P V I Z W Q P V I Z W Q P
V I Z W Q P V I Z W Q P V I Z W Q P V I Z W Q P V I Z W Q P
V I Z W Q P V I Z W Q P V I Z W Q P V I Z W Q P V I Z W Q P
V I Z W Q P V I Z W Q P V I Z W Q P V I Z W Q P V I Z W Q P
V I Z W Q P V I Z W Q P V I Z W Q P V I Z W Q P V I Z W Q P
V I Z W Q P V I Z W Q P V I Z W Q P V I Z W Q P V I Z W Q P
V I Z W Q P V I Z W Q P V I Z W Q P V I Z W Q P V I Z W Q P
V I Z W Q P V I Z W Q P V I Z W Q P V I Z W Q P V I Z W Q P
V I Z W Q P V I Z W Q P V I Z W Q P V I Z W Q P V I Z W Q P
V I Z W Q P V I Z W Q P V I Z W Q P V I Z W Q P V I Z W Q P
V I Z W Q P V I Z W Q P V I Z W Q P V I Z W Q P V I Z W Q P
V I Z W Q P V I Z W Q P V I Z W Q P V I Z W Q P V I Z W Q P
V I Z W Q P V I Z W Q P V I Z W Q P V I Z W Q P V I Z W Q P
V I Z W Q P V I Z W Q P V I Z W Q P V I Z W Q P V I Z W Q P
V I Z W Q P V I Z W Q P V I Z W Q P V I Z W Q P V I Z W Q P
V I Z W Q P V I Z W Q P V I Z W Q P V I Z W Q P V I Z W Q P
V I Z W Q P V I Z W Q P V I Z W Q P V I Z W Q P V I Z W Q P
V I Z W Q P V I Z W Q P V I Z W Q P V I Z W Q P V I Z W Q P
V I Z W Q P V I Z W Q P V I Z W Q P V I Z W Q P V I Z W Q P
V I Z W Q P V I Z W Q P V I Z W Q P V I Z W Q P V I Z W Q P
V I Z W Q P V I Z W Q P V I Z W Q P V I Z W Q P V I Z W Q P
V I Z W Q P V I Z W Q P V I Z B L O Q P V I Z W Q P V I Z W Q P
V I Z W Q P V I Z W Q P V I Z W Q P V I Z W Q P V I Z W Q P
V I Z W Q P V I Z W Q P V I Z W Q P V I Z W Q P
```

THOMAS

After ten hours of driving, four bathroom breaks, and one roadside diner with halfway decent food, we made it to Colorado. The ride was surprisingly relaxing. I didn't want music, I didn't want to talk, and thankfully Emma didn't push for conversation. I didn't even want to think. Thinking was the only thing I've been doing, nonstop, for the past four days. Well, two years, if we're being technical. I wanted to sit back, eyes and mind on the path ahead, without a single passing thought.

Thank God Colorado was a beautiful state. I found myself studying the scenery for most of the drive. The mountains, the trees, the smell of the air, it was all incredible. Even Emma commented on the view, her gaze fixed on the picture outside her window.

We made our way into the town of Buena Vista, Colorado. It was another small town east of Colorado Springs, and it was similar to Kittanning. And Kenton. And Lawson.

There seems to be a trend happening.

Maybe demons like small towns because it's easier to connect with people. It's easier to weave a web in a small group since everyone knows everybody and word spreads fast. Secrets in a small town don't stay hidden for very long.

I pulled the truck into a local gas station and placed the pump in the tank. Emma stepped out to stretch, her tank top lifting as she raised her arms, my eyes instinctively moving to the bare skin of her stomach.

"Do you know where she's at?" I asked, turning my head away to look at something, anything else.

"She works at a massage parlor."

My eyebrows shot up, reaching up my forehead. "She's a masseuse?"

Emma nodded. That was a first. I guess I was still stuck in the mindset that demons could be found in obvious places like strip clubs and bars, but in reality, they can be found everywhere.

Even during your massage or your dentist appointment.

Evil doesn't seclude itself, it doesn't hide in a dark corner, and it doesn't only prey on the damaged. It follows all of us, everywhere, all the time.

We checked into a hotel nearby, and even though this visit with Astrid shouldn't take long, I wasn't up for driving anywhere else tonight. My legs were sore, and my back needed a good stretch. After a hot shower, I pulled on my jeans and black sweatshirt, then stepped out of the bathroom. Emma was lying on her bed in only her underwear and tank top, scrolling through her phone, not even sparing a glance at me.

"You ready?" I asked, sitting on the edge of my bed while slipping on my boots.

She gave a hint of a smirk and continued looking at her phone. "I'm not going."

I froze. She's been a thorn in my side this whole time, insisting she follow me everywhere, and now she suddenly wants to stay back?

"Why?"

Dropping her phone to her side, she turned her head to look at me. "She'll sense me coming from a mile away. Actually, she probably already knows I'm here. If she sees me, especially with you, she probably won't tell you anything you want to know."

I finished tying up my boots and stood to leave. "Fine. Is there anything specific you want me to talk to her about?"

She shook her head. "You got this. I trust you."

Trust. *Right.*

Letting the door shut behind me, I left the room and walked down the hall to the elevator, breathing a sigh of relief. Maybe stepping away from Emma for a few hours will benefit us both.

After a quick fifteen-minute drive, I pulled into the parking lot of a small, rustic-styled building. It had wooden log siding, surrounded by trees with an incredible view of the mountains. If there wasn't a sign out front, I would've thought this was someone's cabin. I stepped up to the door and let myself inside, a gentle chime ringing as I walked over the threshold. Upon entering, the smell of natural oils and something herbal flooded my lungs, signaling a cough but also relaxing me. It wasn't the fresh air of the mountains, but I didn't mind it at all. There was a fireplace to the left, with wood stacked inside but unlit, along with a few lounge chairs and end tables. To the right was the front desk, and a woman stepped out from a back area and up to the counter.

"Hi, can I help you?"

I offered a polite smile. "I'm here to see Astrid."

"Do you have an appointment?"

"No, I was hoping to squeeze something in today." It was the quickest lie I could think of.

The woman frowned. "Oh, I'm sorry. We don't take walk-ins."

Just as she finished her sentence, another woman walked out into the waiting area.

"I'll take him, Justine."

Dressed in an all-white lace sundress, the woman stepped toward me. Her dark skin shimmered under the dim lighting, and her sleek, dark brown hair fell in waves over her shoulder. She had an array of silver necklaces, all different lengths, decorating her chest, along with matching bracelets stacked on her arm and rings on her fingers. When she approached, she brought a soft, Earthy scent with her. She seemed calm, relaxed, and completely unaware of who I was.

"Hi, I'm Astrid." She extended her hand, and I shook it.

Fuck, I remember her. The sight of her sent me right back to the memory. She was working at Stoney's the night of my twenty-first birthday. Laila was bartending for her while she was on her break.

"Thomas," I replied, trying my best to not show any recognition in my expression.

"Hi, Thomas. What are you interested in today?"

"Just a simple massage. I've been driving a lot lately, and my back feels tight."

Astrid grinned, her smile straight and perfect. "Simple enough. Come with me."

I followed her down a hallway and into one of the private rooms. The walls were lined with different color-stained wood, with every corner illuminated with either a candle or dim, warm light. In front of me was a single white bed centered in the middle of the room, and on a hook to my right was a white robe. Astrid motioned to it while setting up her things on a table placed along the far wall.

"Go ahead and get all the way undressed. Then, whenever you feel comfortable, you can make your way onto the bed, starting on your stomach."

I paused at her softness. She had a glow, a tenderness to her. If I hadn't remembered her from Stoney's and if Emma hadn't said anything, I never would've guessed she was a demon. Ever.

I stripped down to nothing, forgoing the robe, and climbed onto the bed face down, laying the white sheet over my lower half. After a few minutes, Astrid turned to me, holding a small cup of oil in her hands. She tilted it, slowly placing the warm oil in a line along my spine, and began rubbing.

Holy *fuck*, these hands.

Holy fucking shit.

The relief that I didn't know I needed was instantaneous. The way her palms kneaded the threads of muscles in my back had me drifting out of my own body. The way her fingers began digging into every dip and groove had me ready to fall to my knees and succumb to her. My body was warding off every urge to resist, giving into the pressure of her touch, letting her take me into the depths of mindless ecstasy. I felt my eyes close, my breathing heavy and slow, my mind blank. She made her way up to my neck, rolling the tendons with the grace of her hands.

I need to do this more often.

Not nearly enough time passed before she told me to shift onto my back. I could've laid there for hours, but I obliged, turning face up while she adjusted the sheet. My body felt like jelly, my limbs and joints so tranquil that I had to mentally force myself to switch over.

Astrid poured more oil gently over my chest. I studied her through my lowered lids, watching as her dark eyelashes brushed against her smooth cheeks every time she blinked. Pieces of her dark hair fell across her vision, her hand momentarily reaching up to tuck the hair behind the ears that were decorated with piercings from top to bottom.

Her hands roamed all over my skin, the oil heated and slick between us. The scent was intoxicating, releasing endorphins inside me that haven't been touched in years. I could feel my cock rising, my body unable to control my desires. I gently cleared my throat and closed my eyes, trying to keep my shit together.

Astrid, not oblivious to what was happening, felt my muscles stiffen, causing her to pause her motions and lean down to my ear. "Don't worry, Thomas. It's your body's natural response." Her breathy whisper was doing absolutely nothing to help the situation. I shut my eyes again, concentrating on my muscles rather than my dick.

Her hands moved up to my shoulders, easing into the curve in my neck. Her left hand brushed against the vertical scar, her fingertips running down the flesh, sending goosebumps down every inch of my body. Her sensual touch lingered over the healed wound, and suddenly the massage felt personal. I blinked my eyes open to see her stare locked onto my scar, studying its depth.

Suddenly, Emma's words came rushing back to me.

Everyone who worked at Stoney's knows Thomas Diesel.

Her mesmerized touch verified it. She remembered me.

"Astrid," I croaked out, my senses still running wild.

She tilted her head in my direction but didn't look or speak to me.

"Do you know where she is?"

Her fingers continued to trace the line, not caught off guard by my question in the slightest. She knew exactly who I was referring to. She shook her head, her eyes raising to find mine.

"I don't."

I exhaled, feeling a small wave of defeat wash over me. Another dead end.

"But," she continued, her stimulating caress moving down my oiled chest. Her head carried up next to mine, her lips close to my ear as her hands slid down my tense stomach. "If I were her, I would've sent that blade all the way through your throat."

Her words rolled off me as I remained still on the bed, her hands slipping under the sheet, grabbing my cock at the base. My hands and arms did nothing to stop her. Her teeth softly grazed against the skin behind my ear, releasing another jolt of pleasure throughout my body. Her grip tightened, slowly stroking the length, knowing exactly what to do to make a growl settle in my throat.

"I don't blame her, though. We all do crazy things for the ones we love."

Her hand squeezed at the head of my dick, my blood rushing to accommodate the need for release.

I looked for Anna, but this time, it wasn't for an escape route. My eyes shot to all corners of the room until landing on her at my side, directly behind Astrid. We locked on each other, my eyebrows lifting in sorrow, and in that moment, I silently prayed to whatever God Anna believed in. I needed her to not actually *be* her. I prayed that she was just an illusion, that she was oblivious to anything happening here on Earth, and that her ghost was only a tool used for my torture. I didn't want her to see me like this, to see what I was about to do, or to see the person I've become without her.

I needed the ghost to be a piece of Laila and not the remnants of Anna.

My stare left her and moved back to Astrid, waiting only a mere second before closing the distance and crashing my lips onto hers. I raised my hand, gripping it in her hair, grabbing a handful as our lips connected in heat. It was the first time I had kissed anyone since Laila, and in the moment, I craved more of the sensation. Her lips parted, allowing me in, our tongues rolling deep in each other's mouths. Her lips were soft and full, tasting like the deepest part of the ocean's water- dark, cold, and secretive.

She ripped the sheet off me, sending it to the floor before separating from my lips and moving lower. I rested my head back down and closed my eyes, not daring to make eye contact with the ghost next to me.

Astrid moved to the foot of the bed, her eyes flaring with hunger, and climbed up on her knees onto the edge. With her hands on either side of my body, her dress hiked up high and her body settled between my legs, she leaned down and took the head of my cock in her mouth, her tongue swirling endlessly.

Fuck, her tongue felt just as good as her hands.

I reached down, my one hand cupping her face gently as her red eyes pierced mine. My other hand gripped her hair, controlling her depth, as I forced my entire length down her throat in one quick thrust. I could feel the ridges on the roof of her mouth rub against the head of my dick, creating a cascading ripple in my body. Her mouth was warm, reminding me of a feeling that I've missed.

I'm only human, and I've wanted closeness with someone for a while now, but guilt always sat in the pit of my stomach instead.

Her hands moved to the spot between her legs, her fingertips circling her clit as I kept my hold on her. I could hear the wetness of her folds, slick and dripping as her hand moved furiously on herself. Her lips wrapped around my base, firm and strong as she eased up and down my length, my fingers threaded tightly against her scalp. She had nowhere to go with no want to leave. I thrust over and over, fucking her mouth as she fingerfucked herself until streams of tears began to spill from her eyes, and her throat made guttural noises.

I shut out the world and all the thoughts that came with it.

If I was going to feel guilty, it wasn't going to happen until my brain caught up with my fire.

I didn't let go until I could feel myself hanging over the edge, my vision beginning to turn dark, my breath hitching deep in the pockets of my lungs. She reached her tipping point with me, her body shaking, her heavy moans vibrating every inch of me. The crest of my cum slammed in the back of her throat, my cock unrelenting, making her swallow the entire shot.

Her lips were swollen and glistening as she slowly let me go, reaching up with her finger to clear a stray drip and licking it off. Her breathing was heavy, along with mine, as she wiped the tears and spit off her face with the backs of her delicate hands.

Hands that were just all over my back, my chest, my scar, my cock.

The lust remained intense in her eyes. I moved to sit up, my entire body still exposed as she climbed off the bed, not saying a single word. She walked over to her table, her actions effortless as her dress fell back in place. I watched her, analyzing her movements, wondering what she was thinking.

Wondering what the *fuck* I was thinking.

The post-orgasm clarity was strong.

I climbed off the table, grabbed my clothes and put them back on, still feeling the blissful effects of the massage in my muscles alongside the regret in my mind.

With her back to me, she spoke. "You want my advice?"

I paused, slightly confused. I'm assuming she was referring to Laila, but after what just happened, I could be wrong. I didn't respond as I pulled my sweatshirt back over my head.

"Don't go looking for her."

I stopped. Her tone was so matter of fact, so confident, I knew there was something she wasn't telling me.

"Why?" I asked.

"She doesn't want to be found. And if she doesn't want to be found, she sure as hell won't be. You're wasting your time."

Obviously, Astrid didn't know about the letters, because those letters aren't from someone who doesn't want my attention. But that was a fact I kept quiet.

I took a few strides to her, my steps quiet and slow, before approaching her back. I remained about a foot away and reached into my hoodie pocket, grabbing a knife I stashed in there before leaving the hotel.

"What makes you think I won't be able to figure her out?" I asked, pulling the knife out of its holder and subtly bringing up the side of my sweatshirt.

She let out a small laugh. "Come on. People have been trying to end her since the beginning of her creation, and she's been able to escape every single time. What makes you any different? You're just a small-town boy from Pennsylvania, eager to get his meaty hands on his trophy. It's not going to happen."

My jaw clenched as she spoke. One minute, she was caressing me, treating me so tenderly, the next, she had her mouth wrapped around my dick while getting herself off, and now she was telling me I was just like everyone else who wanted to stop Laila. I wasn't good enough, smart enough, strong enough. I was worthless.

I held the knife in my right hand, crossing it over my body so the blade was against my left hip. I pressed hard, cutting my skin in a deep line, my muscles tensing as blood instantly dripped from the wound. I barely winced, her words leaving more of a mark than the sharp steel.

"She's not like you, Thomas. She's not human. She's smarter than you'll ever be."

I coated both sides of the blade in my dripping blood, covering every inch of it, and dropped my sweatshirt back down. I closed the gap between us right as Astrid turned to face me.

I didn't wait a single second before sending the blade right into the center of her stomach.

Her knees locked as she stood completely still, her mouth falling open as her eyes looked to mine, the irises losing color by the second. I leaned in close, my hand still clutching the handle of the blade, my lips pressed on her delicate ear.

"You've underestimated me, Astrid."

Her white dress began to turn red, the liquid spreading through the lace. There was a small trickle of my own blood dripping from my nose, but I was so enraptured in Astrid that I barely noticed. Her head tipped back as her arms dangled lifelessly at her sides. I pulled the blade out of her stomach as her body dropped to the floor, her bones collapsing with a loud thud. She lost all signs of life- no breathing, no pulse, no blinking. Nothing.

She was dead.

Years of research have come to this.

I killed a fucking demon.

And damn, did it feel good.

I brought the knife to my lips, a sinister smile pulling at the corners, and licked a streak of blood off the silver blade.

EMMA

"You can drop me off here," I said from the backseat, flinging the door open before the driver could stop at the curb. I jumped out, my cowboy boots steadying me before I had the chance to lose my balance.

"Five Stars. One hundred percent tip," I shouted enthusiastically before slamming the door of the Uber. I tried to remain somewhat calm as I trotted inside, skipping past the reception desk and waiting area and into the hallway of doors, knowing exactly where to go without ever having stepped foot in here before. I slid my hand along each door, feeling the wood for the energy I was looking for. The first few rooms had nothing inside, but upon touching the last door, there was a sense that overtook me, the feeling unquestionable. The intensity and vibrations were strong.

I grabbed the doorknob, those feelings growing even more powerful, and swung open the door.

And what a fucking sight it was.

Astrid lay on the floor, her white dress stained crimson, her body splayed out with her arms and legs in all different directions. Her body was completely lifeless, not a single demon or human cell alive in her.

And then there was Thomas, dressed in his boots, jeans, and black hoodie, standing over her, bloody knife in hand.

He did it. He killed her.

His hair was a mess, his nose was bleeding, his face was flushed, and his breathing was rapid.

He was a killer.

And all that made me want to do was throw him down and fuck him right there.

He turned to me, his eyes dull and cold, not affected in the slightest by what he had just done.

"Emma?" He narrowed his eyebrows, like he was questioning if what he was seeing was really me. "What are you doing here?"

I shook my head. There was no time for questions. "You need to leave. You need to get out of here as fast as you can." I walked into the room and grabbed Thomas' sleeve, hurling him out into the hallway. "Go out the back, get in your truck, and go. I'll take care of this."

"What about you?" he asked, the knife still dangling in his hand. I didn't know he owned a knife. I didn't know he brought any weapons along for the ride at *all*.

"Don't worry about me. I'll meet you back at the hotel."

I shut the door in his face and locked it. I waited until I heard the back door click, ensuring he was actually leaving, then walked up to Astrid. I squatted down to get a closer look. Her body lay still, unmoving, her dark hair fanned out under her, and the sight satisfied an itch I didn't know needed to be scratched.

"It's a shame it had to come to this, Astrid," I said to her corpse, lacking any form of sincerity in my tone. Thomas killing Astrid was a move I did *not* see coming. At all. I knew he had drive and motivation, but I didn't know he had it in him to kill to get what he wanted. A sliver of pride surged through me.

I was *proud* of him.

Astrid was a bitch anyway. She got what was coming to her.

After a few minutes of doing what I needed to get done, I walked out of the private room and back to the front desk. There was an older woman in the back, and when she spotted me, she came rushing out. Before she could say anything, I stopped her.

"Have you seen Astrid?"

"Excuse me?" She was clearly pissed off at me for barging in here and bypassing her.

"Astrid. You know, the woman who works here? And who was just with my boyfriend?" I held up my phone, flashing the map on the screen to the woman. "I tracked his phone here before he turned it off. He told me he was going out with his friends, only to find out he's been fucking Astrid this whole time. It's not the first time they've done this, either."

The woman's eyes widened. Thank God she was buying this.

"And now they're not here. And his truck is gone. I swear, if they've run off together…" My words trailed off as I bit my lip and dropped my phone to my side in defeat.

"I saw the man in here earlier," the woman began. "He was asking for her. But when Astrid came out, it seemed like they were just meeting."

I nodded, trying my best to push out some damn tears. "Yeah, they do that every time to throw people off. They like to act like they don't know each other. It's a kink he likes. He used to do it with me."

"Oh, dear," she said, looking down toward the hallway, unsure if she wanted to comfort me or find Astrid to confront her.

"You know what? Fuck it. If you see either of them again, tell them they can go fuck themselves."

The woman inhaled as I turned on my heel and walked out of the building, the door slamming behind me. I walked out to the gravel parking lot, turning to sneak a quick peek over my shoulder and smirked. She didn't follow me out. She bought it.

Stupid, brainless humans. So fucking gullible.

Me: Meet me at the pool.

I pressed send, the message to Thomas instantly going through, and began walking toward the pool doors. My phone vibrated to notify me that he replied.

Thomas: Why?

I rolled my eyes. Why does he have to fight me on *everything*? Why can't he give in and trust me? He says he will, or that he can try, but he never makes any effort. Even the small things, like meeting me down here, he has to question. It's getting irritating, and if he keeps it up, I don't know if this whole deal is worth the trouble.

I ignored his text and pushed my way through the doors, pocketing my phone. The pungent smell of chlorine and the humidity of the room hit me full force, making my body instantly break out in a small sweat. The floor was wet, but the room was empty, with no kids or families or lifeguards on duty. Flimsy, plastic pool chairs were scattered throughout the room with used towels resting on most of them. I scrunched my nose. It definitely wasn't a five-star pool, but it would have to do for tonight.

I stripped down to my bra and underwear, pretending it was good enough for a swimsuit, and jumped headfirst into the deep end. Raising my arms, I began swimming in a breaststroke, the water flowing smoothly over my hot skin as I completed a few laps.

My mind was here. It wasn't with Astrid, it wasn't with Thomas, it wasn't with Lilith.

It was right here, with me, in the water.

As I reached the far edge, I heard the door close behind me, the sound cutting through the echo of the empty room. Gripping the stone edge of the pool, I turned to see Thomas, his hands tucked into his front jean pockets, his sweatshirt from earlier switched out with a grey t-shirt.

He looked to me, and I to him, a smile forming on my lips.

And after a stretched-out moment, he lifted a small smile back.

"Get in," I said, letting go of the side, treading water.

He shook his head. "No."

I swam closer, keeping my shoulders beneath the surface, my hair floating in thick strands around me. "Just get in."

He rubbed the back of his head, looking around the room. "I don't have anything to swim in."

"You're wearing underwear, right?" I asked, even though I knew he was. I could see it when he lifted his arm. "Get in," I told him a final time.

He simply stared at me, expressionless, cocking his head to the side.

"Please?" I shot him a broad smile, causing him to force out a laugh. I knew he couldn't say no to my manners.

Finally giving in, he walked to the side, took off his shoes and undid his belt, letting his jeans fall to the ground next to my pile of clothes. Then, reaching to the back of his neck, he pulled his shirt over his head, leaving nothing except black boxer briefs that hugged his muscular thighs. My gaze traveled up, soaking in the picture of his toned stomach, when I caught a glimpse of the long, horizontal cut along his hip. The wound wasn't bleeding anymore, but it was still fresh, still red, and still open. He stepped to the edge, his bare feet inches from the water as I swam up to him. I looked up, my eyes wide with expectation, and he looked down at me, his eyes filled with the same darkness I've come to know, engulfing him more with each passing day.

He dove in, the waves of the water crashing into me, and swam the length of the pool before coming back up for air. When he stood, his chest and shoulders rose above the surface, his skin wet with rolling water droplets. He pushed back his loose hair with his hand, shaking the excess water off before swimming back over to me. I watched the muscles in his arms as they worked, pulling tight and flexing with every movement.

I could feel my pussy get wet even through the water.

He reached my side of the pool and stood beside me, his elbow resting on the cement floor next to us.

"How'd you know?" he asked me, and I turned to face him.

I'm assuming he's talking about knowing that Astrid was in danger or dead. I shrugged. "I could feel it."

He gave me a puzzled look, not understanding fully.

"Remember how I told you that Levi and I had a connection? And how he always knew where I was? Well, it's not just with Levi. All demons can feel each other and sense when we're nearby. But we can also sense when one is in danger or when something's off."

He nodded reluctantly, his mind still trying to make sense of it. "So, if we were near Laila, you'd be able to feel her?"

"Yes," I spoke through a slight wince. "But it's different with her. She's good at hiding, and always has been. It's not that easy to simply…feel her." Lifting a hand, I motioned to the area around us, referring to our hunt. "Obviously."

"What else can you feel?"

My eyes flicked over to him, my lips toying with a smile. "If you're referring to what happened between you and Astrid, no, I couldn't feel it. But I knew it was going to happen before you even left the hotel."

"You did?" he asked, his body stiffening slightly. "How?"

"Thomas," I began, his name light on my tongue. "It's what Astrid is known for. Pleasure."

I watched as he swallowed, his throat bobbing with his unease. Astrid was at the top of the list when it came to lust, but her pleasure went well beyond sexual gratification. She always had the most comfortable bed in her apartment, she obviously was the world's best masseuse, and she made the most incredible version of a Sex on the Beach drink. There was a reason why she was a great bartender at Stoney's. She knew exactly what gave people pleasure. She perfected it.

Of course, she always put her own demonic flair on it as well. She would indulge in someone's pleasure for a bit too long, force them into doing something they didn't want to do in the projection that it was their idea in the first place. Coercion, misguiding, delusion, the whole nine yards.

I don't feel bad. She deserved what she got.

Then again, we all deserve the Hell we create.

"So, what did you do with her?" Thomas questioned.

I took a sharp inhale, debating on whether I should give him the long or short version.

"I made it all go away. I cleaned it up and cleared it out."

"Just like that?"

"Just like that."

Thomas studied me, his eyes scanning my face. "But it's barely been an hour."

I gave him a look, one that told him all he needed to know. I didn't need to remind him of who I was. I didn't get on my hands and knees and scrub the blood away. I didn't throw Astrid over my shoulder and carry her body out. I didn't exert any energy to cover up what he did.

All I did was make it disappear, then straighten up the room and all her belongings.

Thomas ran a hand over his face and then through his hair, slicking it back with the water.

"So, what *can't* you guys do?" he finally asked, turning his back so it was flush with the wall.

I waved my hand through the water, the flow seeping through my fingers, thinking momentarily. "Our powers are pretty limited when we're Earthside. When we're in Hell, we are unstoppable. But when we're here, we have restrictions. We can't teleport like most humans think we can. We don't just pop up and come and go wherever and whenever we want. I had a take a fucking Uber to get to you."

Thomas dropped his head and laughed, his smile lighting up, sending a wave of heat down my legs.

"And we can't read thoughts. Sometimes, if I touch you, I can see what's in your head, but I can't look at you from across the room and know what you're thinking."

"You can't?"

I shook my head.

He looked over to me, his eyes haunted by a thought that I couldn't read. The water rippled around us, the sound of the light splashing ringing throughout the empty room. His body moved slowly, and before I knew it, he was in front of me. He planted his arms on either side of me, trapping me in his cage, his shoulders dipping below the water so we were level with each other.

"You sure you don't know what I'm thinking?" His deep voice rumbled against the water around us.

My eyes moved down to his lips, and the urge to lean into them was stronger than ever before. Right now, my wants outweighed my plans. I wanted him. I've wanted him since the first time I saw him at Stoney's. The way he carries himself, the way he looks at the world around us with distrust and reluctance, is unlike any other man I've seen. He knew what he wanted, as unhinged as he may seem, and was willing to do whatever it took to get it.

I moved closer, our chests barely touching and our legs tangling with each other, kicking the water below. Our eyes were teasing each other with fluttered blinks and clouded thoughts, neither one of us daring to cross the line first. I reached my hand out under the water and placed it on his hip, covering the raw cut on his skin. He didn't flinch, his vision steady with mine.

"Fresh blood of a first-born male," I whispered, my face inches from his. "You did it."

His breathing picked up, his jaw tight, his tense hands gripping the edge of the pool behind me. How he got his information on how to kill a demon correctly didn't matter because it all played in his favor. He took a gamble, risking the end result if it *didn't* work, knowing that shit could hit the fan if Astrid didn't die and decided to retaliate. Even if it was a shot in the dark on his end, it worked. And he didn't try to ask me beforehand if his information was correct. He was *that* confident.

Watching him in the balance of the waves, my kicking keeping me afloat, I let my fingers linger over the cut, feeling the separation of flesh created in an act so beneficial to me. To him. To us.

And then he did something I did not expect. He closed his eyes and pressed his forehead to mine.

I could feel his exhale against the surface of the water, as if the weight he was bearing was beginning to roll off his back. He knew how to kill, he now had solid proof. Although we weren't fully there yet, not close to being finished, it was a huge leap in the right direction.

My eyes closed in solidarity, but my mind was racing at the intimacy. It felt like his trust was finally placed in me. He killed one of my own, and I helped by covering it up here on Earth. I could've easily turned my back on him and cast him down to Hell with a swipe of my hand.

But I didn't.

He had shown me what he was capable of.

We are here, together, with one common goal.

And we will see it through to the end.

Then, just as fast as the moment came, Thomas pulled away and moved aside, lifting himself out of the pool. Water came splattering down loudly on the concrete as he walked to a stack of clean towels and picked one up, using it to dry his face. I followed suit, climbing out and grabbing a towel to dry myself with.

Thomas bent down to dry his legs, then tilted his face to me with an evil smile.

"I didn't know demons could swim."

I dropped the towel, watching him bite back a laugh, and began to shove him back to the pool, trying to push him in. Just as he teetered over the edge, he grabbed my arm and pulled me in with him, taking us both under the water. Once we both caught our breath, I splashed the water on his face. He jumped to me, wrapping his arms around my chest, lifting me and throwing me toward the other side of the pool.

Great. Now this stupid fucker was making me laugh.

THOMAS

"Remind me who we're looking for again?" I asked, pulling my truck into another parking lot of another building in another small town. I couldn't even remember the name of this town, all I know is that we're in Nevada. The trips were getting repetitive, the towns were blurring together as one, and the tasks at hand were growing monotonous. As much as I loved my truck, I needed a day away from the pedal. My leg was cramping from the drive, my back was sore again despite the massage, and the whites of my eyes burned red from staring at the long stretches of highway. All I wanted was one day to relax, but we couldn't afford it. We were on a hot streak, meeting people that could take us a step closer to Laila. And all I had to do was place my eyes on Anna, wherever she may be, to be reminded of why I'm doing what I'm doing.

"Polly," Emma said, her eyes scanning the lot, taking in the high number of cars around us. I pulled into what seemed to be the last empty slot in the back row.

Polly. That was another familiar name. I tried to rack my brain of the times I was at Stoney's, trying to remember if I had ever encountered her.

It's still a mindfuck to think that all these demons were surrounding us in our little town for years and years, and no one ever had the slightest clue.

I looked over my shoulder at the large building. It was bare, the brick exterior was a pale shade of tan, with little to no décor or landscaping to clue me in on what was inside.

Emma and I both hopped out of the truck at the same time, meeting at the tailgate. Her blonde hair was mussed gently, hanging down past her shoulders. She dressed in her signature cowboy boots, dark jeans, and a nice white top, making me feel somewhat underdressed in my boots, jeans, and plain black t-shirt.

Right as I was about to head inside, my phone buzzed in my pocket. Messages were rare these days, so I pulled it out, pausing to lean against the truck. It was a text from Soren.

Soren: Can I ask you something?

I hesitated. Of course she could ask me anything. We had that unspoken connection, that shared experience that she probably won't find with anyone else. I welcomed her need to confide in me, but I was reluctant to keep in contact, knowing that she could be used against me in the future. But I didn't want to give in to the reluctance, so I texted back.

Me: Of course.

Within a minute, with the typing bubbles coming and going, she texted back.

Soren: Do you think he knows?

I tapped my finger on the side of my phone, thinking, as Emma huffed in annoyance.

"Can we go?" she asked impatiently, and I ignored her.

I thought about her question, her implications, and began typing an answer before she texted again.

Soren: About the kiss, I mean. Do you think he knows what I did?

Me: I wish I had the answer for you, Soren.

And that was the truth. I wish I could tell her I know what happens after we die, but honestly, I wasn't sure. Even though I had proof of an afterlife, the evidence being a blonde woman standing across from me, I still wasn't sure what went on once we took our final breath. I didn't know if all of our questions were answered, or if only some of them were, or if we were left with more questions than answers. There was a deeply rooted feeling in me that sensed that Anna knew everything, even though she was in a different realm than me. But that's only because she was tied to me, and I was tied to Laila. I can't say the same about Soren and her brother.

Enough time had passed with no response from Soren, so I pushed my phone into my pocket, vowing to check in again with her later.

Emma straightened as she watched me put my phone away, relieved at my attention landing back on her.

"Got your wallet?" she asked, looping her arm through mine, my arm making no effort to return the courtesy. I still wasn't completely comfortable with her embraces, especially when she was this touchy. Last night at the pool was the exception. I was on a high from killing Astrid, succeeding in a trial run of what's to come down the road with Laila. Emma and I connected in a rare but fleeting moment, not only as friends, but also as something deeper. What it was, I wasn't sure, but as unexplainable as it was, I felt it. There was a bigger picture here, so as she tightened her arm around mine, I ignored it and let it slide.

Narrowing my eyes, I turned my head to look down at her. "Yes. Why?"

Her reply was a smirk as she pulled us both to the entry doors. Once inside, I knew exactly why she asked. The giant room was filled with hundreds of different machines, half of them formed in perfect rows, the other half grouped in small circles, scattered throughout the area. There were bells, chimes, and miscellaneous sound effects all ringing at once, with different colored lights flickering everywhere I looked, creating a chaotic and overstimulating environment. A heavy smell of cigarette smoke lingered in the air, swirling in the space around us, filling my lungs. I looked up to the second floor, my eyes catching glimpses of tables covered in a light green felt.

We were in a casino.

She was right when she told me off for assuming that everyone from Stoney's simply moved to other strip clubs across the country. So far, none of them had done so.

Emma pulled me farther inside, bypassing the welcome desk and entering the main floor.

"Where are we going?" I asked, studying the rows of slot machines and the people sitting in front of them. I've been in casinos before, but I'm a man of my wealth, and I don't like to invest in something that has no benefit in the long run. My money is my money. The idea of gambling has never been appealing or an issue for me.

Emma led me to the stairs, and I followed her up to the second floor. There were about twenty tables, all spaced out, with five chairs placed at each one. Most of the tables were filled with men, some wearing sunglasses and some smoking their cheap cigars, all with cards clutched in their hands.

Emma elbowed me, jerking her chin to a specific table. "There she is."

I followed her gaze as we made our way to the table in the center of the room, both of us grabbing a seat and sitting down next to each other. The spotlight above us beamed down, illuminating the green felt. Poker chips of every color were in stacks to the side, and a red deck of cards was placed in the center. Three other men sat at the table, already playing.

"Buy-in is fifty dollars."

I looked up to see the dealer leaning in, speaking directly to me. It didn't even take me half a second to see that she was absolutely beautiful. Her hair was completely black except for two streaks of white hair framing her face. Her eyebrows were sharp and defined, with a bare line cutting through the right one, leading my eyes in a path to hers. She had a silver nose ring piercing and full, pink lips. Just like the rest of the dealers, she wore a plain black t-shirt and black dress pants. She stared at me, her blue eyes haunting, waiting for me to give her the money.

I don't remember seeing her at Stoney's.

I glanced at Emma, who nodded impatiently. I reached into my back pocket, pulled out my wallet, fished out a hundred-dollar bill, and tossed it onto the table. Polly took it and placed it in a box under the table.

"Good to see you, Emma," she said, her British accent low and hushed. Emma gave a half smile right as an older man walked up to Polly, his front flush with her back as he whispered something to her. She cocked her head slightly, leaning into his words, gently giggling at whatever he had to say. His fingers gently brushed up the length of her arm before stopping at her bicep, his hand curling around her tenderly. She nodded to whatever he said, then he dipped away, glancing to Emma without making eye contact with me. Emma's eyes flared red, and her breathing turned heavy as she watched the man leave.

She knew him.

She kept her emotions at bay before changing the subject. "You know how to play, right?"

I gave her a side-eye glance. I may not be a gambler, but I knew how to play fucking poker.

"I'm serious, Thomas. They don't baby you here. If you're stuck, you're fucked."

"I'm fine," I spoke through my teeth, my eyes on the chips in front of me. I pulled out ten more hundred-dollar bills from my wallet and placed them on the table, now understanding why Emma made me go to the ATM before coming here. Polly took them and gave me the equivalent in poker chips, and I, in turn, split them with Emma.

A few rounds passed, with me winning nothing and Emma only winning once. Our bets were low, along with our confidence, as I was watching my money dwindle down to nothing.

That is, until I was dealt two kings.

I threw a hundred-dollar chip in, raising the stakes. I could feel Emma's eyes on me as she threw her cards in and folded. Two out of the three men at the table folded as well, until it was only me and the man directly across from me. Our eyes met briefly, his face studying mine, looking for some kind of bluff. He hesitated but matched my bet, throwing a chip into the middle.

Polly dealt a burn card, then three cards. Six of diamonds, seven of clubs, and a king of spades.

Three of a kind.

I raised the bet another hundred dollars, the black chip clinking against the others in the pile.

The man looked back at his cards, his decision lingering in the space between us as the rest of the table was silent. He could easily have a five and four, or eight and nine, leading him into a straight and winning if the next card drawn is the one he needs.

He threw in his chip.

I kept myself unreadable as Polly pulled a burn card, then drew another card, laying it down with the others.

Five of diamonds. Shit. I could only hope that he already had a five in his hand, the dealt card doing nothing in his favor if he was, in fact, aiming for a straight.

But if he didn't, if he had an eight and nine, his hand would beat mine.

I looked at Emma, her arms crossed and her body leaned back against her chair. I looked to Polly, who patiently waited for my next move, her eyes fixed on me. Then finally, I looked at the man across from me, his poker face strong, his hands resting on his cards.

What did I have to lose? Besides the money sitting in the middle of the table, there wasn't much I had that I could give. My girlfriend is dead, my job is gone, and I have no one or nothing in my life besides the demon sitting next to me, the apartment building back in Pennsylvania, and the truck out in the parking lot.

And even those things are not promised.

I picked up a hundred-dollar chip and tossed it in the center, adding a green twenty-five-dollar chip in with it, just for kicks.

The man across from me did the same.

Including the blinds from the start of the round, the center pot held six hundred and fifty-three dollars.

To the average person, that amount of money is significant, and I respect that. But to me, even though I valued my money, I could lose it and still be fine tomorrow. But that doesn't mean I want to lose.

Polly pulled the last burn card and tossed it aside. Then, with her hand gently on the top of the stack, she drew the final card.

A king of *mother fucking* diamonds.

I flipped my cards over, revealing four of a kind. The man across from me huffed, his hand revealing a jack of clubs and a three of hearts. He had nothing. He was bluffing.

I pulled the stack of chips toward myself, relieved that my money was still my money. The three men apparently had enough for tonight, as they got up and left the table without so much as a wave. Now, it was only Emma, Polly, and I surrounded by a room of other tables and gamblers lost in their own games.

The appeal of playing wore off, the novelty of winning fleeting, the game no longer enticing. I ran a hand through my hair as I gathered my chips, ready to leave as well, before a voice stopped me.

"Are you willing to risk it all, Thomas?"

Polly watched me with her arms open and her hands gripping the edge of the table. I blinked, waiting for her to elaborate.

"Word on the street is that you're looking for her, right?" she asked, leaning forward. "How much are you willing to wager for a chance at information?"

I stole a glance at Emma, who looked just as invested as I felt. Polly was offering some sort of clue, a hint to finding Laila. But I wasn't naïve. I knew there was a catch. A cost.

"You want my chips?" I asked.

She shook her head, her shoulders shaking with a laugh. "No. I don't want your money. We can still raise the stakes with chips, but those aren't the winnings I have in mind."

Her smile quickly faded as she kept her blue eyes on mine.

"I want what's important to you."

I swallowed the lump in my throat as she began shuffling the deck of cards. Here I was, playing games with a demon, betting more than just poker chips.

"Same game. You and me." Her accent rang through my ears as she passed out four cards, alternating between me and her, pushing Emma out of the equation. "You win, you get your intel. You lose, I get what's yours."

I forbid myself from picking up the cards in front of me. I had questions, and I wasn't even sure if I wanted to play.

"How do I know you won't cheat? You are a demon, after all." I didn't even bother lowering my voice. I didn't care who was around to hear, and by the look of amusement on her face, I don't think she cared either.

"I play fair and I lose well. I may be from Hell, but I'm not a liar."

I gave her a disbelieving look, knowing she was probably full of shit.

She rolled her eyes. "I'm serious, Thomas. There are other sins I specialize in. Cheating is not one of them."

I took a deep breath, still not entirely convinced. "That goes for more than just the game, right? You have information on Laila that will actually be useful to me?"

She nodded.

"Okay," I said, the hesitation still thick. "What's in it for you?"

Polly's eyes moved over to Emma, who was still leaning back in her chair. "I want her."

"Deal." The word came out faster than I intended.

Emma smacked my arm hard, my willingness to offer her up stinging her pride, then moved forward, locking eyes with Polly. "Not possible. Neither one of you own me. I can make my own choices."

"You're right," Polly began. "But I can make sure Thomas cuts all ties with you. You'll never have a hand in his little quest again."

"I said 'deal.'" I reiterated, even though the thought of ditching Emma had me feeling a shred of unease. She saved my ass at the massage parlor. She's brought me to multiple demons in a path for more leads. It wasn't like me to use people and their help, then abandon them for my own gain. It didn't sit well with me, but I pushed it away, clearing my throat and trying to get this game moving.

Both Emma and Polly stared at me as I shifted in my chair.

"No," Polly spoke. "You offered her up too quickly. I need more."

"I don't have more."

Polly's lips turned up in a knowing smirk. "Sure you do. What's in your pocket?"

She already said she didn't want my money, so I knew she wasn't referring to my wallet. I tapped my front pockets and felt a small lump. I pushed my hand in, grabbing what was inside and pulling it out.

My mother's ring.

I never put it back in the box after Levi took it out.

I clutched it in my palm tightly.

"No."

Polly paused, a hint of defiance in her eyes. "How far will you go to get what you want, Thomas? What are you willing to risk to take the next step? Are you willing to offer up the things you love and care for? Or do you want to sit in the unknown for the rest of your life, drowning in the fact that you could've changed the outcome?"

I looked down at the silver ring in my hand. With the light from above, the ring still had its shine, it's coating no longer dull. Why do all the fucking demons want this ring?

I felt the silver against my skin and tried to tell myself that it was only metal. It was just a simple piece of jewelry from my dad for my mom and nothing more. I'm sure if my mom knew what was happening, she would tell me that the ring doesn't matter and that it was worthless. To give it up. But for some reason, I felt tied to it. This was the last thing I had from my mother that left me, passing away over ten years ago.

I searched the room, looking in every direction for Anna. I needed to see her, to look in her eyes, to have her ground me. But as I looked, my head spinning, I couldn't find her. There were too many people around, too many lights and noises distracting me from what I longed for.

My eyes slammed shut. I needed this. I needed to find Laila. It was the whole reason why I was here.

I threw the ring onto the table, the diamond weighing it down, sending it spinning.

Polly smiled wide and lifted her cards. "Here we go."

I curved my cards up, not fully taking them off the table before letting them fall back down.

Jack of diamonds and four of diamonds.

Fuck. Not a good way to start.

Polly nodded to me, allowing me to bet first. I studied her, my vision fixated on the shimmer in her eye. She kept her face completely neutral, and I hadn't the slightest clue whether she was happy with her cards or not.

I picked up a hundred-dollar chip and tossed it in front of me. Money doesn't matter in this round, but I wanted her to know I was in it to win. I needed that information.

Of course, Polly matched me without a hint of doubt. She has nothing to lose.

She dealt a burn card, throwing it aside, then laid down three cards on the table.

Five of hearts, two of hearts, and king of diamonds.

Fuck me again. Besides the potential of a straight or flush, I had close to nothing, but maybe I could get away with a bluff. I picked up another chip and threw it in the middle, hoping the next two cards would give me something. Anything.

Polly matched it, pulled a burn card, then drew the next card, laying it with the others.

Three of diamonds.

If the next card is a six, I'll have a straight. If the next card is a diamond, I'll have a flush.

If the next card is neither of those, nor something that can be paired, I'll have nothing.

Emma's stare heated into my side as my thoughts ran rampant. Was the risk worth it? My odds were incredibly low at this point.

But the ring was already on the table. I was already playing her game. I couldn't stop now.

I threw a fifty-dollar chip in the middle.

Polly did the same, drew a burn card, and then pulled the final card.

A nine of clubs.

Fuck. I had nothing.

I flipped my cards over to reveal my loss. Polly showed me her hand. A jack of hearts and a five of spades.

She won with a simple pair. I lost by so little. I almost wish she would've had a royal flush, ensuring me I couldn't have won with anything. Feeling like I was so close made it all worse.

"Sorry, Thomas." Polly grabbed her winnings, stuffing the handful of chips into the pocket of the small apron tied around her waist. The older man from earlier, the one who whispered in Polly's ear, approached our table, seemingly coming out of nowhere. He must've been watching us the whole time. Polly placed the ring into the palm of his outstretched hand. He gripped the metal, his fist dropping to his side, and walked over to a side door, away from the rest of the poker tables. I watched as he scanned a key card over a grey box on the wall, a small light turning green as it allowed him access to wherever he was going.

What the fuck? Why was that ring being treated as some sort of lost treasure? I'm pretty sure my dad bought it for my mom at a random department store, probably marked down on clearance.

The background noise surrounding me faded out as I sighed and hung my head. I lost the ring, and I wasn't getting any information. I took the risk and lost. Now, we were back to square one.

I grabbed whatever chips I had left and got up from the table. Emma did the same, sending Polly a vicious glare at the same time. A small wave of amusement filled my insides, knowing that she had my back, even against one of her own. She was protecting me instead of siding with her home team.

We walked away as more men came over, filling the seats we were just in. I looked over my shoulder to see Polly watching me, the corner of her lips twisted up, her gaze lingering over my body.

THOMAS

An hour later, Emma and I found ourselves walking around the outside of the casino. The sun was set, the sky completely dark, but the air was still dry and warm, making me regret pulling on my sweatshirt once we exited the casino. The surrounding desert heat felt completely different from the Pennsylvania air I've known my whole life. It was a nice change, getting out and seeing the country, even though I wish it was under different circumstances.

We came upon a door, a plain, black entrance with no signs, no lettering, no numbers, nothing. Just a door, a handle, and the same grey security box as the one I saw inside. I jogged up to it and jiggled the handle.

"Locked," I said to Emma as the cold steel held tight under my grip.

Emma shook her head. "No, it's not." She shoved me out of the way and grabbed the metal, the handle opening on her first attempt.

I stared at her as she pulled open the door, not waiting for me before entering. I didn't need to ask how she did that because I knew. I didn't need an explanation to know.

My mind traveled back to the final night at Stoney's when Laila locked the doors with a simple flick of her wrist.

I knew.

We quietly stepped down a long hallway, dim lighting illuminating the coffee-colored walls and matching tile. From what I could see, it was an extremely clean and polished area, completely different from the main areas upstairs. Our footsteps echoed off the long stretch of tiled floor as we passed by numerous rooms, their doors made of frosted glass. I could see the silhouettes of people moving, but it was impossible to see who was inside. Emma placed her hand on each one, her fingertips sliding along gently, careful not to give herself away to the people in them.

"Can you tell what they're doing?" I asked, my voice low and hushed.

She shrugged. "Yes and no. I can't see it clearly, but I can feel the nature of what's going on."

After resting her hand on the first door, she looked at me, a grin appearing.

"What?" I asked.

"Kinky."

I ignored her, but couldn't help a quiet laugh from escaping.

She came to another door, her hand resting for a moment before moving on. "These must be the VIPs. More gambling, more money. A *lot* more money."

The next door was about fifty feet away, with Emma doing the same thing as the other ones, my steps close behind. "Same thing. But those people are betting with things they can't in public."

I paused, looking at the door. What the hell did that mean? They were betting with what? Their houses? Their cars? Or, *fuck*, organs? People? Souls? My mind was racing with the possibilities, and after everything I'd seen in my life, I came to expect anything and everything. Sometimes, nothing was off limits.

Emma pressed on without me, my fists curled at my side, before I jogged to catch up with her. Every door was missing what we were looking for. They were all filled with either sex or gambling, until we came upon the last door. Unlike the others, it wasn't frosted glass, but a simple, heavy wooden door. It was dark, stained, and blank, and there was another grey box on the wall next to it. Only people who had special access to it could enter.

Emma put her hand flat on the door. "It's empty."

"Let me in," I commanded, and Emma pushed on the handle, opening the door for me.

The lights were off, but with the moonlight filtering in through the shaded window, I could tell it was an office. The walls were lined with dark wood paneling, and a giant, rectangular desk sat in the center, with a computer, lamp, and chair accompanying it. There were two lounge chairs across from the desk, a ghost standing in the far corner, and a generic painting of purple flowers on the wall, but there wasn't much else. No paperwork or filing cabinets or anything of the sort. He must be a paperless kind of guy.

Emma shut the door as I walked around the room, my eyes scanning high and low, looking for anything out of the ordinary. The room was immaculate, almost as if it was just a showroom at a furniture store. It didn't look like anyone worked here, and if it wasn't for the nameplate on the desk, I'd think we were wasting our time. I picked up the polished metal plate, eyeing the brushed nickel.

NOMA

I glanced up at Emma, who was leaning with her shoulder against a wall, her arms crossed. "Noma?" I asked, turning the nameplate to show her.

She nodded. "Noma. That's his name."

The man from the poker room on the second floor. The man that has my ring.

This is his office.

"Is he a demon?"

"Yes."

My mind tried to put the pieces together. "Then why did he use a key card for entry at the poker tables?"

Emma shrugged. "Appearances, probably. Shits and giggles, maybe?"

I placed the nameplate back down, angling it back to the way it was before. My eyes did one last sweep of the room before coming to a stop on the wall next to Emma. There was a seam, a line running from ceiling to floor, almost invisible to the naked, untrained eye. But there was a slight space in the middle, causing the top half to be about a fourth of an inch off center from the bottom half. If I didn't build houses for a living, I wouldn't have noticed it. I walked up to it, studying the gap, my fingers trailing the line. It was smooth, but it was a dead giveaway.

Emma watched me as I gently pushed the wall, the paneling popping open with a soft click. And once I pulled back the wall, I saw exactly what I wanted to see.

A safe.

It was a small, black safe with a numeric keypad on the front. It doesn't get any simpler than that.

And I had a feeling I knew what was inside.

Taking a step back, I rubbed my jaw, my heartbeat accelerating. "Can you—"

"Thomas," Emma said, cutting me off and stepping away from the wall, a realization suddenly hitting her. "He's coming."

Her eyes widened, and her posture straightened with foreboding. She could feel him drawing near. I knew I only had a few seconds to decide what to do before he would step foot in this office.

I shut the wall to the safe and pushed Emma to one of the lounge chairs. "Sit," I whispered to her with force, and she plopped herself down. I heard footsteps on the tile outside the door as I hustled over to the corner. The door opened slowly, the wood wedging me between it and the wall. I pinned my back against the paneling as hard as I could.

"Emma," Noma spoke cheerily, and I could hear the smile on his face.

Emma glanced over her shoulder to him, her back to the door. "Noma."

The way her voice trailed off at the end of his name caught me off guard. Something wasn't right.

He paused, his breathing thick as he took a step into his office, his dress shoes clicking on the floor. I still couldn't see him. All I could see was the desk, the empty lounge chair, and half of Emma. I could see her lean over and rest her elbow on the arm, giving me more to watch, but she never made eye contact with me.

I steadied my breathing and tried to calm my heart rate.

Noma took another step in, the left side of his body coming into my line of sight, blocking my view of Emma. I watched as he tilted his chin up, placed his hands in his pockets, and took a deep breath.

"Did you bring a friend?" he asked Emma, and I knew it was over.

I kicked the door, sending it flying shut, and lunged toward Noma. He spun around and tried to grab me, but I jammed my right forearm into the crook of his left elbow. This set him off balance, allowing me to throw my other arm hard into his throat. He tipped forward, coughing and trying to catch his breath, and that gave me the opportunity to go back to his left arm and twist it over his shoulder, making him collapse on the floor. All in a matter of seconds.

I pinned him down onto his stomach, pushing all my body weight onto him. He was a big guy, so it took extra effort to keep him from flipping me off his back.

"Fuck, fuck!" Noma exclaimed, his words like background noise to me.

"Emma," I said, looking up to see her standing by the chairs. "Come here."

I kept my hands pressed on him, his arm still contorted over his shoulder as she approached, her eyes hinting to desire.

"My pocket," I said, nodding to my sweatshirt. She reached in and pulled out my knife, sliding it out of its case. I leaned down and bit my sleeve, pulling it up with my teeth and exposing my right forearm.

As Emma looked into my eyes, I gave a single nod, and she slowly slid the blade horizontally along the outside of my arm. Noma was still shouting as blood spilled down past my wrist and onto my hand. She wiped the blade with my blood, making sure all of it was completely covered, then moved to hand it to me.

With a singular, fluid motion, I grabbed the handle of the knife and sent it directly into Noma's spine. He let out an aching scream with whatever air was left in his lungs. Then, after a few moments, his body stiffened, his movements slowed, his shouting stopped, and my pressure released.

He was dead.

And Emma helped me do it.

Once time had slowed and his body remained limp, I shifted my weight off of him, letting myself sit on the floor. I looked at the man, the knife buried to the hilt in his back, and exhaled. This, all of this, was still new to me. The demons, the chasing, the killing. I wasn't sure if I would ever get used to it, but damn, did it feel fucking good.

I bent my knees up and rested my arms over them. Blood trickled down my skin to my palm, and I made no effort to stop the bleeding. Part of me felt like I deserved to bleed for what I'd done. I looked up at Emma, who squatted down next to Noma, studying his body. With a tilt of her head, she pulled the blade out of his back, wiped the blood off using his suit jacket, then placed it back into the sleeve.

As she handed it back to me, a voice spoke, causing me to jump.

"Well, that was interesting."

Polly. She stood in the doorway, her arms crossed as she took in the room before her. Noma was face down, dead on the floor, with Emma and I on either side. I quickly shoved my knife back into my hoodie pocket before she could see it.

Her heels clacked on the floor as she moved closer, her eyes darting to the dead body in front of her. She kicked his foot, sending it rolling over to its other side.

"Hm. Shame." Her words were coated with sarcasm. She clearly didn't care that he was dead, which played in my favor. She wasn't mad that I killed him.

She walked around his body and moved toward me as I remained on the floor. She had changed her clothes since the poker game; she was now wearing silver strapped heels and a black silk cocktail dress with her hair tied up in a high ponytail. Once she moved past me, my body still faced toward the door, she broke the silence.

"I'm assuming you're here to take back what you've lost."

I stayed silent, looking down at the floor under me. I could hear her walk behind the desk, the room suddenly illuminating as she switched on the lamp.

"I admire that about you, Thomas. You're willing to get what you want, even if it's not rightfully yours."

I gritted my teeth. The ring was mine, even if I lost it in some stupid fucking card game. If she thought I was going to hand it over and walk away, she was wrong.

"You'll do whatever it takes to overcome the odds, even if you don't finish first."

She made her way around the other side of the desk, her heels clicking past Emma, circling back to me. She stopped at my feet, my gaze still on the floor as she kneeled down, trying to get into my vision.

"But did you?" she began, her voice hushed through her thick accent. "Did you get what you came here for?"

I watched my blood drip off my fingers and onto the floor. I came here for more information on Laila. But so far, I've lost my mother's ring and gained more blood on my hands. Both literally and figuratively.

My jaw locked as I finally looked up at her, her piercing blue eyes like ice before me.

"I'm not like you," I grumbled. "I don't lose well."

She exhaled a laugh, her eyes briefly flickering over to Emma and back. "I know. That's why I'm going to help you."

I arched an eyebrow. What? I had just lost her game not long ago, and she's willing to help me anyway?

"Thomas Diesel, the forbidden apple of Lilith's eye."

Reaching out, she placed her pointer finger under mine, catching a drop of blood. She stuck her finger in her mouth, sucking the crimson right off with a smack.

"Mmm," she let out a moan. "No wonder why she likes you."

I rolled my head back, tired of these stupid fucking mind games. I wanted to get to the point, get what I wanted, and leave.

"Tell me what you know."

With a smirk, Polly stood back up to her feet, giving me her hand. Rejecting it, I stood up and pulled my sleeve back down, drying and soaking up the blood with the cotton fabric.

"Come with me."

She pulled me behind the desk and pushed me down onto the chair. Emma moved back to one of the lounge chairs, watching us like she wasn't even there.

"Since you seem to be so needy, I'll give you another opportunity. Satisfy my needs, and I'll satisfy yours. Let me taste you more. Let me see what all the fuss is about. Then, we'll talk."

"No," I stated firmly. "Talk first."

Polly raised her eyebrows. "You're a man that handles his business before his pleasure. I like that." Her voice was coated with lust as she looked down to me, her eyes greedy. "Too bad you're the one that lost, remember? I hope you don't think I'm just going to hand everything back over to you. Come on, Thomas. Show me what you're willing to do to get it back."

What the fuck was going on? Why was this even being discussed? All I wanted was to get her information, no matter how insignificant it may be, get the ring, and go. I leaned forward, my elbows on my knees, my head tilted up to her. "Tell. Me. What. You. Know."

I could see the debate in her fierce eyes as she placed her hands on her hips. My eyes trailed down her body, not shying away from the fact that I'd take whatever she wanted to give me, in terms of both her and Laila. But as I watched her battle her decision, I knew that whatever information she had must've been worth something, or else she wouldn't hesitate to tell me. Either that, or she has some sort of tie to Laila that could hurt her if she breaks it.

No matter what, I'm here for the information, and I'm not leaving until I have it.

I could see her tongue run over her teeth, her mind racing. Her silver, shimmering earrings dangled as she shook her head.

"It's funny you think she's still around, playing your silly cat-and-mouse game. Not only does she have the entire Earth at her fingertips, but she also has all of Hell in her clutches, too. So, tell me, Thomas, why would she make herself so easily accessible to you? Or to *anyone*, for that matter?"

Polly glanced to Emma, sending her a look of pity before she leaned down, placing both hands on either side of the chair, gripping the armrests. I kept my eyes level with hers as she leaned in, letting her body hover over me, a secret tickling her lips.

"And what makes you think she's still in the country?"

The question came out, and I froze.

Polly knows where Laila is?

More importantly, she left the country?

Fuck.

I knew it was a possibility. It always has been, and I've never been oblivious to it. But there have been leads, with John and Soren, that made me believe she hadn't gone too far off.

Or maybe Polly was bluffing.

"What do you mean?" I asked, narrowing my eyes.

"You fucking Americans think the whole world revolves around you." She lightly shoved my forehead, making my head tip back. "She could be anywhere on planet Earth, and your small brain thinks that she's still hanging around a dingy bar that your daddy falls asleep on, on 'Main Street in Kittanning, Pennsylvania?'"

Her voice instantly flipped into a mocking, valley girl, American accent when she said that location. I jumped up from my chair, grabbed her by the throat, and walked her backward until she was against the wall. She smiled, loving the fact that she pissed me off, and my fingers tightly squeezed her neck.

"I never once said she would never leave the country," I spoke against her jaw, my nose brushing along her cheek. "In fact, I've always entertained the idea that she could be long gone, somewhere I'll *never* find her. She might be in the fucking Amazon rainforest or on Mount Everest, for all I know."

My grip tightened, forcing her to squirm underneath me. I discreetly pulled the knife out of my hoodie pocket and tucked it into the back of my jeans, pulling my sweatshirt over to cover it. Once it was secure, I pressed myself flush against her, her breasts hard against my body. I could feel her nipples through our clothing, making my own body react in ways I wasn't expecting.

"She might even be back in Hell, settled in her red velvet throne, laughing at the fact that I have no way of getting to her, and no way of knowing."

I pinned her body against the wall even harder, thrusting my hips into hers.

"Every single one of you demons is the fucking same." I looked over to Emma, including her in that statement and hoping she got the message, then looked back to Polly. "Don't insinuate that I'm ignorant. Because I'm anything but."

Her hooded eyes glanced to mine, relishing in the fact that I had her where I wanted her, and she had me where she wanted me. Apparently, we were both getting what we wanted tonight.

She swallowed, trying her best to clear her throat before speaking. "I have something for you."

My hand remained strong on her, not loosening any muscles in the slightest.

When I didn't move, she continued. "From Lilith."

My breathing stopped, only momentarily, before catching myself. "What is it?"

Her eyes flickered over to the wall next to us, where the safe was. "It's in there."

I knew it. I knew there was a reason why I was still here, why I even came here in the first place. There was no way I was about to let go of Polly, so I looked over my shoulder to Emma, who was still sitting in the lounge chair, looking completely uninterested and unfazed by everything.

"Open it."

I could tell Emma wanted to make a jab, or say something funny, but my eyes gave her a look that told her to save it. We needed to get this over with.

She stood up and walked to the wall, popping it open and revealing the black safe. There was no need for any wizardry, voodoo spells, or anything of the sort. All she did was grab the handle and open it, almost as if it was never locked.

I watched as she pulled out my mother's ring, her hand holding it up to show that it was still in the same condition. Then, Emma reached into the safe again and pulled out something I didn't expect to see.

A white envelope.

Another letter.

Emma shut the safe, then the wall cover, and sauntered over to us, holding both items up to me. Right as I went to grab the ring, Polly snatched the letter out of Emma's hand. I pocketed the ring quickly as Polly moved to shove the letter down the front of her dress. I removed my hand from her throat and tried to go after the letter.

"Ah, ah," Polly spoke, clutching the fabric of her dress over the paper. "Don't think you can get it that easily. You did lose the bet, after all."

With her one hand still gripping her dress, she placed her other hand on my chest, her palm warm through the fabric, and pushed me back to the desk chair once again. I didn't resist, I didn't fight back. I sat down, only wanting the letter.

Polly slowly pulled the envelope from her dress and placed it on the desk, smoothing the bend. Then, she took a step to me, leaning down and placing her hands on my thighs. My eyes instantly went to the dress that was loosely hanging over her breasts, exposing herself.

My cock pulsed, growing at the sight. I turned my head to Emma, who had her arms crossed.

"I'll meet you outside in a bit."

Without any reluctance, she turned to go, but Polly stopped her. "No. Stay."

My head snapped back to Polly. *What the fuck?*

She moved even closer, her soft lips speaking on mine. "If you want this letter, she has to watch."

My eyes subtly looked to Emma, who kept her expression blank as I nodded. She obeyed and sat back down. I wondered what was going through her head. Was she annoyed, hesitant, bored? Was she turned on or disgusted? Has she done this before?

Who am I kidding? She's a demon. Of course, she's done this already.

I, on the other hand, have not. I've never participated in anything involving more than me and another woman, even if the third party was only watching.

And I couldn't say I wasn't turned the fuck on.

Feeling Polly's breath lingering on my lips, I reached up and grabbed her ponytail and broke the tie, which forced her hair to fall down in waves. My hand pulled the back of her head, fisting her hair as I gave in and kissed her. I closed my eyes, let the feeling take over, and forgot everything my mind was telling me I was doing wrong. I let my flesh kick into drive while my morals moved to the backseat.

Polly's lips were tender but firm as her tongue dipped into my mouth, our desire growing more heated by the second. Trying to keep my focus on myself, I dismissed the stare of Anna and the presence of Emma, concentrating on the fact that I was getting what I wanted in more ways than one. But then her hands moved under my sweatshirt so that they were on my skin, feeling every bit of my chest, and I was right back into the desires I'd been trying to tame. Our kiss deepened as I kept one hand in her hair, the other trailing down her neck and onto her shoulder, taking the strap of her dress and pulling it down. She took the hint and quickly undid the zipper, letting the dress fall to the floor, revealing her bare, slim body underneath. No bra, no underwear. She planned this.

My lungs inhaled, squeezing at the need for satisfaction. Polly moved her hands to my belt and undid it, unbuttoning my jeans as well and pulling them down. I pulled my sweatshirt over my head, taking my shirt with it, mindful of keeping my knife at my back, wedged between myself and the chair.

Waiting for her next move, I leaned back, my elbow propped up on the chair as my finger rubbed my lips. My right arm was still coated in my blood, creating the illusion of my power. I had the ability to destroy her, and she knew it. Her eyes moved from my arm to the fleshy, vertical scar on the side of my neck, and I could practically hear her heartbeat through her chest.

It was almost as if I was some sort of myth to these demons, and they had to see me, taste me for themselves.

The only thing that separated us was my boxer briefs, which were tented from my rock-hard dick. Polly grinned, looking down at my cock through the fabric with fire in her eyes, animalistic and hungry.

I heard the sound of Emma's cowboy boots as she got up and walked around the desk, placing her back against the wall, opting for a better view. For a moment, I almost forgot she was here, but a part of me was glad she still was.

The electricity between Emma and I was there from the beginning, only growing stronger with each day and each obstacle. And even though the passion was intense in this moment, in this room, the three of us surging with heat, I felt it with Emma more than I did with Polly.

Our eyes connected, and a brief smile tugged on her lips.

My attention was brought back to Polly, who reached for the waistband of my boxer briefs, pulling down and letting my cock spring free. I could feel the wetness of my pre-cum, ready for release as she gripped me in her hands, her touch warm and strong. She moved to kneel, but before she could place herself between my legs, I grabbed her arms.

"Not yet," I rasped, and she looked at me with doe eyes. Bringing her up, I pushed her up onto the desk and placed her feet on both armrests of the desk chair. Her legs were spread wide, herself on full display as I took in the sight of her beautiful body. I let the knife behind me settle down lower, still tucked between myself and the cushion, keeping it hidden as I slowly leaned forward. Although, based on the look on her face, I don't think she was focused on anything but her own pleasure.

Moving to the inside of her thigh, I gently bit down on the skin, leaving a trail of bites as I made my way up her leg. I could feel her tense under me, the tease too strong, the need for more escalating too fast. I found my way to the center of her legs, her pussy wet and glistening, begging for my touch. Polly leaned back on her elbows as my lips grazed her skin, my breath warm against her clit. My tongue slipped out, barely making contact, beckoning a cry from her throat. I did it again, leaving her in the balance of wanting and needing, aching and pleading, before finally pushing into her, letting it all go. My lips devoured her, consuming her, drinking all of her. Her deep, breathy moans stirred inside me, adding fuel to my fire. Her taste was like nothing I'd ever tasted, with the sweetness dripping from my chin as I craved her more by the second.

Angling my chair, I made sure Emma had a good view of everything I was doing. I could hear her heavy breathing, and that's when I decided to look out of the corner of my eye to her direction, making eye contact with her as I pleasured someone else. When our eyes connected, I could feel her gaze pierce through me, her needs radiating off of her like the heat of a flame, and I just knew she was soaked under those jeans. Her eyes watched my tongue as I licked Polly's clit, circling the flesh, then continued to study me as I added my fingers. I slipped one inside her pussy, never taking my lips off, then added another, a loud cry echoing from Polly as I caressed her walls. Her knees began to shake and her hips began to buck as I could feel herself close around my fingers. I pressed my thumb on her clit, alternating between it and my mouth, and that's all it took for her to come spiraling down. Her hands moved to the back of my head, pushing my face into her as she arched her back, her shoulders rubbing against the desk. Her body shook with release, and I smiled against her, knowing that even though I lost the bet upstairs, I'm getting what I wanted down here.

Once she came down from her orgasm, she lifted her head to see me. Her face was red, her hair was disheveled, and her breathing was coming in quick, short spurts, but her expression showed deep satisfaction.

And Emma's did as well.

Polly slid off the desk with ease, her legs on either side of me as she hovered over me. I knew what she wanted. The look in her eyes said it all as she remained in dangerous territory. My dick was straight and her body was above it, waiting for the go-ahead, but I couldn't bring myself to commit. Before my cock could convince me otherwise, I grabbed Polly's hips, pushed her away from the treacherous position, and opened my knees. She sank herself down to the floor, placing herself between my legs, accepting the fact that she wasn't getting me fully. But she was getting more of me than most.

Her skin glowed as her post-orgasm high still filtered through her flesh. She sat on her heels, eyeing the thick shaft pulsing before her. A hint of a sultry smirk played on her lips before she reached in and stroked my length. I let my head fall back onto the chair, enjoying the feeling of her grasp tightening and loosening, her skin smooth on mine.

Then I felt something warm and wet, and I looked down to see her lips wrapped around the head of my cock.

"Holy shit," she muttered between licks. "You taste so fucking good."

I did my best to keep my moans in my throat, but when she pressed her tongue flat on my base, I couldn't help but let a small grunt slip through. She took me in her mouth, her head sliding up and down slowly, my length filling her entirely as I felt myself tap the back of her throat. She didn't stumble, she didn't gag, she simply took all of me, her blue eyes watching me without a single blink.

I could hear Emma to my right as her breathing became even more rapid and heavy than it was before. Fuck, she was turned on, too.

I kept my eyes on Polly as she coated my cock with her spit, her head bobbing as her tongue swirled around the head. She smiled and her teeth gently grazed on my skin, almost causing me to tip over the edge right then and there. I shot forward, still keeping the knife behind me and out of Polly's vision, and grabbed her hair once again. Her head reared back, but her smile stayed.

"You need to slow down." My voice rumbled as I clenched my jaw. "You've clearly had centuries to perfect this, but I'm an imperfect human. I will come before you have a chance to take your next breath."

Polly did nothing except smack her lips as I let her go and sat back in the chair. With slow, sultry movements, she resumed the pleasure, her lips even more warm and swollen than before.

Fuck.

I moved my hand to her face, brushing my thumb across her cheek before moving lower. I cupped her breast as it filled my hand, my fingers pinching her tight, hard nipple. She let out a moan, her throat vibrating against my throbbing cock, sending electric sensations all through my body. When I looked down, I could see the area between her legs, the shimmering skin still wet, slick, and dripping. Dammit, it would be so fucking easy to lift her onto my lap and slip inside of her.

And I can't believe I was actually considering it.

I heard the sound of a zipper, and I looked to my right to see Emma's jeans down past her hips. She had her own fingers hidden in her underwear, deep in her pussy, fucking herself. She and I made eye contact as her lips parted, barely easing into a small smile. I could picture her mouth being the one wrapped around me, her tits open and bare, and it was a vision I wouldn't mind seeing come to life.

My mind was catastrophic at the exhilaration of it all. The feeling of Polly's heated mouth on my cock, the sight of seeing my spit and her cum dripping down her thighs, and knowing the fact that Emma was getting off on this too.

I could feel myself so close to finishing.

Sliding forward in my chair, I pulled Polly up for a kiss as I grabbed the knife from behind my back, carefully and silently sliding it out of the case while her lips mixed with mine. I brought the blade down to the underside of my thigh. I cut hard, creating a new, fresh horizontal line on the back of my leg, the blood instantly dripping onto the floor. I coated the steel, making sure to never break my kiss from Polly. I even pressed my cock against her stomach, thrusting up and down to mask the other movements I was making.

Once I knew the knife was covered entirely, I broke the kiss and forced her back down on my cock. She happily obliged, her passion for me hotter than before. I held the knife at my side while Polly wrapped her lips around her teeth, adding pressure to her repetition and pushing me past my limit.

My eyes rolled back as the wave crashed into me, my body tensing and jerking from the natural ecstasy. I could feel my blood pulsing not only in my cock, but also in the new cuts on my arm and thigh. Polly drained me and sucked in every last drop, and I could hear Emma beside me moaning, reaching the same orgasm that I just experienced.

The demon slid her mouth off my hard cock for one last time, her mouth filled and dripping with my cum. A small dribble fell down as I took her by the chin, gripping her tight, forcing her to look at me.

"Swallow it," I demanded, her crimson-red eyes locking with mine. As she did what she was told, I lifted the knife from my side and stabbed her deep in the throat. Her swallow had yet to make it all the way down, so when I pulled the blade out, the red of our blood and the white of my cum swirled together, painting a pretty picture on the sharp steel. I released my grip, and she instantly fell to the floor, her body and soul no longer an issue.

I killed her before I could torture her into giving me Laila's exact location, if she even knew it. Then again, who knows if any of that would work, or if she would even tell me the truth. My torture tactics were probably like child's play to her, and even though I had Emma with me and on my side, I probably wouldn't have been able to break through to her. And for all I know, Polly might have an alliance with

Laila, and her false information may have misled me. Then, if she *did* know where Laila was, she could easily give her warning that I was onto her, trailing her scent, letters aside. Getting one step ahead of her and killing her when she didn't expect it was what I wanted people to know about me.

I do not fuck around.

I do not wait for others.

I am in control.

I looked at the knife, studying it, aware of the fact that it was keeping me on track. It was proving to be more useful than I had ever imagined it to be. It was taking demons out of my way, sending them back down to the depths of Hell, all while leading me to the one I wanted. I brought it to my lips, my tongue sweeping the side of it, taking a taste of what I deserved.

I felt a stream of my own blood fall from my nose as Emma shuffled over to me, her jeans back up over her hips but still unbuttoned as she swung her leg over my lap. My dick was still bare and somewhat hard as she straddled me, her and I both ignoring my nosebleed as a sense of clarity rushed into her eyes, and I could tell that she needed that as much as I did. I ran my fingertips lazily over her back as she draped one arm over my shoulder, tilting her head to the side in adoration.

"My offer still stands, you know."

My heated gaze fell over her lips, reveling in every bit of desire I had for her.

Her offer of fucking me with no consequence. It was something I thought about more often than I should.

I felt insatiable.

"And you're not leaving here with the taste of her on your tongue."

Emma brought her other hand to my lips, the one that was just knuckle deep in her pussy, and pushed her fingers in my mouth, bypassing the metallic blood from my nose. I ran my tongue over them, sucking her, tasting her cum, wanting more.

That's when it hit me.

I. Wanted. More.
Fuck. I'm in over my head.

ANNA

STISWPVIZWQP

THOMAS

My back rested against the frame of my truck as I looked up to the cloudless sky. There was so much out there, so much that I was unaware of in this life and beyond. I'll never know all the answers, and that's a fact I'll have to settle with. The stars were everywhere, speckled in every spot my eyes could see. The moon hung high, the silver crescent creating a halo against the midnight blue. I thought back to the night Laila kissed me for the first time on my eighteenth birthday and the vision that came with it. The woman sitting on the crescent moon, cutting herself on the curve, letting herself bleed.

Keeping my face up toward the sky, I closed my eyes, picturing my own growing number of cuts on my body, and it was slowly beginning to make sense.

She made herself bleed when she found me, and I'm making myself bleed to find her.

Emma opened the back door of the casino and made her way out, not a single hair out of place. Meanwhile, I was covered in dried blood, my hair was a mess, and I'm pretty sure my shirt was on backwards under this hoodie.

"All good," Emma spoke, her voice crystal clear as I watched her approach the truck. After everything inside, she forced me to get dressed and leave, allowing her to clean up the mess I made. I followed her orders, tucking my knife away and grabbing the letter on the way out.

Apparently, whatever she did in there didn't take much effort because only a few minutes passed before she joined me here.

She went to walk to her side of the truck before I stopped her.

"Where do they go?" I asked, turning my body toward her but still leaning against the truck.

She blinked.

"The demons," I clarified. "Where do they go after I kill them?"

Taking a step toward me, she sighed. "They go back to Hell."

I nodded hesitantly, not sure why the answer didn't satisfy me. It couldn't be that simple, could it?

After a moment, she continued. "They go to Hell's graveyard, which is the bottom tier. Basically, they're the dog shit on someone's shoe. They endure the ultimate torture: The Void. They have nothing, they experience nothing, and they sense absolutely nothing. The only thing they gain is insanity. If they somehow make their way out of that, then they can make their way back up to the top, of course, but it takes time. A long time. Centuries."

My lungs deflated at the severity of the things I've done. The things I've changed both Earthside and other side just in the past two days.

"And that's if Lucifer even lets them out of the grave in the first place."

She resumed walking back to the passenger side and climbed in. I lingered for a moment, the weight of the consequences weighing heavily on me. My actions were causing someone's eternal torture. Was it right that I was playing God, sending these demons to their demise?

But they were *demons*. How could it *not* be the right thing to do?

Everything Laila said to me about Anna, about saving her and bringing her back from the dead, voiced in my head. If it wasn't right to keep someone alive when they weren't meant to be, then it couldn't be right to end them when it wasn't their time, either.

I shook my head. These aren't people I'm killing, and I needed to keep that in mind.

"Hey," Emma called to me through the open window. I turned around and got into the driver's side of the truck. "Don't sweat it. This isn't new to them."

"They've died before?"

"Maybe once or twice. But they're used to the things that happen in Hell."

I stared straight ahead, my mind on my thoughts rather than what my eyes could see.

"Plus," she added, shifting her shoulders to me. "You'll be long gone by the time they would ever have a chance to get their hands on you. You're safe."

Great. I wasn't even thinking about their vengeance.

Until now.

"How do you know?"

"Because we have a deal, remember?"

Right, the deal. I kill Laila, Emma reigns Hell, and I'm locked out of the depths forever. I help her, and she looks out for me.

If only it felt that simple.

I glanced over to her, the blonde locks of hair swept over her shoulders, her cheeks flushed from her orgasm minutes ago. Her words felt like music in my ears, but then I remembered what she was known for.

Deception.

But, for some reason, this didn't feel like a trick to me.

She leaned forward, her tongue slowly slipping between her lips, and my eyes moved to her mouth.

"You're untouchable, Thomas."

Emma and I pulled up to a motel that was right off the highway. At this point, my body felt sore and exhausted, even though my mind was wide awake. All I wanted to do was find a bed to sleep in. Emma begged me to drive another hour so we could stay in Las Vegas, but the last thing I wanted was a hassle on where to stay and what to do, and I knew she would end up roping me into some sort of late-night activity. I told her we could take a day to go and explore tomorrow, even though she's been there over a thousand times. It was called "Sin City" for obvious reasons, but it really was the perfect place for demons. They don't need to sleep, nor does the city, allowing them twenty-four-seven access to their prey.

It was stereotypical.

So, for now, we're settling for a small, one-story motel. It was covered in neon lights and broken window trim, accompanied by an old, worn road sign and one other car in the lot. Emma and I walked into the tiny, musty office of the motel. An older man looked up at me from his book.

"I'd like a room, please."

He nodded, then looked down at his binder, moving at a glacial pace as he scanned through pages of who-knows-what. I placed my forearms over the counter, tapping my fingers on the top, waiting patiently. Emma glanced around the room, her bag crossed over her chest, her demeanor oddly calm.

The man moved to the wall, his glasses on the edge of his nose, and pulled a key with a red keychain from a hook. "Looks like you guys got the last room."

He handed me the key with a toothy smile, my hand pausing before moving to grab it. There was only one other car in the lot. Either everyone staying here was out to dinner, all at the same time, or this guy was lying, trying to make this place look more popular than it was.

"Only one bed, though," he added with a not-so-subtle wink.

I looked over my shoulder to Emma, who obviously couldn't care less. I really didn't want to share a bed, but I considered it. I just wanted to sleep.

"Is there a couch?"

"A small one. And there's a bar on the other side of the building if you need a drink."

Emma came up next to me and pulled the key out of my hand. "It's fine, Thomas. Relax. I can sleep on the couch."

She did everything but roll her eyes at me as she walked out of the office. She was annoyed, but at what? I wasn't sure.

I pulled out my wallet, fished out two fifty-dollar bills, and handed them to the man. "Thank you." I rushed out after Emma, who was already making her way to our room. She looked down at the keychain, which had a white number four engraved on the red plastic. She stopped at the fourth door and pushed her way inside, not needing the key.

"Emma," I started as she switched on the light and threw her bag on the couch. I followed her in and shut the door behind me. Immediately, I was hit with the typical mildewy smell of a motel room as I scanned the area. It was incredibly small, with dark brown colored walls, a matching bedspread on a full-sized bed, and a loveseat that could barely fit two people. The bathroom was in the corner, the toilet and sink squeezed in next to the standup shower that hosted Anna's ghost, and I shook my head.

We should've kept driving.

"Emma," I repeated.

She looked over her shoulder at me. I placed my stuff down on the bed.

"You're not sleeping on that," I said, pointing to the couch.

She laughed quietly, then turned back to her things, unzipping her bag. "It's fine. I don't sleep anyway, remember?"

I exhaled, squaring my shoulders. "You're not sleeping there."

"Thomas," she began, throwing a shirt down in frustration. "I get it, okay? I understand that you don't want to sleep next to me, or want me here, or even like me. You've made that *very* clear since the beginning. But guess what? I wasn't made to be liked, and I don't need you to fucking like me."

I watched as her eyes flared red, making the hairs on my arm stand on end.

"I need you to *trust* me."

Her chest heaved with anger before she turned back to her bag.

I wanted to trust her, I really did. I wanted to let go, but I couldn't, simply because of who she was and what I've been through. I wanted to believe that her desire to rule Hell outweighed her need to deceive me. And when I think about myself in comparison to the big picture, the eternal vision, it makes sense. I'm just a stepping stone that she's using to get what she wants. And now that I've thought about it, she's been honest about that from the beginning.

But what if she gets what she wants, then goes back on her word to betray me?

I guess that's where the trust comes in.

"Let's go get a drink," I said quietly, motioning to the door. The grungy bed was inviting me to lie down, but my mind was still working in overdrive, and I knew I would only end up staring at the ceiling for hours anyway. Plus, alcohol might help me fall asleep later, as long as I don't drink too much.

I opened the door and held it as Emma slipped on a sweater and followed me out.

"So, let me get this straight," I began, the glass bottle of beer dangling between my fingers. "Your favorite fruit is a *lemon?*"

Emma smiled wide, nodding excitedly. We sat at the bar of a small side room of the motel, which only held four stools, three tables, and an electronic dart board. Two other people sat at the table behind us, lost in their own conversation as a speaker on the other side of the room played some eighties rock music.

I have to say, with a place this small and unknown, I've never felt more hidden in my whole life.

Emma ordered just a plain Sprite, no alcohol, but with an added wedge of lemon, and I ordered whatever beer they had available. I asked her about the lemon wedge, and that's when she told me it was her favorite fruit.

"Out of all the fruits in the world? A lemon?" I repeated, taking a swig of my drink. "Why?"

She didn't hesitate a moment before standing on the rung of the barstool to reach over the counter, the bartender out of sight as she grabbed a whole lemon. She tossed it to herself, catching and gripping it firm as her eyes studied it, the bright yellow rind complimenting her tan hands.

"The peel is bitter and often unwanted, yet people use the zest for cooking so many things. The juice is sour, but only for a moment before turning sweet."

She turned the fruit in her hand, a look of adoration in her eyes.

"It's deceptive."

With a wink to me, she dropped the lemon back over the counter, letting it roll against some glasses. Of course, I should've known she would be narcissistic enough to compare herself to a fruit.

I could feel a sliver of a smile appear, but I pushed it away before Emma could notice. As she took a sip of her drink, I leaned in closer to her.

"Can I ask you something?"

She nodded, swirling the ice in her plastic cup with a straw.

"If there's a Hell, that means there's a Heaven, too. Right?"

Emma stopped, her chin tilted down as she kept her eyes on her drink. "Yes."

"And it's good there?"

She kept her voice level. "Of course."

I swallowed more of my beer, letting the cool liquid ease down my throat. We sat in the sound of the music for a minute before Emma spoke up again.

"That's where you'll be going. As long as we keep our deal, that is."

We both looked at each other at the same time. I raised my eyebrows, thinking about the things I've done in the past forty-eight hours and how they shouldn't warrant me a trip upwards. Even when I look at my life before that, with the strip club, my relationship with my dad, and my relationships with Anna and Laila, I don't think any of it would be pleasing in the eyes of God.

But right now, at this moment, I don't know who I'm trying to please.

"How is that up to you? Doesn't God have to be the one to allow people into Heaven?"

Emma shrugged. "He's not going to turn someone away if they have nowhere else to go."

"So, Heaven is full of Hell's rejects?" A laugh slipped out, one that I couldn't hold in. "Come on, Emma, that sounds ridiculous. I don't think that's how this works."

"Why not?"

I gave her a disbelieving look, and she countered with an inquisitive one, waiting for me to answer her. I ran a hand over my face.

"You're telling me God and Lucifer negotiate over each and every soul and decide on where to put them?" I immediately shook my head, refusing to believe the idea. "God has more power than that."

"You think God has more power than Lucifer?" she questioned me.

"Of course, I do," I began. "He's all-knowing, all-powerful, always good, you know, all that."

Emma's lips turned up in a smile. "You're right. That He is." She took a quick sip of her drink, eyeing me before continuing. "But so is Lucifer. He's all-knowing. All-powerful. And always evil."

The song that was blaring from the speaker ended, leaving the room in a brief silence before a new one began.

"In order for there to be good, there must be evil. The scales must be balanced. If God held all the power, everything would be good, and only good. And in turn, there would be chaos, because humans are flawed, evil exists, and darkness appears every single night."

My eyes remained on hers as she spoke.

"You hear it all the time in church services. The devil is always watching, always trying to move in on the weak, always trying to distract those from God. He's always there, in the shadows, waiting to rule. But it's all the same with God, only with different intent. They are power equals."

Listening closely, I caught each and every one of her words and drank them in. Surprisingly, what she was saying didn't sound completely wrong. Lucifer had all the knowledge and power he needed, except for the opposite reasons.

"Balance, Thomas."

Good and Evil. Heaven and Hell.

I narrowed my eyes. "So, there's no purgatory either?"

"Yes, there is. But in order to be in Purgatory, both God and Lucifer have to agree on placing that person there. If one doesn't agree, they don't go. Then, it's either Heaven or Hell."

I eyed her as she took another sip of her drink, digesting her words. And before I could ask, she answered for me.

"No, Lucifer will not let you into Purgatory. I'll make sure of it."

Good to know that not only do I have Emma on my team, but now I have Lucifer as well. I almost had to laugh at the sound of it all, choking on the thought of Lucifer vouching for me. *Lucifer.* I'm sure if the people behind us overheard our conversation, they would definitely think we were fucking psycho.

I swallowed the last of my beer, then raised my bottle to the bartender, asking for another.

"You really think you have a lot of pull down there, don't you?"

"Not yet," Emma smiled gently, a subtle shake of her head. "But once Lilith is out of the way, I will."

I was put at ease with her confidence. That was something that couldn't be faked. She really wanted this, she wanted her power.

"Speaking of Lilith," she began. "Did you read the letter?"

"No," I said as another beer bottle was placed in front of me, and Emma furrowed her eyebrows.

"Not yet," I corrected. "I will. But I already know what's there. Some stupid, Confucius shit. Something she doesn't mean. It's all just part of her game."

Emma nodded. "Maybe. Or maybe it's something that could be useful to you."

Right after the sentence left her mouth, her confidence faded, and her lips instantly fell. Her shoulders straightened, and her eyes drifted over my shoulder. I turned to look, following the path of her vision, but there was nothing but a blank wall there.

"Emma?" I asked, continuing to look around the bar, not seeing anything out of the ordinary.

She groaned as she pushed her drink away and hopped off the stool. "Give me five minutes, okay?"

"What? Why?" I pulled my wallet out of my back pocket, trying to find bills to leave for the drinks. She put her hand over mine, stopping my search.

"Seriously, Thomas. Give me five minutes. We have an unwanted visitor," she said as she headed out the door, letting it shut behind her.

I took a deep, annoyed breath. Trust. I have to trust her. The look on her face said she wasn't lying, that there actually was someone else here.

But then again, maybe that was just part of a bigger plan.

I ran my hands over the front pocket of my jeans, making sure the ring was still there. It was.

After drinking most of my second beer, I checked the clock again. Seven minutes had passed, and she wasn't back. Did she say she was coming back? I couldn't remember.

Fuck it. I threw some money on the bar and left. The desert air was warm and dry as I walked around the building, my hands on the knife in my hoodie pocket. When I came to the front of the motel, the yellow neon overhead lights brightening the strip of doors ahead, I saw two people standing at my truck. One was Emma, her bright blonde hair cascading down her back, facing away from me with her elbow resting over the side of the bed. The other, I couldn't quite see from where I was standing. I moved closer, keeping my steps quiet and slow.

"What don't you get? You don't need to be checking up on me all the time," Emma said, sounding annoyed.

I inched closer to my truck until the second person came into view.

His black hair was slicked back, a piece of it falling over his forehead as he dug his hands into his pockets. He pulled out a small baggie and offered it to Emma, who then shook her head.

"Fucking hell, Levi. Would you cut the shit?"

Levi.

The demon who I found rummaging through my truck the other day.

He opened the baggie and tilted it on the edge of my tailgate, dumping out a white powder. After he nudged it into a line with a credit card, which was probably stolen, he leaned down and snorted it, his finger pressed against one nostril.

This fucking asshole was doing cocaine off my truck.

"Everything good here?" I stepped into the light and approached my truck.

Emma jumped at the sound of my voice, spinning around to meet my eyes. "Fuck, Thomas. You scared me."

I gave her a sinister smile, cocking my head to the side. "I did, did I?" I let my gaze linger over her chest, watching her catch her breath. "Good to know I'm capable of that."

"Oh, so you'll let this fucking Abercrombie model check on you, but you won't let me? When *he's* the one that's the actual threat?" Levi yelled, wiping loose powder off the bottom of his nose. He reached into the same pocket and pulled out a carton of cigarettes, popping one out and sticking it in his mouth.

"Threat?" I asked, my head still to the side as my eyes flickered from him back to her.

Emma stared at me while Levi lit the cigarette and kept talking.

"Yeah, a threat. She's been hanging around you this whole time while you've been killing others like us. I'm not capable of hurting her, nor would I ever want to. But you," he took a step toward me, blowing smoke in my face. "You could."

He was right. I could.

I've done it three times now. I have the lines etched in my skin to prove it.

Emma stepped in front of me, in between us, keeping me and Levi apart.

"Would I have a reason to hurt Emma?" I asked, my fists tight and my eyes locked on Levi.

She was just as vulnerable in this relationship as I was.

I could kill her, just like she could turn around and kill me. Just like how Laila killed Anna.

I remained tall, keeping myself clear and firm in the conversation. If Levi wanted Emma to betray me, or if Emma had some sort of plan against me, I had a feeling that Levi would tell me. He didn't seem like the kind of person to sugarcoat anything, especially with people he didn't care for.

"Levi, you need to leave," Emma stated firmly.

I took a step closer, my body flush with Emma's back, nudging her as my stare remained on Levi. "I asked a question. Does Emma need to fear me? Would she give me a reason to kill her?"

"Dammit, Thomas!" She shouted, turning around to face me, thrusting her palms into my chest. I stumbled back but caught myself. "Stop! And you stop, too. Both of you need to put your dicks away." She turned to face Levi, who sucked on his cigarette, inhaling with a painted grin on his face. "You don't think I can take care of myself? I've done it this long without any problem." She stuck a pointed finger in his chest, continuing. "You don't know half the shit that's going on here. One slip-up from me, or you, or some other dickhead could ruin this whole thing. I can fill you in some other time, but for now, find some other girl to peg you and stop *fucking* following me."

Levi dropped his smile as he pulled his cigarette from his mouth and balanced it between his pointer and middle fingers. In an instant, he gripped Emma's biceps and threw her against the truck, but she didn't bat an eye at his rage. She simply stared at him, her irises a fire red as he kept her pinned, a small stream of grey lifting from the smoke in his hand.

"Don't you ever talk to me like that again, *bitch*. I have looked out for you since day one, and now you're siding with this fucker? Over me?"

Levi pushed himself into Emma, getting in her face. I slipped off to the side of the truck, out of sight.

"You would be nothing without me. How many times have I saved you, huh? How many times have you called me, needing me, wanting my hard dick shoved in your aching cunt? Begging for my cum to drip out and down your thighs, you desperate *fucking* whore. And now, you're dumping me for what? Lilith's play toy? Some mortal human named '*Diesel?*'"

His words were hushed on her ear, and her head reactively tilted, trying to squeeze him away. She clenched her jaw, her arms still pinned to her side. "Watch what you're saying."

Levi chuckled, showing his chipped, crooked teeth. "Right, right." Then, with a jostle, he pressed his fingertips into her even deeper, the skin on her arms probably bruising under her sweater. "You will always be *mine.*"

I watched as he licked the side of her face, his tongue trailing from her jaw to temple, his nostrils flaring at her taste. Then, he lifted his hand and took one last drag of his cigarette before turning it around and extinguishing the burning end against the wet flesh of her face. A crease formed as Emma scrunched her nose but silently took everything he was giving her. A red, circular burn instantly appeared on her cheek as he threw the cigarette butt to the ground.

I stepped out from the side of my truck, my knife covered in blood from the fresh cut on my left forearm. I rushed to them, coming up on Levi's side, not sparing one second before plunging the blade deep into the side of his neck. His eyes rolled to the back of his head as his body collapsed to the ground.

Fucker.

Emma's mouth dropped open as she stayed glued to my truck, her body frozen in awe.

"Thomas," her voice was quiet as she looked at me with wide, clear eyes.

It wasn't fear or panic that she showed. It was apprehension.

She knew I was sparing no one without a thought.

You fuck with me? *Gone.* You fuck with Emma? *Done.*

I saw her eyes move to my left arm, the sleeve of my sweatshirt pulled up high, showcasing a deep gash on the inside of my forearm. Blood continued to flow as I watched her, my pulse beating in the adrenaline that filled me.

I *will* take down anyone who stands in my way. I *will not* hesitate.

I leaned down to pull the blade from Levi's neck before Emma stopped me.

"Let me," she said, stepping away from the truck and moving to where I was standing. She squatted down, placed her hand on his shoulder for leverage, and pulled the knife out with a swift motion. With the sound of his flesh tearing and the blood pouring onto the concrete, I noticed a white envelope sticking out of his back pocket. I quickly leaned down and pulled it out, safely tucking it away into my sweatshirt without looking.

Emma stood to face me, keeping the blade in front of her face, eyeing the red shimmer of the fresh blood. The lights from the motel reflected onto the liquid, flashing me gently as Emma rotated the handle in her grasp. She smiled at the sight before bringing the knife to her lips, sliding the blade slowly into her mouth, tasting the salty blood of the demon at her feet.

The corner of her mouth sliced open as she slid the blade in further, not a single wince of pain on her face. As she pulled the knife back out, the sharp edge continuing to cut her lips, she opened her mouth and let her tongue swirl around the tip, creating little marks on her tongue as well.

She was tasting not only Levi's blood, but mine and hers mixed together also.

Emma licked the blade completely clean, her spit leaving a shiny finish on the steel. Flipping it around, she handed it back to me handle first, and I took it and placed it back in its holder. The knife fit snugly against my back as I tucked it into the waistband of my jeans. Emma wiped her lips clean with the sleeve of her sweater, the corner of her mouth still split open and bleeding, but she didn't seem to care.

The fact that there was a dead demon right next to us would've been worrisome in any other circumstance, sending me running, but right now, it felt like the most unreal thing in the world. I felt powerful, I felt high and drunk on it. Here I was, completely fucking relentless, with someone in my corner that understood parts of me that I couldn't understand myself. Emma was opening doors for me that I didn't even know existed, and she was confident in not only me, but in herself that she could take me to where I wanted to be.

I trusted her.

EMMA

The one demon that has stuck by my side for almost all eternity was gone. All it took was the blood of one human to send him back down into the chains of Hell, where the torture is the highest, the hardest, and the most intense. I sighed, knowing I'll probably never see him again. He was lying on the slab of pavement behind me, like a dead animal on the side of the highway, his blood in a puddle beneath him.

And I didn't feel a single ounce of anything.

No sadness, no grief, no anger, no pain. Nothing.

Not that I *could,* anyway. We aren't capable of feeling much. Desire, rage, and excitement are the things we can feel, and most events we experience on Earth can trigger some sort of variation of those.

But not now. I don't care about anything right now, other than the human standing in front of me.

I could feel myself holding in a giddy laugh. Who would have ever thought a mere human could keep me in line like this?

For some reason, his drive keeps me driven. His focus keeps me focused.

And it wasn't because Lilith laid claim to him.

Maybe that was a reason for my motives in the beginning, to climb higher with the one person that could get her attention.

But now, things are different.

I can see the allure of him. Of course, he's beautiful on the outside; anyone could see that. But it's also in the way he shoots me a knowing look, a glance that cuts right through me, sending me into the highest levels of temptation. The way his breathing steadies me, constantly keeping me balanced.

Maybe it was because I could almost taste the beginning of my reign in Hell, but this, standing here with Thomas, was different than anything I had experienced before.

It felt like a reign on Earth.

I looked over my shoulder to Levi, his body limp and pathetic. It almost felt like a relief, having him gone. He was one less thing to have on my mind.

"I'll take care of this," I said to Thomas without looking at him. "Go."

There was a brief moment of pause before I heard him turn and go, his footsteps heavy on the walk to our room. I heard the sound of the motel door click as I kneeled back down to Levi's body.

"Sorry it had to end, pal."

But not *too* sorry.

I knew that if the tables were turned, he wouldn't be sorry either.

I ran my hand along his face, feeling the heat of his skin slowly begin to turn cold. I made my way down to his pants pocket and reached in, pulling out the carton of cigarettes he had shoved inside. I plucked one out, grabbed his lighter and lit it, the end glowing bright orange. I didn't put it between my lips, simply because I fucking hated the taste of tobacco. All I did was hold it, watching the ash grow as the paper faded back. Once there was a decent amount of heat and smoke, I tapped the ash off, grabbed Levi's chin and tilted him to me, and shoved the searing cigarette in his eyeball. Fumes of burnt tissue surrounded me as his eyeball began to liquefy. I then relit the cigarette, watching the fire burn the cheap paper again, then did the same to his other eye. I did this over and over, using multiple cigarettes and alternating eyes until I was content. The scent of the melting organ filled my nose and lungs, satisfying me in ways Levi never could.

I stood up, dropped the cigarette butts to the ground, and squashed them with my boot. Looking down at Levi, his eyes now two black holes, I smiled.

Fucker.

Now, it was time to clean up Thomas' mess.

With one last look at Levi, I closed my eyes, inhaling deeply.

Then I opened them, and he was gone.

Just like that.

The body was gone, the smell had vanished, the burn on my cheek disappeared, and the pavement was clean.

Like no one was ever here, like nothing had ever happened.

I walked past the truck and under the yellow lights that illuminated the doors until I came to ours. I stood outside, staring at the number four that was screwed onto the surface before placing my hand on the doorknob. With my touch, I could feel Thomas on the other side of the door.

He was waiting for me.

I couldn't tell if he was angry, or worried, or relaxed. All I could feel was him waiting.

Taking another deep breath, I opened the door slowly to see him standing, facing me, his hands in his jean pockets. He still wore his black sweatshirt, both sleeves doused in his own blood, with his face flushed from the rush of the kill and his hair a tousled, light brown mess. I clicked the door closed behind me, and without a single word spoken between us, he rushed to me, closing the gap and pinning me to the closed door. My stare locked onto his as his eyes never left mine, not for a second, filling me with an erotic heat between my legs. He placed his palm flat on the door above my head, bringing his other hand to my jaw, his thumb stroking it gently.

I could see the passion pouring out of him. His body was tense with need and aching for release.

The other demons could get him off, sure. It was easy to suck him dry and make him come, but none of them connected with him on a deeper level. Humans craved intimacy, and Thomas was no exception. The other demons only satisfied what he allowed them to see, but with me, I could feel myself in his soul. We had that connection, we had that bond, and I knew that he felt it too. What the other demons did with him was all on the surface.

With me, intimacy is spiritual.

His fingers lightly lifted my chin, his touch almost *too* gentle for my liking, before taking a moment to drink me in. I knew exactly what he was thinking. This was wrong. What he was feeling, what he was thinking, it was all wrong. This went against all his morals and everything he was taught.

Now was his chance to stop something he would later come to regret.

To stop everything before it even started.

But he didn't.

His lips crashed onto mine without fear, without any trepidation in his choices. And fuck, his kiss was *anything* but soft and easy. It was passionate, erotic, and intense. My lips pressed hard onto his, the craving for him growing stronger every moment we were connected. Our mouths fit together perfectly, with our noses brushing against each other as we tilted our heads, needing to be closer. His hands moved down to the backs of my thighs, and he lifted me up effortlessly, with my legs wrapping around his waist and my arms locking around his neck. He carried me to the bed, never breaking our kiss as his hands remained clutched on my ass. I could feel his legs hit the mattress, his body leaning over and dropping me down onto the bed. I immediately ripped off my sweater and jeans, revealing a white lace bra and matching thong. I moved to take those off as well before Thomas stopped me. He ripped off his hoodie and t-shirt, his chest tight and toned, his golden skin smooth as I let my hands roam. I looked at his arms; the left was still dripping fresh blood from the gash he made to kill Levi, and the right was patched with dried blood from killing Noma, the wound slowly beginning to dry and recover. But both were muscular and tethered with veins, strong and ruthless in the fight for his vengeance.

Fuck, those arms were hitting a certain spot in me.

Thomas leaned down and began kissing my neck, the feeling sending jolts through my body. His lips made their way to my collarbone, his teeth digging into my skin as his hips pressed into mine, the bulge in his jeans obvious. A small moan escaped me as his breath heated my chest.

This was the one, absolute best thing about being in a human body. Sex.

Even though I'm a demon, I'm still in a human body, which means I'm still capable of getting off just like everyone else. But sometimes, since my soul is attached to another realm, since my spirit is not of this Earth, my senses are heightened and my body takes me to places no mortal human can go. That's why demons are always known for lusting after others or fucking until their bodies give out. We can feel things that no one else can, that no one else could come close to understanding.

Thomas made his way lower, his mouth trailing over my bra before he reached up and pulled it down, exposing my breasts. His hand grabbed one, his fingers rolling and pinching my nipple as he took the other in his mouth, his tongue licking and his teeth scraping. I fully removed the bra and arched my back, the feelings already beginning to be too much as goosebumps lined every inch of my skin.

Even though I didn't want him to stop, he moved lower, trailing kisses the entire path down my stomach, ending at my thong. His fingertips trailed the hem before yanking it down, tearing it off my legs, and throwing it on the floor. He kneeled in front of me, on the floor, his hands under my knees, spreading me wide. I had no shame, no shyness. I just wanted pleasure, and I wanted it from *him*.

His mouth started on the inside of my thigh, and my legs started to shake from the desire my body needed to give in to. He licked my leg, his tongue gliding up the skin before meeting my center, his lips gently brushing against my clit. The stubble that lined his chin grazed me, heightening the sensation that I was already giving into. I grabbed his hair, my hands tugging anything I could find, and pulled his face into my pussy harder. His tongue danced in and on me, taking me higher as my body suffocated him. He didn't falter, he only increased his intensity as his name rolled easily off my lips.

"Oh my God, Thomas."

He moved his thumb into the mix, rubbing my clit in a circular motion, matching the path of his tongue. My eyes drifted back into my skull, and I could feel myself bite my lower lip, breaking the skin and making it bleed. With the taste of my own blood, I almost came right then and there. My pull on his hair tightened, and I could see the muscles in his shoulders constrict, his pain my pleasure and his pleasure my pain.

Unable to bear it anymore, I grabbed his face and pulled him up to me, wanting to delay the inevitable orgasm and make this last as long as possible. His face glistened with my wetness as I kissed him, tasting all of me on him, including the blood from my lip. His lips suctioned to mine, his hunger growing with the different flavors of me as he crawled on the bed over me. I could see the look on his face, the one that said he was ready to go all in. I shook my head.

"Not so fast," I pushed my palm into his chest. He stopped, a flash of puzzlement sweeping over him before I turned and pushed him down on the bed, flat on his back. I swung my leg over his body, straddling him, feeling his dick pulse under me.

"Your knife?" I asked, my hand out and palm up. Thomas moved his hands to his back, pulling the knife from the waistband of his jeans. There was a brief moment of hesitancy before he placed the handle into my palm. I smirked, knowing full well that that was a trust move, and pulled the knife from its holder. I eyed the clean blade, the silver shimmering under the dull motel lighting, then looked at Thomas. I turned the blade to myself, the tip pointing at the notch between my collarbones. Thomas blinked, his eyes wide as he waited for my next move. Slowly, I dragged the knife down my chest, in a line between my breasts, all the way down to the top of my belly button. A trail of skin parted, the crimson blood dripping down in a race, my breathing growing rapid with the pain and pleasure mixed as one. I could see Thomas' gaze studying me, watching the streaks of blood run down my warm flesh, my nipples hard and pointed.

It was an invitation to him, to drink me, to take me in fully, to become a part of me.

Wrapping his hands around my back, he sat up and pulled me closer. I let my arms rest on his shoulders, tossing the knife to the floor as he leaned down, his tongue flat on my skin, and began to lick upward. I shuddered, the feeling complete bliss as he lapped up the blood, the red liquid filling his mouth, his throat moving to swallow it. He made his way up, his face nuzzled in my chest as he continued, drinking me in. I let my head fall back, a deep groan creeping up from my lungs, my pussy so fucking wet from the rush. He got to the top of the cut, right at the base of my throat, and he pulled my body flush against his, his bloody lips planting kisses all over my shoulders and neck. My hips began to trust mindlessly as the pressure in his jeans remained firm. I looked down at him right as he stopped to look up at me, his nose, mouth, and chin all covered in my blood. I kissed him again, tasting it all, him and I as one.

I pushed him back down on the bed, his torso bouncing on the mattress as I reached for his belt, unbuckling it and moving it out of the way. I unbuttoned his jeans and slid them down, his body lifting to help me.

"You don't think I'm going to sit back and let the others know how you taste without me knowing myself, are you?" I asked, tilting my head to the side as I gripped the band of his underwear. He grinned, and I smiled back, both sets of our teeth stained vibrant red. I pulled the fabric down, his cock bounding free, hard as a fucking rock.

I leaned down, letting my breasts rub against his length, my excess blood coating his skin. At this point, the blood was spread all over me, like paint on a canvas. I used the tip of his cock to paint my breasts, the blood mixing with his pre-cum to cover my nipples. He bit down, his jaw tense and ticking as he tried to suppress his euphoria. It took everything in me to keep my composure, to take it slow, and to not slam his hard cock deep inside me.

Moving myself lower, I wrapped my hand around him and moved to the bottom of his shaft, my tongue sliding from the base to the tip. Thomas groaned, and I looked to him, his face still bloody, my eyes not leaving his as I spit on the tip of his dick, letting the red saliva drip down his entirety. He watched my every move, his composure struggling to stay in check as his breathing grew ragged. I stroked him gently, wanting to build the tension, even though I knew I could set him off in a matter of seconds.

I tightened my grip on his cock, his skin wet and slick with each pump. I leaned down, my mouth opening for him as I teased him, my tongue lingering on his tip. I took him in, swirling him around from cheek to cheek, playing with the head of his dick. Adding in a little playfulness, I used my teeth to softly scrape all the way down, then suck all the way up, popping off the tip like a lollipop.

I grinned, a small moan slipping between the spaces of my teeth. "No wonder why they couldn't get enough of you. You taste like Heaven."

Thomas picked his head up to look at me directly. "You know what Heaven tastes like?"

I squeezed his cock in my hand, the appendage jolting at my touch. "Of course I do. You have to know what Heaven is like in order to handle Hell."

He threw his head back down on the pillow as I sucked on him again.

"And you, my angelic devil," I said, popping my lips, "taste like the raindrops from the clouds of nirvana."

Thomas let out a deep rumble as I continued to work my mouth, his body signaling that he was near the edge. With one final lick, not wanting him to finish just yet, I let him go and crawled up to him, my blood still coating both of our faces and my body. I reveled in the image of us. It was something only a devil could love, both of us so unhinged and deranged, the act so primal and raw.

Our lips connected once again in a kiss that couldn't be defeated. I rubbed my body all over him, spreading the flowing blood everywhere, the drips falling down his sides and onto the bedsheets. I circled my hips onto him, his cock nestled under my bones. By pulling me tight and palming my ass, his desire to become closer was obvious. He was basically trying to crawl inside my skin.

I moved to the side of his head, my red lips close to his ear. "Weren't you ever taught to not play with the devil?"

His mouth closed in on my neck, sending a rare chill down my spine. His hand threaded through my hair, smearing blood throughout the strands as he spoke through clenched teeth. "Your demons play well with mine."

I let out a breathy laugh. He only knew of the Earthly side of me and my powers. If he knew about the things that I've done in Hell, I think things would be a little different.

With a light lift of my hips and a quick adjustment from Thomas, he thrust hard at my entrance, sending himself straight in. I closed my eyes, letting out a heavy whimper as he filled me completely. Hearing his breathing increase in pace made my insides heat, knowing he was feeling the effects of my body intertwined with his.

"Fuck, Emma," he whispered so quietly I could barely hear it over the waves of pleasure in my ears.

I knew this was his first time having actual sex since his girlfriend died.

Who, by the way, was watching us over in the corner of the room.

The thought of her standing there made my clit throb.

I love putting on a good show.

I rocked my hips, lifting and dropping, sliding his cock in and out slowly, feeling every inch of him surround me. I succumbed to every feeling that approached, letting the action speak for itself as Thomas worked in me. I sat up, fresh blood still glistening on my front as I rode him. My knees took the power, lifting and dropping me on his dick, the sounds of us slapping together filling the room. His hands were gripped on my hips, his fingertips digging into me, leaving little red welts in their wake.

I could feel the instant my soul elevated from my body, taking me to the highest realm of existence. There was a beam of light shining through my vision, illuminating my bliss, giving me the maximum amount of oxytocin. It filled me, almost to the point where I needed the overflow to expel, whether it be through my cum, my blood, or even vomit.

As I said, demon sex is an entirely different ball game.

I've had sex for centuries, millennia even, and about ninety percent of the time, it has satisfied me and left me content. Most of the men and women I've been with, demon or not, have been excellent partners. There have been a few that were lacking the drive and desire to get me off, instead wanting their satisfaction only, and I've never wasted my time with them more than once.

But *Thomas*.

Thomas reminds me why humans are so susceptible to love.

Why they crave each other's closeness in the form of intimacy.

Why they rely on each other for more than just orgasms.

And look, here I am, telling Thomas to use me for release instead of focusing on the connection.

A part of me ached at the thought that I could not feel that same connection that Thomas does. I wish I could know the feeling of missing someone, or enjoying someone, or even falling in love with someone. But all I can do is see how it looks from the outside and try to portray what it would be like on the inside.

And the closest thing I can do to conjure up any sort of feeling is to have sex.

I looked down at Thomas, his skin glistening with a layer of blood and sweat, the scar on his neck turning a shade of light red. My fingertips grazed on the vertical line as I closed my eyes again, the feeling of the raised bump sending me back to that night at Stoney's. I could see Lilith, standing before Thomas, completely covered in her own blood. She has his knife in her hand, a knife different than the one he carries with him now, and I could see the fury in her eyes.

She was mad. Furious.

Not only was she angry, but she was hurt.

And we all know how the saying goes.

Hurt people hurt people.

In a quick, fluid motion, I saw her hand swipe down Thomas' neck, creating the scar that my hand now touched.

I pulled away, not wanting Thomas to know what I was just watching. But by the continued movements of his hips and the groans trapped in his throat, I don't think he noticed a thing. My palms caressed his chest, feeling his toned, firm muscles under me, taking me back into the moment. Then, before I knew it, Thomas wrapped his arm around me and flipped me over to my back. He propped himself up on his knees as I lifted my hips off the bed, allowing him a deeper angle. His body thrust into mine, the lust cutting through me like a dagger. I took in the sight of him, his body like a fucking god as he took his power, taking over his dominance, losing himself in me. In us.

"Emma, *fuck*, you feel so *fucking* good."

I smiled at his words, watching as the beads of sweat mixed with the blood painted on him.

His vision caught on something to his right, and I followed his gaze to the corner of the room where the ghost resided. He squeezed his eyes shut, tucking his chin down as his movements slowed, just barely, as his momentum fell off tempo.

"Thomas?" I asked, faking my confusion. "What is it?"

He didn't answer, but instead continued his thrusts.

"Thomas, is it her?" I asked, even though I knew it was. I lifted my hand to his chin. "Look at me."

He ignored my request.

"Please."

He paused his body, squinting his eyes open, peeking at me. His eyes locked on mine.

"Focus on me, okay? Only me."

He gave a slight nod before beginning to fuck me again. Thankfully, he remained hard, the erection still strong and hitting all the right spots. I let him shift to the side, angling his back to the ghost.

"It's just us, Thomas. You and me."

I sat up and pulled him out of me, only for a moment as I turned my body around. With him still on his knees, I backed myself up to him, my ass pressed against his hips. Reaching down, I guided him back into my swollen entrance, the area still soaking wet for him. His hands grasped my hips, our rhythm steady as he came back to me. I reached up and over my shoulders, my hands sliding around the back of his neck, bringing his face to mine. We kissed as we fucked, the sensations transcending what I could've imagined.

His hands slowly moved to the cut down the center of my torso. He trailed his middle finger up, collecting more blood on the tip until he reached the top. Then, as his mouth pulled away from mine, he stuck his finger in his mouth, his taste for me insatiable.

He couldn't get enough.

With that same middle finger, he brought it down to my clit, rubbing it, the feeling accenting the movements of his throbbing dick. I moaned, feeling the climax approach, my back arching against his chest.

Fuck, holy *fuck*.

His other hand came up to my throat, gripping the front with ease, squeezing my trachea tight. His pumping became more furious, speeding up with the rumbles of his throat.

"Fuck, Emma, I'm going to come." His voice came out broken and full of edge.

My pussy squeezed at the mention of his orgasm. I held it tight, milking him for all he had as he let it all go inside me, still holding my throat. The waves of my euphoria hit me at the same time, my body rocking and jerking right alongside his. Our lungs were panting in unison as we both came down from our high, our bodies tired and defeated as he released my throat.

Remaining at my back, Thomas dropped his forehead onto my shoulder, still trying to catch his breath. I smirked, knowing everything that just happened was something he needed. Not just for himself, but for us, for our mission. He needed clarity, he needed release, he needed relaxation. And if he needs it all again later, I'd be more than happy to do it all again.

I reached over and touched his bicep, beginning to turn to face him, but he instinctively moved away from me. It was a subtle movement, but it was enough for me to notice. Leaning back, his body resting on his heels, I watched as he rubbed his blood-coated jaw, refusing to make eye contact with me.

"Thomas?" I asked, and this time I was genuine.

He simply shook his head as he silently got off the bed, his back to me as he found his boxer briefs off the floor. I crossed my arms, making the vertical cut, and all the blood from it, disappear. He hesitated before turning back to look at me, and as soon as he saw that I was healed and clean, an insincere laugh escaped him. He looked down at his chest and saw his own skin still completely covered.

"I'm going to shower. Get some rest." He nodded to the bed that I was still sitting on, clearly wanting some distance from me. It's fine, I can take a hint.

He walked into the bathroom, shutting and locking the door behind him, taking his ghost with him.

Once again, I was here, wishing I could feel something.

THOMAS

What the fuck have I done? What in the actual fucking *fuck* have I gotten myself into? I let my dick think for itself for one fucking minute, and the next thing I know, I'm balls-deep in Emma, listening to her moan my name through her pretty little mouth. I regretted everything the second we finished and I pulled myself out of her. Dammit, I shouldn't have crossed that line.

But God, did it feel fucking *phenomenal.* Just the thought of her naked, bloody, and wet for me is getting my cock hard again.

Fuck. No. *Fuck.*

I ducked my head down, letting the water from the shower run over and off my face, closing my eyes at the feeling. I had completely washed the blood off about ten minutes ago, but I couldn't find it in me to turn the water off. I wasn't ready to face what was on the other side of the door.

I even fucking came inside her without thinking. Who, in their right mind, would come inside a fucking demon? Who knows what I just unlocked? I never thought twice about protection with Anna, even though we talked about it on multiple occasions, only because if she were to ever get pregnant, it would be the best thing to ever happen to me. It would be an absolute dream to start a family with her.

Fuck.

I slammed my hand on the white tiled shower wall, a thrash of pain running up my arm at the thought of Anna and the life we could've had. The life that was stolen from her.

With the water still running down my face, I turned to look at the bathroom door, where Anna stood, watching me.

The steam surrounded us, making it hard to see her through the clouds.

But nothing had changed. Her expression remained blank, her strawberry hair still moved with an unknown breeze, and her scar still stretched across her forehead. She still wore my shirt that dropped to the middle of her thighs, and her eyes never left me.

Even as I fucked someone else.

I forced myself to make eye contact with her, to face her, and to face what I had done.

And if I'm being honest, I'm angry at the way I would do it again.

As much as I was in love with Anna, I have to accept the fact that she is gone. I'll never get to kiss her, fuck her, hold her ever again. I have to move on, I have to live my life, I have to find happiness.

But having her here, watching me at every moment of every day is making it fucking hard.

I have to right this. Her soul needs to rest.

She needs to find peace as far away from me as possible.

There was a soft click of the bathroom door as I watched the handle twist. I straightened and turned my body, letting the hot water beat against my back, warming and relaxing my muscles. The door opened, and in walked Emma, still naked. The giant cut on her torso was gone, along with all the blood that came with it. She made it disappear moments after we were done fucking. She was now perfectly fine as she stepped into the bathroom, watching me as I let the water roll down my body. I switched my focus to the floor, eyeing the drain at my feet. Emma moved her hand to the glass shower door, about to slide it open before I spoke.

"No."

She looked at me, her breathing steady.

"Emma, don't." I clenched my jaw. I don't need her in here with me. I need space. I need to clear my head.

Emma's eyes moved down to my cock, which was already half-hard at the sight of her. Her lips pulled up into a smile as she eased open the door and stepped inside. The spray of the warm water bounced off me and hit her skin, creating goosebumps all over, causing her nipples to harden. I closed my eyes, wishing this away, wanting to hold myself strong in my willpower.

But the desires of my flesh were stronger than the urge to resist.

I felt her step closer, her smooth legs against mine, the water flowing between us like a river. She pressed her body against me, her breasts slippery against my torso, making me fully hard. My cock raised against the bottom of her stomach, making her bite her bottom lip with a smile. I reached up, my thumb grazing her lip, and pulled it out from her teeth. Her hands rubbed all over my body, the water rushing over my shoulder to the valley between us.

There was no use resisting anymore. I had already tasted the apple, I might as well eat the whole thing.

"Is this what you want, Emma?" My hand trailed down to her jaw, coaxing her now wet skin. "You want me to fuck you into oblivion? You want to keep me all to yourself?"

My hand moved down her neck as she stared at me, her eyelids lowered.

"You want to scream my name every night as others scream in torture below us?"

Emma let out a dark laugh, the thought pleasing to her. And it didn't even faze me.

"What about Laila? You think when she finds out about us, she'll be okay with it?" I asked it as more of a threat, knowing there was no way this would go over smoothly.

A hint of a smile appeared on her lips. "You'd be an idiot to think she doesn't already know."

I paused, knowing Emma was right.

I have your blood, Thomas.

Laila's words rang in my head from that night at Stoney's. She tasted my blood, forever entangling me to her. That's how Anna's ghost was always with me. That's how she knew.

She knew about the other demons, the killings, the orgasms, and finding the letters.

She knew where I was and where I was going.

It was all a game to her, and I was simply a pawn.

What a fucking joke.

"She's tied to you, Thomas." Emma trailed her finger up my chest, the simple movement creating heat. "Just like me."

I blinked as her words stilled me. I thought back to the sex earlier, and how I tasted her warm blood. Then I thought of the moment I killed Levi, and the vision of Emma licking the blade clean.

She has my blood, too.

We are connected. We are tied.

And this time, I'm not bothered by it. Maybe it's because this isn't out of hatred or wrath like it was with Laila. This isn't a punishment.

We are a team.

With my hand still lingering over her neck, my other hand slid between her legs and onto her wet center, slick from both her arousal and the water. I pushed one finger in, then another, easing in and out slowly. My thumb pressed on her clit, causing her to release a moan, a grin forming on my lips. Her eyelids fluttered closed as she tipped her head back.

"Tell me you want this, Emma," I whispered into her neck, my lips on her exposed skin like a predator on its prey. My fingers continued as I kissed her throat between breaths. "Tell me you want me. Only me."

She hiked her leg up, wrapping it around my waist, giving me better access to her entrance. I finger-fucked her faster, not trying to be gentle in the least bit. I needed her to tell me I was the only one she was working with. I needed her to be with me and only me. I needed her validation and exclusivity.

But she kept her lips closed.

I pulled my fingers out, causing her to whimper in their withdrawal. I lowered myself slightly, creating the right angle before moving my rock-hard dick to her pussy and slamming it inside, not wanting to wait for another second. Emma gasped, the movement making both of our heads spin.

I can't believe it felt this *fucking* good.

Her head moved to my shoulder as my arm wrapped under her ass, basically lifting her to fuck her.

"Tell me, Emma," I whispered in her ear, pushing her wet hair away with my free hand. "I know you feel it."

Her loyalty to me these past few days has been telling. I know she has a motive, and she needs me to achieve her highest ranking. But the look in her eyes tells me there's more to it than just me helping her meet an end goal.

I thrust in and out, my cock throbbing at the feeling of her tight, slick walls wrapped around me. She let out a deep moan, her tits bouncing under the water like the fucking temptress she is.

"Tell me."

I grabbed the back of her neck as I turned us around, so that she was fully under the water, and I was getting the excess. My grip was firm as I kept her face under the stream, not letting her move away to catch her breath. My cock was still buried deep inside of her, and I could feel her muscles contracting at her panic.

I knew she couldn't die, not by this. That was evident. But that didn't mean I couldn't do a little torturing of my own.

"Thomas," her voice came out garbled as the water filled her mouth.

I felt her buck backward, trying her best to find her way out of the water. But my hold remained strong, keeping her exactly where I wanted her. Her leg dropped from my waist, but I kept my arm under her, not letting her fall away from me. Her toes barely touched the shower floor as she scrambled to get her footing. I could see her eyes open, the blue irises transitioning to a shade of red as she continued to push back.

Her fingertips dug into my arms as I held her tight against me. It had to be uncomfortable, breathing in all that water and feeling it enter your lungs. Maybe it felt like glass in her chest.

Maybe it even burned.

"Tell me, baby," my voice was dark and rough as I squeezed her neck harder, my dick filling her fully, feeling the climax approach. Something stirred inside me as I saw her struggle to fight, watching as she lost control, and I gained it.

Her mouth opened again as she gasped for anything other than water, her blonde hair soft and soaked down her back. I felt her squeeze around my length, her body growing stiff and rigid as she let out a cry.

She was coming.

The realization sent me to the same place as I let myself go inside of her, the waves rocking my body with hers. I let my cum fill her, the creamy liquid coating every inch of her insides as I drained it all.

All I had was one taste, and now I couldn't stop.

I let go of her and she instantly fell to the shower floor, her lungs expelling every bit of water that she had ingested. She coughed and vomited, all of it spiraling down the drain under her. Her hands propped her up as her hair fell over her face. I turned the water off once everything was gone and the floor was clean.

Emma looked up at me, her eyes filled with something I couldn't recognize.

It almost looked like pride.

"You and me," she said, still trying to catch her breath, a smile flashing over her face. "It's only us."

I squatted down to her level, holding out my hand for her. She took it and I helped her stand, her legs slightly wobbly as she got to her feet. I held her, steadying her, and looked down as she raised her chin to me. Without a second to spare, I leaned down and kissed her.

It's only us.

After a minute, she pulled away and stepped out of the shower, grabbing a towel from the clean stack against the wall. She wrapped it around her body, tucking it in at her chest. Then, with a quick glance back at me, she smiled and walked out of the bathroom, walking past Anna on the way out.

THOMAS

My leg bounced up and down as I stared at the letters in front of me. There were two envelopes that still needed to be opened. As I sat on the edge of the motel bed, I grabbed the first one, the one that we found in Noma's office. Suspense filled me with an unknown dread as I ripped the seam and pulled out the paper.

There is no better feeling than being where you know you belong. Finding that effortless life is like opening your eyes only to see that you're actually waking from a coma. One day is good, but the next day is better. Let yourself go, along with all other expectations, as your mind wanders through a cloud. Fill your days with things that will keep you exactly where you need to be. Knowing your path doesn't mean you need to slow down. Only those who fight for what they want will know what to do. Through your actions, you will inherit your belief.
I will be here.
The light has been darkened.

Now come find me.

My heart is with yours in the place unseen.

I put the paper down on the bed beside me, my eyes wide with disbelief.

Now come find me.

This is it. She's actually telling me to come to her.

She's summoning me.

I scanned over the sentence one hundred times.

Now come find me.

Holy fuck.

"Anything good?"

Emma sat down on the bed next to me, and I handed her the paper. She scanned it, soaking in every word that was handwritten in front of her. With a quick exhale, she handed it back to me, then got off the bed. She walked over to her bag and began to shuffle through her things.

I watched her, confused. "Well?"

She paused on one of her t-shirts before looking at me, as if it was all so obvious. "Let's go find her."

Raising my eyebrows, I let out a huff. "Yeah, obviously. That's what we've been doing."

Emma rolled her eyes and turned back to her bag, grabbing her Harvard sweatshirt and pulling it on.

"Do you have any idea where she could be?" I asked.

"No," Emma responded, untucking her hair from the sweatshirt and fanning it out behind her.

Fuck, she was beautiful, and I couldn't help but feel caught up in it all. After our shower last night, I passed out on the bed with her lying next to me, her body fitting into the curl of mine. It was as comfortable as a motel bed could be, but it was the best night's sleep I had in a while. I forgot how nice it was to have someone next to me, just being there with me.

But when I woke, I felt like I had one hundred needles stabbed into my chest. This isn't what I should be doing. This can't be where my focus lies.

I needed to get my head on straight, and I needed to stop drinking the poison off her lips.

Feeling tethered in my regrets, I looked out the window and watched the purple and orange sky turn to a light shade of blue. It's just past sunrise, and we are back to reality, deciding what the next step should be.

On the nightstand to my side, my phone vibrated with a quick buzz. I turned and pulled out the charger, eyeing the screen. There was a message from Soren.

Soren: Hey, sorry to bother you so early. Ever since I saw you, this whole thing has been on my mind constantly. I can't stop thinking about Brock and if I made the right choice or not.

Before I could even finish reading it, more messages came through.

Soren: I thought I did, but after we talked, I'm not sure.
Soren: Actually, never mind. Sorry if I woke you.

Without hesitation, I began texting her back.

Me: First, don't ever think you're bothering me. You're not. I know how hard it can be to feel alone in this, so if you ever need to talk, let me know. Don't bottle it up.
Me: Second, don't doubt yourself. You made the right choice. Don't let anyone tell you otherwise.

After watching her typing bubble come and go for a minute, she responded.

Soren: Thank you.

Lowering my head, I closed my eyes as I gripped my phone. This was so unfair. Soren, someone who was innocent and blameless in this whole mess, has been so fucked mentally by Laila's games and my questioning that she was beginning to distrust everything. Maybe if I had kept my nose out of her business, this wouldn't be happening. I could picture her, wide awake and lying in bed, unable to sleep through the night because of the weight of the war in her mind. She took that extra year of her brother's life and now sees it as something tragic.

She doesn't deserve this. John doesn't deserve this. Anna doesn't deserve this.

The need to protect Soren was growing stronger by the day. I couldn't change the past, but I can keep it from happening to anyone ever again.

She needs to keep that extra year close to her, simply for her own sanity.

But then I looked at Emma as she sorted through her jeans and remembered the things we did last night. The things *I* wanted to do, the things *I* initiated.

And I know that Soren can't be involved in a life like this. She deserves better than that.

With no more texts from Soren, I placed my phone back onto the nightstand, tucked the letter back into the envelope, and laid it on the bed. I grabbed the next one, the one from Levi's pocket. There was something different about this one, but I couldn't place my finger on it. The envelope was the same, the weight was the same, but there was something off, aside from the front being completely blank. Maybe it was in the way I found it. Maybe it wasn't meant for me. I don't even know how Levi came to have it. All I knew was I had to tell Emma about it. We were in this together, and she already got mad that I hid the first one from her. And if the roles were reversed, I'd be pissed if she hid something from me.

"There's another one," I said, my voice hushed, even though it was only the three of us in the room.

Emma snapped her head to me, her face contorted into confusion. "What?"

I held up the envelope, flaunting the white paper.

"Where did you get that?"

"It was in Levi's pocket. I found it after I killed him."

Her eyes remained unblinking as they moved from the letter to my face. "Open it."

Sliding my thumb into the seam, I ripped it open at the fold. I pulled the paper out and opened it.

Don't trust her.

I blinked, staring at the three words in front of me. It was definitely meant for me, from Laila. It was in the same handwriting as the other letters. I looked to Emma, who was eyeing me suspiciously, then back to the paper. I could feel my pulse quicken, trying to think of a way to handle this without it exploding back at me.

"What does it say?" Emma asked, her hands on her hips.

I rubbed my index finger along my lip, trying to stall for time, but there was no way around it. I handed the paper to Emma so she could read it herself. She took it, looked at it for a few seconds, then handed it back.

"Typical."

I furrowed my eyebrows, surprised that she wasn't angrier. "What?"

She shrugged a shoulder, then went back to organizing the clothes in her bag. "She knows we're close to finding her. And she also knows we're friends. She's trying to get in your head." She closed the zipper and walked back to the bed, acting completely casual as she stood in front of me. "It was a weak attempt, but I figured she would try it at some point."

I inhaled Emma's scent, her skin and clothes and hair smelling like citrus. She took the letter from me, placed it on the bed, then wrapped her arms around my neck. I grabbed her hips as her body fit perfectly between my legs.

"Honestly, I'm surprised that's all she wrote. You would think she would try a little harder."

I nodded in agreement, even though I didn't agree. Emma may know Laila better than I do, but Laila knows me better than Emma does. Laila was simple and straight to the point. She didn't need to say anything else, because she knew those three words would get through to me. Even if it was just a little bit.

Those three words made me question things.

Emma leaned over, pressing herself to me, letting her lips hover over mine. "By the way," she began, changing the topic. "I didn't know you had it in you, Thomas. I haven't had sex that good in a long time."

Her lips reached mine, bringing me out of my thoughts and back into my body, the feeling just as good now as it was last night. She slid her tongue into my mouth, my lips opening to welcome her as she pushed me back onto the bed. My hands slid under her clothes, her skin smooth under my touch.

Just as she crawled on top of me, the motel door busted open without any warning. We both turned our heads in that direction as the fresh sunlight poured into the room. There stood a man, looking to be almost seven feet tall and about three hundred pounds of straight muscle, looming in the doorway. He was fucking massive.

The man stepped into the room, with his bald, tattooed head reflecting the daylight, in turn contrasting against his dark clothing. Emma moved backward, crawling off of me.

"You didn't think Levi would come here without reinforcements, did you, darling?"

His eyes were on Emma as she stepped back. "Why are you here, Shade?"

Shade? I looked back and forth between them both.

Who the fuck was Shade?

Before I could sit up, Shade moved to me with one quick stride, his body pouncing on top of mine. He pinned me to the bed with his weight, and I immediately felt like I was suffocating.

Then, in the blink of an eye, I felt pain on the left side of my face. He punched me square on my cheekbone, and I could feel the bone chip under my skin.

"Fuck!" I yelled before he hit me again, this time in my left eye. A rush of blood came to the surface, and I could immediately feel my face begin to heat.

He punched me again, and again, and again. His swing was unrelenting as I tried to fight my way out from under him. I squirmed, I kicked, I thrashed, but with his weight on my arms and body, there was nothing I could do to free myself.

Over and over, his fist connected with different parts of my face.

He hit my mouth, my skin splitting open with the blunt force.

He hit my jaw, popping it out of place.

He hit my temple, making stars appear as my vision turned black.

He hit my eye socket multiple times until I couldn't see out of my left eye. It was swollen shut as my pulse beat in the depths of my skull.

He switched hands, striking the other side of my face, the force popping my jaw back into place.

"Get off of him!" I barely heard Emma yell through the ringing in my ears. Shade stopped, and I turned my head to look out of my watering right eye. She was standing to my left, her hand at the base of Shade's throat.

She was holding my knife, the blade completely covered in blood.

With only one eye to see out of, I tried to blink the water away to get a better view. Shade instantly backed off of me, stepping away from the bed. Emma held the tip of the knife at his throat as he pulled his hands up in surrender. I tried to sit up, but the new pressure in my face kept me flat on the bed.

"Get the *fuck* out of here, Shade, or I will make you fucking regret it."

I felt a wet, stinging sensation in my calf. I lifted my leg to see the bottom of my jeans pushed up, exposing my skin. There was a horizontal line on the side of my leg. Emma must've cut me while Shade was on me to get fresh blood on the knife. I didn't even notice. I would smile if my face didn't hurt so fucking badly.

"Chill the fuck out, Emma. I'm just here to set this asshole straight."

I groaned, the pain in my head catching up quickly. And due to the fact that I couldn't breathe in anything except for blood, I knew my nose was broken. Part of my mouth felt puffy and tight, and I knew that my lips were busted and bleeding.

I could feel Shade's eyes on me as he slowly stepped to the door. He hesitated for a moment before dropping his hands and turning his back to us. "This isn't worth dying over." His words quivered in his breath, and whatever he was feeling, whether it be fear or nerves or dread, it was noticeable. I shifted my head, watching him leave the room as Emma slammed the door shut behind him. I exhaled through my mouth. Who would've ever thought that demons would be scared of *my* blood? Shit, this was almost comical.

Emma's footsteps came to the side of the bed. I closed my good eye, the need to pass out creeping up on me.

"No. Stay with me, Thomas." She tapped the side of my face, leaving a light sting on my cheek.

It felt like I was using an unnecessary amount of energy just to find my voice. "Can you fix me?" I asked through broken breaths, my lips barely moving in their swell. I felt blood ooze down my chin from my bleeding lip.

Emma sat down on the bed next to me, the back of her hand brushing against the better—but still broken—side of my face. "I can't."

Her words sounded defeated, like she was disappointed that she couldn't take better care of me.

Why were demons even on Earth if they couldn't do anything more than unlock some doors, clean up crime scenes, and give gifts of revival?

She sighed. "But I know someone who can."

I let out another groan, my head rolling away from her hand. I wanted to say so much, but all I could muster up were noises from the pit of my lungs, lungs that were slowly filling with blood and other bodily fluids. We didn't have time for another demon to come here, and we didn't have time to find a hospital. We especially didn't have time to sit and wait for a doctor to fix me.

I was screwed.

It felt like someone had taken a sledgehammer to my face and crushed my skull into pieces.

It felt like I was going to die.

But I knew I wasn't going to because I couldn't.

Laila wouldn't let me.

All those times I tried to kill myself, she never let it happen. She surely won't let me die from some guy beating the shit out of me, no matter how badly I was injured.

Although, suffering wasn't out of the question.

My good eye scanned the room in search of Anna. I found her over in the corner, standing still, staring at me. Out of all this madness, she's the only thing that stays constant in my life. I gave her a piece of a pathetic smile as my face continued to throb, my chest aching in rhythm to my pain.

God, how the fuck did we get here?

Everything that happened so far led us to this moment, to this dingy motel room, my face in pieces as I stared at the ghost I was meant to be with.

I deserved this. I deserved everything that I was getting.

I deserved Laila's punishment. All of it.

I closed my eye, wishing the pain, and my life, away.

Please, Laila, let me go.

EMMA

Thomas' painful moans filled the tiny room as he lay on the bed, his legs hanging off the edge, bent at the knee. His face was a puffy, purple, contorted mess, with blood and swelling covering almost every inch of it. It wasn't *too* terrible, definitely not as terrible as he's making it seem, but we definitely needed someone to help him before things got worse.

I sat beside him, my arm propping me up as I watched his breathing. It was slow and steady, but it was also wet and bubbly from the blood swimming down his throat. I could see him slipping in and out of consciousness in his body's fight to control his pain.

Eh, okay, *maybe* it was pretty bad.

I tapped my fingers on my leg, eyeing the door every couple of moments while waiting for the person I was expecting.

"Stay with me, Thomas." My words hung in the air as I kept my sights on the door.

His response was no response, lifting a small amount of worry in me, and at that moment, I knew. This worry wasn't a selfish worry. The hope for him to stay alive wasn't because I needed him for my own benefit, but because I couldn't stand to think about how much pain he was in.

Squeezing my eyes shut and scrunching my nose, I couldn't believe what I was thinking.

Is this what it feels like to care about something? To *feel* something?

I wasn't created to feel or gain any sort of heartfelt emotion.

So, what is it?

"What's your favorite color?" I asked, trying to keep both our minds off the pain. There was a tired minute that came and went before he found the energy to answer, his finger lifting and tapping the bed slowly, as if he was pained to respond.

"Green." His voice was quiet and hoarse, filled with both physical and emotional hurt.

"When's your birthday?"

"Fuck my birthday." He coughed and winced at the same time.

…Okay then.

"What's your favorite animal?"

He paused, either from thought or from pain.

"I'll tell you mine," I whispered, leaning into him more. "Black panthers. First of all, they're sexy as hell."

That got no reaction, except for a roll of his head.

"Second, they are extremely stealthy, with their big paws, the effortless stride, and their sharp claws. Their color conceals and hides them, and if they find you during the night, it's game over."

I watched as Thomas closed his eye again. His breathing slowed down even more, with each rise and fall of his chest coming in longer intervals. My eyes roamed over his body as I watched him give up.

Okay, okay. I take it all back. This was really, *really* bad.

"No, Thomas." I completely turned my body to him, my hands gripping each shoulder. "No. Come on. Stay here."

Fuck. *Fuck.* His lips parted, his exhale long and deep, letting the life slip off his tongue. Then, after a small groan, his hand slowly lifted off the bed and reached for me. I leaned into his touch, his skin soft as he feathered over my cheekbones. It was a movement so delicate, so intimate, that I held my breath at the gentle stroke. A soft knock sounded at the door, pulling my attention away from him.

"Fucking finally," I spoke under my breath, guiding his hand back down to the bed as I stood up and walked to the door. I didn't bother looking into the peephole before swinging it open, revealing a tall, slender woman. Curly, dark brown hair fell into a long braid that rested over her shoulder, leading my eyes to her tight, white tank top and white shorts that complimented her dark skin beautifully. With her was a small, cream-colored bag that hung in the crook of her arm.

She only spared me a fraction of a glance before walking past me and into the room, completely shifting the atmosphere with her pure, clean ambiance. Gold glitter layered over every inch of her skin, sparkling in the sun's reflection, creating an ethereal illusion.

"Is this him?" she asked, approaching the bed and staring down at Thomas. She placed her bag on the floor as I nodded. He didn't acknowledge her, possibly unaware that she was even here.

"Thomas," I padded back over to the bed and gently pushed his shoulder, making his head roll. "This is Lara. She's going to help you."

Thomas slowly moved his face in our direction, showing more life now than he did for me moments ago. Peeking his better eye open, he tried to speak, clearly struggling to get his words out. "Lara? As in… are you… Lara Croft?"

I snorted, unable to keep my laugh quiet. Lara ignored me as she kept her sympathetic eyes on Thomas. But now that I looked at her, she did have some resemblance. The white shirt, the braid. The fact that she was badass.

I grinned. Hey, whatever keeps his spirit alive.

"Tell me what happened," she said to me while studying his face intensely.

Moving back to the open doorframe, I sighed and leaned against it, crossing my arms. "Shade stopped by."

The room fell silent as Lara turned to look at me. "Shade? Why was he here?"

"All these four-letter names," Thomas rasped, primarily to himself. "I can't keep track of them all. Emma. Lara. Anna."

"Anna?" Lara looked at me, wanting an explanation.

"Look, it's a long story," I clipped, answering her original question as my tone grew short. "I can fill you in later if you're interested, but you don't seem to be the nosey type, and I'd rather get him fixed up first."

Lara looked back to Thomas, easily accepting my answer without a fight. She sat down on the bed next to his head, crossing her legs at the knee. Her gold rings glistened in the sparse sunlight as her hand hovered over his face, waiting a beat before gently laying it on his forehead. She let it rest there for a few seconds, then slid it down to his swollen eye. Thomas lightly groaned at the contact but didn't fight against the touch of her on his body.

The irises of Lara's eyes turned a bright, shimmering gold as her spiritual energy flowed through the tips of her fingers. She repeated this process over each part of his face, healing every inch individually. I watched as he was put back together before my very eyes, her hand fixing what Shade had broken. He remained completely still as he began to look more like himself again.

Her hand rested on his nose, and soon enough, there were no more sounds of wet breathing. Using both hands, she pushed her palms flat on his chest, removing all the fluid in them.

Standing on my tiptoes in the doorway, I looked at his face.

He was entirely back to normal.

He was healed.

Becoming more attentive to his surroundings, Thomas blinked a few times, gaining his vision back slowly. He looked to me, then to Lara, who remained on the bed next to him. He tried to stand quickly, but Lara stopped him.

"Be careful. Be slow."

Her voice was soothing, like the quiet flow of a stream, keeping him planted in his spot.

"You are healed," she said, keeping the same smooth, comforting tone. "But you must use caution. Your body will feel weak for a few hours. Listen to it. Be mindful."

Leaning down, she reached into her bag and pulled out a clear, square glass bottle with a gold, circular lid. It looked like a mix between a flask and a perfume bottle.

"Drink this." She handed the bottle to Thomas, the clear liquid sloshing around inside. He took it reluctantly, keeping his gaze on Lara.

"What is it?" he asked, and my heart tripped at the sound of his voice. He sounded normal, thank God.

"It is water from the Golden Falls of Paradise."

Thomas' eyes widened in disbelief as he looked at the bottle, as if he was holding a winning lottery ticket. He untwisted the cap and brought the bottle to his lips, drinking about half its contents.

"It will restore your strength and improve your health."

He licked his lips as he looked back down at the bottle, his expression filled with wonder. "Holy shit," he said with a wide smile. "This is amazing."

Other than a simple flicker of a grin, Lara ignored him. She stood off the bed, grabbed her bag, and headed for the door. "I wish you well, Thomas." She paused at my side as her body faced the outdoors, her head turned to me.

"Are the scales balanced?" Lara asked me, quiet enough so Thomas couldn't hear. He was too preoccupied with his new fancy water bottle to care anyway.

I laughed softly at her choice of words, but her expression remained serious. It was her way of asking if we were even. She was always so proper, so correct, it would drive me absolutely crazy if I saw her constantly.

And it didn't help that she was so damn beautiful.

About two millennia ago, she and I had some fun. It wasn't anything serious. It was as simple as both of us being in the right place at the right time, with minor temptations to settle. We weren't in love, and we didn't have any deep connection. And given the fact that she was an angel, and I was *not,* it didn't last long. Her morals came to light, and she regretted everything. Ever since then, I've held it over her head, keeping our little secret tucked away in the shadows. She was the one who never wanted it to be known, and I could respect that as long as she was willing to come when I called. To do something for me when I needed it most.

And that time was now.

I needed Thomas to help me get to where I wanted to be, and he was no use to me if he was broken. So, I used our past relationship as a lure to call Lara here and heal him.

Call it blackmail, if you will, but I call it deception. It's what I'm known for, it's in my blood.

Our eyes connected, the glow of my red meeting the shimmer of her gold, and I knew this was the end. "Yeah, we're good."

Lara nodded. "Goodbye, Emma."

She walked out of the room and down the path of doors, the sunlight casting a warm glow on her sparkling skin. I shut the door, walked to the window, and pulled the curtain aside. She was nowhere to be seen, like she simply vanished into thin air.

Which she probably did.

After a moment, I heard Thomas inhale, breaking the silence. "So, care to explain?"

I opened the curtain completely, letting the sunlight beam in, and turned to face him. He had moved himself so that he was stretched along the length of the bed, a pillow wedged between his head and shoulder, laying on his side as he swirled his water bottle in circles.

My heart lurched at the sight of him—healed, strong, and back to normal—conflicting with everything I've always known.

"That was Lara," I said simply.

"I know."

"She's an angel."

"I know."

I narrowed my eyes, scrunching my nose. "How'd you know?"

Thomas lifted his water bottle. "There's absolutely *nothing* like this in this world, Emma. And I'm pretty sure there's no demon that can get water from Paradise."

I rolled my eyes, annoyed that he was right. She was an angel, and angels were the only ones with access to the Golden Falls of Paradise. And, if we're being technical, demons couldn't get into Paradise, period.

Sometimes, the obvious answer is the correct answer.

"But my question is, why was she willing to help me? Or, actually, help you?"

I sighed, turning back to the window. I peeked out one last time, with no sight of Lara. Not that I was expecting to see her.

"She owed me one. That's all." I shrugged, keeping my reasons short and brief. Thomas didn't say anything, and I didn't care to expand further. I had no hard feelings for Lara, at least not anymore. That slate was finally wiped clean.

Another minute passed without another word from Thomas. I turned around to see him fast asleep on the bed, the water bottle clutched in his hands. His body has been through a lot lately, so to see him pass out didn't surprise me. He needed the rest.

After shutting the curtains and walking to the door, I wrapped my hair up in a ponytail and pulled on my cowboy boots. I quickly opened the door, locking it from the inside handle before quietly shutting it, making sure to not let in any sunlight.

The sun was scorching, the sky was cloudless, and the heat was dry. I walked into the dirt parking lot, past Thomas' truck, my boots kicking up dust with each step.

I had somewhere I needed to go.

I had someone I needed to talk to.

EMMA

I stared at the black, iron gates before me, trying to focus through the nighttime darkness. The rods were rusted at the pointed tip, giving the illusion of dried blood trickling down. I reached up and touched the rust, felt the grit between my fingers, and smiled.

There's no place like home.

I pulled the chain off the bars and dropped it to the ground, the black grass under my feet catching the metal with a *thud*. The gates disconnected, and I pushed one side open and stepped through, into the land called The Black Field. The setting before me was eerily quiet. No screams, no whispers, no haunting noises tickling my ears. Just the sound of muffled, suppressed silence. Under me, there was a slender dirt path guiding me to where I wanted to go. On both sides of the path, there were vast, empty fields with more black grass, the long blades dancing in the cold breeze. There were dark, black forests outlining the edges of the fields, the trees and leaves all black as well, expanding out farther than any eye could see.

Trust me, you don't want to know what's inside those forests.

I kept my steps along the path, moving farther along, and looked up at the picture above. What was supposed to be the sky was actually just a giant, dark slat of nothing. No stars, no moon, no illumination of any sort. Since I knew this place like the back of my hand, it wasn't an issue for me, but for a first-timer, it was incredibly hard to navigate the path without the ability to see where you were going. And even for those who have been here before, those who wake up here every day, the path was everchanging. There was no consistency.

Even *I* get unnerved sometimes.

The wind around me was harsh, almost causing me to lose my footing with each step. The path and its surroundings were here to make a person feel alone and exposed, in turn making them feel vulnerable. Most people grow scared, they freeze, they curl into a ball, or they panic. Some people run back to the gate, only to run for miles, unable to find where they started. Some run to the woods, looking for a way out, only to run into their own torture. Some run straight forward, looking for a way to fight, or a way to survive.

Spoiler alert. They *always* lose.

This place isn't just flames and chains and burning and pain. That's just the Hollywood version. It was fear, it was seclusion, it was insanity. It fucked with your brain just as much as it fucked with your body.

It was Hell.

I walked about a half mile before coming to a small patch of black grass that I'd come to memorize. To anyone, it would look the same as the rest of the grass, but to me, with the four short blades in the middle of the square, it was my landmark. I kneeled down, moving the grass with my hand, and saw a small, black box. With the grass to the side, the box raised from the ground and opened a red laser. The laser scanned my eyes, then moved back down into the grass. A rectangle in the path in front of me slid open, allowing me access to a set of underground, descending stairs.

The black box was meant for demon access only. There have been precisely four humans who have found that black box, and every time that box scanned their eyes, it immediately knew they were not a demon, and denied access. The box sent out two fishhooks and pierced them directly into their eyes, pulling out their eyeballs in a split second's time.

And that was just day one of their Hell.

I guess you could compare Hell to a theme park. There were different sections, and in those sections, there were little subsections, each specializing in its own type of torture. Souls were usually confined to one specific section for the rest of eternity, but sometimes, Lucifer will move people around, just to liven things up.

I love when he gets in those moods.

I made my way down the stairs, the stone steps dark and dusty. As I descended, I passed a few black, ghost-like beings, their backs pressed to the walls.

The Shadow People.

They were the ones who have been here since the very beginning, the first people to encounter Hell in their afterlife. They've been here for so long that their souls have depleted into nothingness. Existence without awareness. They wander the halls of Hell, exploring every inch, even though they know it all by now. If they find a new soul, someone who is freshly dead, they will cling to them, hoping to gain some humanity back. But they just end up tearing down the new soul instead, feasting on whatever they can obtain.

They weren't anything remarkable, or even terrifying. They were simply beings. They didn't have eyes, faces, or mouths. When they were here, they existed as a black entity, with no soul, no aura, nothing.

Just a black, multi-dimensional shadow. Searching for you. Following you.

They left all the demons alone, though, since they knew they could never get anything out of us no matter how hard they tried. Plus, the second one tries to touch me, I immediately send them to the other side of Hell, with other souls they can swallow.

Once at the bottom of the staircase, I followed another path. There were holding cells on each side, with dark grey cobblestone enclosing each room. The only way to see in or out of one of the cells was a small, four-inch by four-inch square located on the heavy stone door. There still wasn't much lighting, making those squares pretty useless, but there was still more light than the empty fields above.

This area of Hell was called The Wasteland.

It wasn't my favorite place to be, since it got its name from the people who reside here. They sit in their empty cells, with nowhere to shit besides the cold floor they sit on. It was a different kind of torture, focusing on entrapment and solitude with absolutely no resources. Without food or water, some of them would grow so hungry and desperate enough to even eat their own shit. All of them end up dying at the end of the day, then wake up the next morning to go through it again. They go through the same cycle, over and over, wasting away in their own waste.

It's pretty fucking disgusting.

But then again, they were fucking disgusting on Earth. So, it fits.

I snuck by the holding cells, passing each square with the illusion that I was simply a soul wandering the halls. Once again, the area was quiet, which wasn't unusual for this section. Sometimes people would scream and fight and try to force their way out. But that brought attention to themselves.

And once you're here long enough, you know not to bring attention to yourself.

I made my way to the end of the path, coming to another sealed stone door. To the naked eye, it looked like part of the wall, but to those of us who know our way around, it was obviously another entrance. I leaned forward, letting my lips hover over one of the stones in the wall. I exhaled, a black vapor of my breath covering the surface. The stone pushed itself back into the wall, disappearing as another black box emerged from the empty space. I reached my hand out, letting my palm cover the box as it registered my handprint. Once accepted, the hidden door in the wall opened.

The sight took me back to a time when I was here with Levi, and one of the souls in the cells was causing too much commotion. He was screaming, yelling, and trying to reach his hand through the square to grab us. He was trying to survive and escape, which was expected. They all try at some point. But this time, Levi wasn't having it. He was already pissed off about something, so he decided to take it out on this human.

Levi unlocked the cell, and as soon as the door was open a fraction of an inch, the human tried to take Levi down. But Levi was prepared to fight, grabbing the human by the throat and placing him in a tight headlock. Levi dragged him over to the hidden wall and used his own breath to unlock the black box. Once it appeared, Levi grabbed the human's hand and placed it on, causing a denial of access. A blade from a hidden guillotine dropped, cutting off the human's arm, causing him to absolutely lose his shit.

Levi threw the human back into his cell, along with his arm, and the human never made another noise again.

I sighed at the memory of Levi. I wonder how he's holding up.

Pushing through the door, I walked down another set of stairs. These ones were spiraled and made of wood, creaking with each step down. There were flaming sconces on the walls, lighting up the way, revealing more Shadow People along the walls. I followed the curve of the stairs, stepping farther and farther down, feeling like I'd been walking for hours. The number of stairs was constantly changing, just like the path of The Black Field. As of now, I feel like I've walked down forty flights of stairs.

Eventually, my foot hit the bottom, the heel of my boot digging into rich, cold soil. I lifted my chin to look up ahead, my eyes locking on a set of black double doors with silver lion-head knockers.

Finally.

There were no walls, no buildings, no trees. There was nothing around me. Just darkness cloaking my skin, earth under my boots, and silence quieting the white noise inside me.

My heartbeat began to speed up from the adrenaline.

I walked forward, my steps quiet but louder than anything else around. I reached the doors and closed my eyes, pressing my warm palm on the heavy metal in front of me.

These double doors were the only doors in all of existence that I could *not* see through and could *not* open with a touch of my hand.

I let my hand rest for a moment before moving it up to the knocker. Grabbing the metal that circled through the lion's mouth, I tapped the knocker three times.

Tap, tap, tap.

After a moment of silence that felt like hours, a voice broke through the doors.

"Enter."

The word was spoken in the native demonic tongue, a language that only we could speak and understand. It was used for many reasons, mainly because it was historic, it was ritualistic, and it was *ours*. But it was also used so human souls could not understand what we were saying, adding to their insanity. All demons could speak and understand every language on Earth, but in Hell, our native language was the *only* language we used.

I pulled open the door, the weight of the metal heavier than I remember. I stepped in and took in the sight.

It was one of my favorite places in the history of the world. The black velvet carpeting was smooth to the touch, always clean and soft and inviting. I took off my boots, careful not to drag any dirt or soil in. The walls were lined with more black velvet, with real, black roses covering the walls intricately and beautifully. I lifted my hand to the wall on my right, feeling one of the soft petals between my fingers. The stems were woven through one another, with the thorns poking through the veil of flowers. The roses added an intoxicating essence to the room, mixing with the natural musk and woodsy smell that already existed. I inhaled deeply, tasting the aromatic scent on my tongue.

God, I've missed this so fucking much.

Straight ahead of me was a large wooden desk about ten feet long. It was made of gorgeous oak wood, stained dark to match the colors of the room. There was a fire going in the fireplace behind the desk, blazing orange and red hues, heating up the space around us. My skin grew goosebumps, feeling the contrast of heat from the flames on my front and the brisk chill of the air on my back. I approached, eyeing the massive desk chair that was facing away from me and angled toward the fire.

"Emma."

Oh, *fuck.* The deep, grumbly voice made me wet every *fucking* time. I squeezed my thighs, trying to keep myself aligned. The chair swiveled around, and there he was, in all his glory.

Lucifer.

I sucked in a breath as I took in the sight of him. He was dressed in dark grey suit pants and a white button-up shirt, tucked in at the waist with the sleeves rolled up to his elbows, showing off his muscular, thick arms. The top two buttons of his shirt were undone, revealing a hint of his golden, firm chest. His face was clean-shaven, his jawbone and cheekbones sharp as he raised his chin to me. His hair was perfectly parted and combed, cut right above his ears, not a single dark brown hair out of place. His eyes were piercing into mine, his grey irises like a wolf's coat in the middle of winter, setting my body on fire.

He was perfect.

"Welcome Home," he said in our native language, his words rolling off his tongue effortlessly. I almost collapsed in a puddle right there, but instead, I cleared my throat and swallowed my desires.

"Thank you." My fingertips brushed the edge of the desk. "It's good to be here."

He leaned back in his chair, the leather cushion tilting at his weight. "It's been a while."

I nodded. I haven't been back down here in about twelve Earth years, which equates to about eight hundred sixty-four years in Hell.

He was right. It's been a while.

"Do you know where Lilith is?" I asked, getting right to the point of my visit.

Lucifer propped his elbow up on the arm of his chair, bringing his finger to his lip. I watched his every move, the way he brushed his soft, bottom lip, the way his eyes scanned my body from head to toe, and the way his chest moved up and down slowly, with long, drawn-out breaths. Each motion sent a tingle of lust down my legs. He could fucking blink at me and I'd be on my knees instantly.

"Should I care?" Lucifer responded. It wasn't animosity toward Lilith, nor was it concern, but more of a question of curiosity.

With a subtle tilt of my head, I moved my eyes down to his desk, avoiding his eye contact. Lucifer was the only soul that could intimidate me. "For the past couple of years, no one has been able to find her. And now, there's a human—"

"Emma, is this of any significance to me?" He raised a hand, cutting me off.

I didn't respond, letting the crackle of the fireplace fill the silence between us. Lucifer was not one to fuck around, and he never got involved in anything trivial on Earth. In fact, he never made his way Earthside anymore. That's what we, the demons, were for. We were the ones that did all the dirty work, that corrupted souls and satisfied our temptations, with Lucifer as the first-in-command as he stayed in Hell. We followed any and all orders from him, but for the most part, he trusted us to be on our own. He gave us our own powers, allowing us the freedom to make our own choices.

I knew I had to figure out a way to get what I wanted from Lucifer.

I had to use my deception.

"Thomas Diesel," I began, and Lucifer stood up from his chair, making his way around the desk and heading to me. "Do you know him?"

"Yes," he said simply. Of course he knew him. Lucifer knows everyone, good and evil. It's a fact.

"Do you know of the things he's been doing?"

"Yes." Lucifer eased his way between me and the desk, forcing me to take a step back. His body heat was hotter than the flames from the fire, making me lose the rhythm of my breathing.

"So you know about Levi? And Polly? And the others?"

"I'm aware." He gently leaned back against his desk, crossing his muscular arms over his chest.

I swallowed, looking Lucifer in the eyes. Right here, right now, I had a decision to make. If I wanted to climb the ladder, stepping on everyone along the way, I knew exactly what to do.

I took that one step forward, the one that Lucifer pushed from me. Our bodies met, my chest flush on his front.

"Then you know that Lilith is next."

Lucifer's eyes were glued to mine as he worked his jaw. He and Lilith were close, very close. They were their own souls, of course, and there were more times than not that they only had their own best interests in mind. But they were here, in Hell, together, before anyone else. They had that bond that *no one* could come between.

And that's what I'm using to my advantage.

"I need to find her. I need to protect her."

My index finger found its way under his hand, the one that was crossed over his chest, under his other arm. He unfolded himself at my touch, allowing me to feel his palm. Reactively, he moved his hand to my chin, lifting it toward his face, studying the skin that belonged to him.

All of me belonged to him, and only him.

Lucifer and I have never crossed any physical lines. We've never had sex. None of the demons have, besides Lilith. That was solely her job, although from what I understand, they haven't been with each other in a while. I'm not even sure when was the last time she's been down here.

Surprising to most, Lucifer is not what he's made out to be. He's not overly sexual like the rest of us, and he's not one to push boundaries, either. He's a businessman, running the world of Hell, keeping everything the way it should be- dark, harrowing, and torturous. There was no time for lusting and pleasure, unless he made the time, which he rarely did. He was the most well-known being of Hell, only because he took the fall for everything. People on Earth blamed him for their wrongdoings and misfortunes, when in reality, the demons around them were the ones to blame.

Lucifer was just the scapegoat.

I'm not saying he isn't evil, because he most definitely is. He is the leader of eternal damnation, creating and molding Hell into a world of his own, placing souls in each area for everlasting torment. But he isn't as prominent in people's problems as most would think.

"Lilith can take care of herself," he said to me, his teeth clamped tight, his shoulders square.

I leaned into his touch as his hand slowly moved up to the side of my face, his thumb gentle on my cheek. I kept my eyes on him, watching as his silver eyes were set ablaze with a hunger he needed fulfilled.

"I know she can," I whispered. "But Thomas, he is dangerous. He is lethal."

I ran my hands up Lucifer's chest, feeling the white cotton of his shirt under my palms. He neither rejected me nor fell into me, without a single crack in his composure. He remained serious.

"I've seen the things he has done. He's not to be taken lightly."

My words were truthful as my hands made their way up to Lucifer's neck, my knees going weak at the brush of myself on his skin. His expression remained the same, his lips full and his breathing steady, as I felt his finger slide into the waistband of my jeans. He gave them a slight tug, pulling me into him even more than I already was, and I had to refrain from acting on it.

"I need to prepare her for what's to come, at the very least."

With the words "to come," I pressed my hips into his, feeling his cock stiffen under me. Just knowing that I could make him hard made my insides scream and my blood rush. Him and I, together, as one flesh. It was all I ever wanted.

And now, I could see that he wanted it too.

Maybe he didn't necessarily want *me*, but I know the look of a man that wants to fuck.

"Very well," he rasped, his tone dark and hushed as he lowered his mouth to my neck. I tilted my head away from him, allowing easier access to my skin. He kissed the area, sending jolts of electricity all throughout my body, heating me in ways no human or demon soul ever could.

This was different.

This was Lucifer.

Sliding my hands down to his belt, I grabbed the buckle. The act made Lucifer pause as he held a finger up, pulling his face away from me.

"These games you and Lilith are playing, they need to end. If I give you her location, promise me that it will end."

I swallowed a newly formed lump in my throat at his words. Promises to Lucifer were never light and never meaningless. They were severe, they were serious, and they were life-changing. If I made this promise and broke it, there would be no recovery.

I'd be obliterated.

But that was the point of all this; I wanted it to end too. I wanted Lilith gone, and I wanted her reign to be over. I wanted this.

I nodded my head, obeying his command.

"I promise."

With a quick glance of distress, Lucifer pulled himself away from me and made his way back behind his desk, taking a seat in his chair. I mourned the feeling of his body against mine, the way it left as quickly as it came, but I knew that if I followed through with this, I would have him all to myself.

Lilith would be gone, and I would be his.

Only his.

It was just another reason to follow through with my plan.

Lucifer pulled out a handheld tablet from the top drawer of his desk. The screen flashed on, and his finger scrolled through, looking for the information he needed. After a minute, he stopped, his eyes dancing back and forth as he read through a few sentences. I had no idea what apps or programs he was using or where he was getting his information from, but there was one thing that was always consistent. His information was never inaccurate.

With a sigh, he placed the tablet down on the desk, leaning back against the black cushion.

Then, he told me exactly where she was.

I fucking had her.

I thanked Lucifer with a slight pang in my heart, knowing I could've satisfied his needs right here, in this moment. But there was a heavy confidence in me that knew this was only the beginning of us. This wasn't finished.

I headed to the door and pulled my boots back on before looking back at Lucifer. He stared at me, watching me, his blood hungry for mine.

I took this opportunity and ran with it.

"Before I go," I lowered my voice, my tone turning husky. "I need one more favor."

THOMAS

My eyes felt crusted over as I blinked them open. For a moment, the room began to spin, forcing me to close my eyes tightly. I squeezed them shut, hoping the balance would right itself if I could only see darkness. I rubbed my eyelids, peeling off the layer of sleep crust that must've appeared while I was sleeping.

Sleeping. How long was I asleep?

I opened my eyes, the spinning now gone, and looked around the room. The small, dank motel room that hosted an insane number of incidents that occurred over the last twenty-four hours.

Or maybe longer? Fuck, how long was I asleep?

And where was Emma?

I slowly sat up, my hands pushing my body backward as every joint in my body ached. The shoulder I slept on was stiff, my knees were creaking as I climbed off the bed, and my ribs felt compressed from staying in the same position for so long.

I knew I was getting old, but why was I so sore?

My feet planted on the floor as I finally stood all the way up with my arms stretched over my head. I pulled at each elbow, feeling the muscles in my biceps scream at me. A quick glisten flashed into my eyes as I looked down to the bed, a square water bottle lying right in the middle.

The water bottle.

The angel who fixed me.

The demon who broke me.

Shit, it was all flooding back to me.

I brought my hands up to my face, afraid of what I might feel. I knew Lara had healed me—at least, I thought I did— but did I still look broken? Were there still cuts and blood all over my skin?

I walked to the bathroom and opened the door, only to catch Emma making her way out. She was wiping her wet hands on the ass of her shorts.

"Woah, hey," she smiled at me, her blonde hair softly framing her face as our bodies barely collided. Stumbling off balance, I caught myself against the door frame, my arm leaning against the wood.

Emma. Last night. *Her blood. The shower.*

This morning. *Her kiss.*

Fuck, I needed to get my head on straight.

"Hey," I mumbled as I rubbed the back of my head. "How long was I out?"

Emma lifted a shoulder in a shrug. "A few hours."

Hours? I felt like I blinked and woke up. But that explains why I was so sore.

"May I?" I pointed to the inside of the bathroom, and Emma stepped to the side. My body brushed against hers as I made my way past, images of our naked bodies together filtering through my thoughts, and I immediately pushed them away.

I faced the mirror, looking at my reflection. My eyes were tired but of normal color. My nose was aligned, my jaw was fixed, and there wasn't a single scratch to be seen.

I was fine.

I could breathe normally, I could see normally, and it felt as if nothing had ever happened.

My eyes locked onto the vertical scar on my neck. It was still there, untouched. A reminder that will never disappear.

Leaning onto the sink, I gripped the edges of the porcelain, my knuckles turning white at the thought of it all. This is my life now, and it will never be the same. Not after everything I've seen, not after everything I've been through.

I thought my life changed on my eighteenth birthday, and part of it did, but nothing compares to the events of the last week.

I could feel Emma's presence in the doorway, lingering like a fog, waiting for me. Turning to her, I saw her expression and knew there was something she wasn't telling me.

"Thomas, we need to talk."

With those words came a million thoughts, both positive and negative, but I couldn't focus on them right now. She was right; we needed to talk and get things sorted out, not only with our plans for Laila but with our plans for each other.

What happened last night and this morning was a mistake. I shouldn't have slept with her, and I shouldn't have veered us off track like that. I gave in to something I wanted short term when I knew it was something that could never be long term.

I wanted a wife, I wanted a family, I wanted Anna.

But Anna wasn't long term, either.

Fuck.

I made my way past Emma and back into the bedroom. Grabbing the square water bottle, I sat down on the edge of the mattress and took a swig, still astounded at the water I was consuming. It was like my taste buds could see the infinite heavens above me, drinking the answer to all the doubts of the world.

Part of me wanted to drink it all, right now, my body already addicted to the way it made me feel. The other part of me wanted to keep it locked away forever, never drinking it again unless I absolutely had to.

Emma planted herself across from me, leaning against the arm of the loveseat. With her boots crossed at the ankle, she folded her arms over her chest. Just from the way she was standing, I knew all my previous thoughts were flying right out the fucking window. She was wearing those white, cutoff denim shorts that elongated her legs, the same legs that were just wrapped around me last night with her heels digging into my back. A black, flowing tank top covered her chest and top of her stomach, the bottom hem stopping slightly above her shorts, exposing the tan skin on her stomach. I couldn't help but imagine pulling those clothes off and throwing them to the floor, licking the flesh on her stomach. I pictured myself making my way up, slowly, cautiously, as I take her nipple in my mouth, my tongue swirling around the tight bud.

A surge ran through my dick. Fuck, I was hard again.

I briefly looked at her face and noticed she was flushed, like she was warm, as if she was cooling down from running a marathon. My eyes flickered to the bathroom door, trying to piece things together.

"Were you…" I started, but then shut down that thought. It was none of my business, and she could do whatever she wanted in her spare time. But a little piece of me wondered if I didn't satisfy her enough last night.

"Are you okay?" I asked instead, hoping for a broader answer.

Emma's demeanor switched on like a light, a bright, wide smile spreading across her cheeks. "I'm better than okay, Thomas." A small laugh slipped through her lips.

Pushing off the couch, she made her way over to me, kicking my legs open and pushing herself between them. Reluctancy took over, since the last time we were in this same position, I had the shit beat out of me. But with my fingertips mindlessly grazing her smooth, soft thigh, there wasn't much I could think about right now. She leaned down and grabbed my face with both hands, with her blonde hair falling over her shoulders, and kissed me. It was deep, it was confident, and it was riddled with optimism.

A few moments of her lips suctioned to mine was all it took for me to lose control again. I wanted her, I craved her, I yearned for her.

Just as I was about to slide my hands up her shirt, she broke the kiss, her smile still lingering.

Then, with her lips hovering over mine, her breath warm on my face, her citrus scent filling my lungs, she spoke three words I'll never forget.

"I found her."

ANNA

GWRLOTOTLWV

THOMAS

"Pretzels?"

My leg stopped bouncing at the sound of someone's voice speaking to my left. I looked up to see a woman with brown hair, pulled tightly into a bun on the top of her head. She dressed in all blue, with a wrinkle-free suit jacket and a matching pencil skirt. Her smile never faltered as she waited for my response, holding a brown wicker basket at her side. The expression on her face looked shallow, like she was going through the motions, not here mentally. I must've taken too long because Emma sent her elbow into my ribs, a brief yet deep stab of pain in my side, reminding me to use my actual voice to answer instead of the one inside my head.

"No, I'm okay, thank you."

The woman looked to Emma, who gladly took two miniature bags and placed them on the tray in front of her.

My leg resumed bouncing as I looked out the small window to my right. When on the ground, the sky seemed endless, so far away, like there was no way I could ever touch it. But from here, sitting at forty-five thousand feet in the air, I felt like I could touch the top of the blue dome. The clouds bundled beneath us, creating the illusion that they would catch us if we fell, like a safety net in the sky.

"Would you cut it out?" Emma hissed next to me, placing a pretzel in her mouth. Her hand pressed on my knee, urging me to stop bouncing. "Are you scared of flying? Are you nervous?"

I shook my head. "No. I just want to be there."

Emma snorted. "Well, you have about thirteen hours left, babe. Settle in. Eat some pretzels."

My gaze moved back to the window, watching us hover over the pure white clouds. As soon as Emma told me she knew where Laila was, I instantly grabbed all of our stuff and threw it in the truck, without asking where exactly she was or how she even figured it out. I didn't care, all I wanted was to end this. There was no more waiting around, no more figuring out our next step. We had the last piece of the puzzle, and there was no way I was going to wait around for another fucking second.

And I didn't care if I was walking right into a bear trap. If Laila was there, I was willing to do whatever it took to take her down, even if it was all a setup.

I was willing to sacrifice myself for the sake of everyone else.

The plane was quiet as some people shuffled around in their seats, trying to sleep as the lighting in the cabin grew dim, the result of the sun beginning to set. We endured a four-hour flight from Las Vegas to New York, where we then made our connecting flight and were now on our way to the final destination. I looked down to the world below, the ocean looking so small through the tiny spaces in the clouds. My eyes moved back over to Emma, who was happily chomping away on her pretzels, oblivious to the severity of what's to come. Since we were the only ones sitting in our row, with people both in front and behind us wearing headphones, I took this opportunity to have my questions answered.

Leaning into Emma's space, I lowered my voice to a whisper. "So, tell me, how did you figure it out?"

Her head turned to me mid-chew, her hand stuck in her miniature bag. "Figure what out?"

I fought the urge to roll my eyes. "Where she was."

Bringing her shoulder up, she shrugged. "Someone had the information we needed, and I got it from them."

She couldn't be more fucking vague, and that pissed me off. I hated being in the dark, but as I watched her, sitting here calmly next to me, I tried to give her the benefit of the doubt. Maybe she was hiding it to protect me.

"Was it Lara?" I asked, unable to hide my need to know.

Emma narrowed her eyebrows. "What? No." She answered as if I offended her, like it wasn't even possible.

"She's an angel, right? Can't she find people? She found us, after all."

"She didn't *find* us, Thomas. I told her where we were, and she came."

"She was nearby?"

Emma dropped her shoulders, sighing, clearly annoyed with my questions, but could she blame me for being curious? This was all new to me.

"No. She wasn't nearby. She's an angel, and angels have different Earthly powers than demons. They can heal people, and they can show up anywhere they want at the drop of a dime. I called, and she came. Simple as that." She shoved another pretzel in her mouth, ending the topic.

"So if she didn't tell you where Laila was, then who did? And when?"

"Holy fuck, Thomas. Don't you trust me?"

I looked around the cabin, making sure that our conversation was still at its lowest volume, not drawing attention. "Yes, I trust you. But you don't want me going into this completely blind, do you?"

Her eyes locked onto mine, and I could see her hesitate. I was right, I shouldn't be caught off guard by anything. I should know every last detail so there was no room for uncertainty.

But then she went back to her pretzels, ignoring whatever battle she was just dealing with in her head.

"My source of information is completely irrelevant to our situation."

Fucking hell. I pressed my fingertips to my eyes, rubbing until I saw stars. Getting anything out of her was proving to be near impossible at this point. I silently cursed airport security for not allowing blades on carry-ons, or else I'd be holding a bloody knife to Emma's throat, giving her no choice but to answer my questions.

Then again, we'd probably draw attention and get kicked off the plane, forcing us to land early and not in the location where we wanted to be.

"Fine," I said, letting it go. "But she can feel us getting closer, right?"

Emma nodded slowly.

"Then how do we know that she's not on the next flight out of there, flying back into the States as we fly out? How do we know she's not avoiding us?"

"Because, Thomas," she started, pointing to the backpack at my feet, "that's how we know."

The black backpack sat nicely between my feet, holding only a few things that I didn't want in my checked luggage: my mother's ring, because I'd rather fucking die than let it out of my sight again, my wallet, my passport, a few bags of chips that cost more than they should, and the manilla folder that held all my research. And in that folder, right on top, were the four letters from Laila.

I reached down and unzipped the bag, pulling out the four papers from the folder. After smoothing out the creases, I placed them on the folding tray attached to the seat in front of me.

I've read them all hundreds of thousands of times, to the point where I had them memorized by heart. And even still, they didn't make sense to me. There was something that I wasn't getting, something that wasn't clicking.

But what?

I put them in chronological order, starting with the letter from Stoney's, then the letter from Soren, then the letter from Polly, and finally, the letter from Levi's pocket, which was the only one that was straightforward and different from the others.

Besides the final letter, the only other thing that stuck out to me was the sentence from the third envelope.

Now come find me.

You don't get much more direct than that. She wanted me to find her. She was waiting for me, hoping I would find a way to her, showing herself in ways that I couldn't figure out.

Staring at the letters on the page and searing them into my memory was beginning to frustrate me. I began to resent reading them, upset with myself that I couldn't figure out what she was trying to tell me.

Or maybe, *maybe* she wasn't trying to tell me anything at all. Maybe these letters were here to fuck with me, to stall me for time, as another twisted punishment in her games.

I was following her trail, always two steps behind her, instead of finding a way to get in front.

I was a pawn in her game, and I was doing everything she wanted without even realizing it.

A few hours passed, and I was starting to give in to the battle to stay awake. The cabin was almost completely dark as the nighttime sky surrounded the path of the plane. Passengers were fast asleep, with only the sounds from the jet engines as white noise.

I pulled off my black sweatshirt and crumpled it into a ball, wedging it in the crook of my neck for a makeshift pillow. These damn seats were so uncomfortable, but I was growing more and more exhausted by the minute. As soon as I got somewhat comfortable, Emma nudged my arm.

"I think the flight attendants are asleep."

I closed my eyes, trying to block her out, but she didn't notice.

"Or, they're in shifts. But I can see one of them up there, sleeping on some sort of cot."

I groaned quietly, hoping she would shut the fuck up and I could get some sleep.

But then I felt her hand slide over to my leg, her fingers gently squeezing my thigh as she made her way up. My dick instantly surged at the affection, but my mind was on the opposition.

"Emma," I gritted my teeth, squinting my eyes open. "What the fuck are you doing?"

She leaned her head back against her seat, letting it roll to face my direction. A sly smile painted her lips as her hand found my growing cock, tracing circles around the tip through my jeans.

"Are you a member of the mile-high club, Thomas?"

Her voice was like silk on my ears, challenging every piece of me to say no to her advances. But for some reason, I couldn't.

I shook my head, lifted it off my sweatshirt, and looked around to make sure no one was watching. There was an older couple in the row across the aisle, but they were fast asleep. The people surrounding us were also sleeping, with the man behind me snoring lightly. There was no one around that was aware of what she was doing, and that made my blood pump faster.

Emma leaned in closer to me, her nose almost touching mine, her teeth pulling in her bottom lip seductively. "Do you want to become a member?"

This was not something I had planned. It wasn't even something I fantasized about.

Until now.

Her lips met mine, her mouth warm and inviting as I moved my hand to her soft, fine hair. I gave a small tug at the base of her skull, a light moan escaping as her head tilted up. Her tongue slid out and she licked my lips, controlling me, possessing me. I gave into her, using my free hand to press hers harder on my cock, feeling it throb under her touch.

There was something about her that dominated me, that made me lose all restraint, that guided me into decisions I would never normally make.

Her hand unbuckled my belt, and I helped her, making sure not to make any noise. I undid my jeans, sliding them down only enough so that my dick sprang free, only in sight if someone were to look directly in our row. Without hesitation, Emma leaned down and took all of me in her mouth, my length seeming even longer with the excitement that we could get caught. It was pure adrenaline putting me on edge, and with her head bobbing on my cock, her warm spit gliding her perfect, plump lips up and down, I almost came in that moment. It was too much for me too fast, so I pushed her off and pulled my boxer briefs up.

"What—"

I cut her off. "Get in the bathroom. Now," I commanded, my voice low.

Emma wiped the excess spit off the side of her mouth and obeyed, the speed of her breathing almost matching the pace of my heartbeat. She fled the row and walked down the aisle to the back of the plane, entering the bathroom and locking it. I waited an antagonizing few minutes, my cock aching for her as I tucked it into the waistband of my jeans, straightening myself up as I prepared to follow her.

Once enough time cleared, my dick not close to letting up, I got up and made my way to the bathroom. A man, sitting in the last row, watched me as I walked to the bathroom. I could've sworn he gave me a hint of a smile, almost as if he was mentally high-fiving me for what I was about to do, but I ignored him and kept going. Just as I reached the door, I heard her unlock it, and I slid right in with her.

And in that instant, I regretted this decision.

Airplane bathrooms fucking suck, that's for sure. There was barely any room for the two of us, and the fact that Anna was standing in the narrow space on the other side of the toilet made things just a little bit awkward. Usually, she kept her distance, standing on the other side of the room where I could ignore her or at least turn my back to her. But there was no way around it now. She was so close to me, with nowhere to go, and I could practically feel the absence of her heartbeat.

Fuck. I'm such a shitty person.

Whatever lust I lost from seeing Anna in the bathroom with us was gained back the moment I saw Emma peel off her shirt. Her breasts bounced free, her nipples hard under the soft, cream lighting. I took one in my mouth, my tongue swirling around the tight bud as my fingers clutched the other. Her head hung back in ecstasy, whimpering so softly as her long, blonde hair fell like a waterfall down her smooth back. I sucked, bit, and licked her nipples as she dropped her shorts, letting them fall to the filthy floor under us. My hands found the back of her thighs and I lifted her, placing her on the edge of the sink, spreading her legs wide open.

Her head came back to me as I kissed my way up her chest, past her prominent collarbones and exposed neck, and then to her lips which welcomed me. Her forehead rested on mine as she pulled my bottom lip with her teeth, biting gently.

"Fuck me."

God, the voice that was fit for only the sharpest vixen, and here I was, with her, eager to feel her. There was nothing faster than me pulling down my jeans and underwear as I fisted my cock, lining it up with her entrance. I rubbed the tip up and down, feeling her arousal cover me, letting my pre-cum mix with it.

And then I thrust deep inside her, feeling every inch of me in her, her walls squeezing me feverishly. My hips slammed against her inner thighs as she wrapped her legs around me, biting my shoulder to suppress her moans. With each thrust, I found myself closer and closer to the edge, watching myself in the small bathroom mirror as a small layer of sweat covered my forehead. I tried to hide my panting, but the feeling of her wrapped around me in every possible way was making my head spin, forcing me to find as much oxygen as I could.

"You and me, Thomas," Emma whispered in the ear closest to Anna, and for a split second, my mind wondered if she could hear those words too.

"That's all it ever will be. You and me."

I squeezed my eyes shut, because with Anna so close to me, all I could think about was the first time I fucked her and made the same promise that Emma is making now. On my balcony, I promised her that I would be the only person to save her. But I failed, and now she was dead, watching me as I pumped my cock into someone else.

But then Emma rubbed her clit on me, grinding into me, and I was right back to where I was. Gripping her hips, I pulled her into me, harder with each movement. My fingers dug into her skin, feeling the bones beneath, needing to be even closer than I already was.

Her skin was slick as I slid in and out, the crown of my dick feeling all the intensity as the base was being milked by Emma. Anna glitched to the space we were just in, next to the door, as I picked Emma up and moved her to the other wall, pinning her back to it. I fucked and fucked and fucked her, my needs unrelenting as my balls tightened, squaring up for the finish. My thrusts turned more forceful, my bones banging against hers, bruising and marking her without even trying. The force of my thrusting was turning brutal and cruel as I unleashed every bit of myself into her. Emma's body stiffened in distraction from the new intensity, probably wondering if I was doing it out of passion, anger, or both. But she quickly snapped out of her thoughts as her arms rested on my shoulders, her hands threaded through the hair on the back of my head, pulling and scratching and kneading.

"Fuck, Thomas, I'm going to come." Her voice was slightly above a whisper, loud enough for others to hear, but at this point, I couldn't give a fuck. I wanted her, I wanted to reach my limit, and I wanted to fill her with every last drop, and I didn't care who knew.

"Come with me," I managed to say, a rasp coating my words as I leaned into her and bit her jaw. With her breath in my ear and her pussy tight, I released everything I had into her as her body jolted, her climax wrapped around me. Intertwined as one, we reached our height together, with the sky above us and the ocean below.

I slid myself out of her and let her feet fall back to the floor. But before we could do anything else, before we could clean up and fix ourselves and head back to our seats, I reached down between her legs, feeling the mixture of both of us pooled between her legs. I placed two fingers inside of her, making her lips part with a satisfied moan, and pulled out a thick, creamy layer of our cum. Studying it, I raised my hand to my line of vision, letting my thumb feel the slippery silk, the polished liquid that was the same color as clouded ice. The coated fingers found their way to Emma's lips as I spread the cum, painting the gloss on her, then stuck my fingers in her mouth, letting her suck the rest off. Her eyes locked on mine, looking at me through her long, dark eyelashes as her tongue circled my fingers, and fuck, I was already getting hard again.

"Wear me on your lips for the rest of the flight," I said into her ear. Her answer was an easy smile, and I knew she liked the games we played. As did I.

Before I had a chance to tuck my semi-hard cock back into my jeans, Emma reached down and brushed the last drop of cum off my dick, sucking it off her fingertip.

"I don't think I'll ever get enough of your taste."

My mouth lifted in a half smile as Emma got dressed. I fixed my jeans and straightened the rest of my clothes. My hair was a mess, my skin was red and sweaty, and if anyone saw us step out together, it would be completely obvious what had just happened. But I found myself laughing at the fact that we were so reckless, and it also felt good to get my mind off of what I was about to face tomorrow.

Once Emma fixed herself up, she looked over the curve of her shoulder to me, sending a wink my way. She opened the bathroom door quietly and turned to squeeze past Anna, leaving me in here, alone with my ghost.

The one that I've been trying to ignore while she has no choice but to watch everything I do.

I couldn't bring myself to look her in the eye.

ANNA

LURGXCHIHQXZEMJGVRRBXWRYRBFQCZX

THOMAS

If you were to tell me five years ago that I would end up in Tanzania, looking for a demon that killed my girlfriend, I would probably turn around and ignore you, tell you you're fucking batshit insane, or, if I was having a good day, maybe even laugh at you. There's no way in hell that I would've imagined this happening to me, not ever. I didn't even know if the afterlife, God, or demons were even real until these past few years.

Even now, I still have my doubts. Like this is all a dream, or that *I'm* the one going batshit insane, and that I'm just imagining it all. I'm having some sort of mental breakdown or psychotic episode.

As insensitive as it may be, it's the only justification I have for myself.

The only explanation is that I'm going crazy. Honestly, it's more believable than my reality.

But here I was, standing in Africa, staying in a resort in Tanzania, looking for the one that has caused me the utmost turmoil in my life.

And there was no distracting me, there was no talking myself out of it. She was here. I could feel her.

I could feel her blood mixed with mine, coursing through my veins, heating each and every cell in my body, setting me aflame.

She was here.

I had the nosebleed to prove it.

By the time the plane had landed, I had gotten about four hours of sleep, and that was enough to reset my body. I was ready, I was prepared, both mentally and physically. But the second I stepped foot on the land, my mind was instantly drawn to the scenery, and I was in awe. The views were absolutely breathtaking, with rolling hills covered in the greenest grass I've ever seen, so rich and healthy and nourished. The sky was so blue and vibrant that it hurt my eyes, with only a few sparse clouds scattered throughout, and even those looked more vivid than those from the view of the airplane. Emma and I checked into our resort, our asses lucky enough to grab a suite at such short notice. It was a beautiful safari-themed resort located in the Ngorongoro Conservation Area, with three African men playing bongos for travelers as we entered, with giant, contagious smiles spread on their faces.

Our room was more than I could've asked for. It was a safari lodge-style suite with stone walls, wooden accents, brown and yellow and dark green paint, blankets and other décor with tribal markings, all creating the perfect African atmosphere. We placed our luggage down in the entryway, not bothering to fight over sleeping arrangements, and I made my way to the balcony. Sliding the door open, I stepped out into the glow of the impending sunset, running my hand over the neatly stacked stone railings. I looked out, the Earth hallowed out and open in front of me, so inviting and enticing. Our lodge was placed right inside the edge of a crater, one that was so large and wide that I would mistake it for hills or small mountains if I didn't know any better. There was a lake right in the middle, one that wild animals frequented for their drinking water. The view was nothing short of incredible, my eyes trailing all the dips and valleys and habitats surrounding me. After almost a full twenty-four hours of travel, seeing this, breathing in this fresh, pure air, made everything worth it.

I almost wanted to abandon all the reasons why I was even here, just to enjoy this creation.

And part of me ached at the fact that I knew this wasn't going to be a peaceful place for me in the hours to come.

I would be leaving here with more heavy memories than happy ones.

The thought loomed over me like a dark cloud, one that wasn't fit for the beautiful Tanzanian sky.

All I could do, right now, was watch the remainder of the sun dip under the horizon, casting a perfect orange and purple hue, the African heat warm against my skin.

And then, once the sun was gone and darkness took over, I would begin the hunt.

With a quiet push, I heard the balcony doors slide open, Emma's light steps approaching my back.

"You okay?" she asked, stepping to my side, her eyes on the crater below.

I took a deep breath and placed my hands on the railing in front of me. It was a loaded question. Was I okay with coming all this way, just to face the unknown? Was I okay with running head-on into the depths of the fire, hoping that everything would work out in the end? Would I be able to catch myself if something went wrong? What was I willing to sacrifice for the greater good?

Better yet, was I messing with the balance of the world? Everyone always wants to take down evil, of course. But do we need the evil in the world to balance out the right? Without bad, what is good? Without good, what is bad?

Who am I to decide?

But I can't let these past three years go. I can't tuck them away into my long-term memory and watch as they fade over time. I was wronged, Anna was taken from me, and more importantly, her own life was taken from her.

And if all I can do is avenge her, then that's something I did right.

My hands gripped the black metal railing as I couldn't find the words to answer Emma. Instead, I looked down to the valley below, my vision instantly catching Anna in the grass, the green blades almost reaching her knees as she watched me, waiting for me.

"Don't give up on it now, Thomas," Emma whispered, still looking out ahead. "You're one of the strongest humans I've ever known, and I don't say that lightly. You have been manipulated, taken advantage of, and tormented, but you still have that fire inside you. You've already come this far. Don't lose the fight. There are so many other people in the world that need you to fight for them."

My eyes darted to the side, giving her a quick glance before looking away. For some reason, this moment was sticking with me, giving me the feeling that I'll never forget this. A demon, watching a sunset with me, giving me a pep talk before I go and kill one of her own. If this wasn't my life for the past week and a half, I'd be wondering what the hell was happening. Aren't demons supposed to be like the little devil on my shoulder, tearing me down, leading me into trouble, pulling me away from things that don't benefit the greater good? I know she wants Laila gone, but it was strange to hear her build me up rather than side with someone who was technically on her team.

We stayed in silence as the sun fell behind the hills, dipping below the horizon, swallowing any light left in the sky. With the sun hidden, the temperature dropped, prompting me to pull on my black sweatshirt over my dark t-shirt. A piece of me didn't want to wear it, since I knew I was going to cut myself for blood at some point, but I wanted to stay dark and hidden, keeping as much of me as unseen as possible.

"Ready?" Emma asked. Her clothes were dark as well, wearing black jeans and a black hoodie, with the hood up and over her bright blonde hair. She still kept on the brown cowboy boots, though.

Just as I was about to say yes, my nose began to bleed again, with heavy drips dropping to the suite floor. The blood was flowing fast, the dark red liquid forming into a steady stream as I pressed the heel of my palm against my nose, stopping the sudden flow.

Maybe I won't need to cut myself after all.

Emma cleaned the floor, and since I didn't want to leave a trail of my blood anywhere in this resort, I tucked an embarrassing amount of tissues in my hoodie pocket, right next to my knife.

The knife I used to change the outcome of the world, and the world after.

I turned it in my palm, rotating the smooth handle, and looked up at Emma. She sent me a look of curiosity, waiting for me to speak my thoughts as I stared at her.

There was something I needed to do first.

"Give me ten minutes," I said, walking to the door of the suite and opening it.

"Thomas, we don't have time. We need to go." She turned to follow me, but I stopped her.

"Just give me ten fucking minutes."

Her face instantly fell as she took my request seriously. Heading out, I left Emma in our room as the door clicked shut behind me, and I walked down the hallway. In minutes, I was down and out of the lobby, making my way outside of the resort. Passing the parking lot and all the cars and golf carts in it, I headed down toward the middle of the crater. Before I could go in too far, I stopped, hiking through the tall grass, turning my head in all directions.

"Come on," I begged under my breath, searching. "Where are you?"

My eyes grew wide, seeking high and low before I spotted her.

Anna was standing off to the side, up on the edge of the crater, about fifty yards away from me. She was slightly hidden by the decking of an outdoor restaurant that was currently setting up for an event. I quietly made my way over to her, stepping through the high grass, keeping my eyes on her the whole time. I wasn't letting her change locations on me, not now. Those evergreen eyes that I've memorized, that have shown up in my dreams time and time again, that have watched me for years now, stilled on me, unblinking in the recent twilight.

Once I was within only a few feet of her, I exhaled.

I still don't know if she can hear me or see me. I hope to God she can't. But I had to take the chance, knowing it would be my last one.

I tried to steady my voice, feeling the catch in my throat before even attempting to speak. I didn't even know where to start. Fuck, I wasn't expecting it to be this hard.

My gaze moved to the scar that ran across her forehead, then back down to her eyes. I mustered whatever voice I had out, as rocky and hoarse as it may sound.

"Fuck, Anna, you have no idea what I'd do to hold you right now."

Her hair bristled in the breeze, small strands flowing against her cheek as I could feel my eyes turning glossy. I dropped my head, knowing I'll never get a word back from her. I'll never get to hear her voice again. I held the back of my hand against my nose, doing everything I could to keep my emotions at bay.

"If I just had one more minute with you…"

I could feel the weight in my chest grow heavier, my attempt to push it away futile.

"Just one more fucking minute. I'd give anything for one more minute."

I kept my vision on her legs, unable to make eye contact with her anymore.

"It kills me that I wasn't there with you that night. I wasn't there to save you." A sharp inhale filled my lungs as I kept my hand over my face. That night was a night I played in my head over and over, never letting it go. I can still picture her foot peeking out from behind the kitchen island, her blue toenails catching my attention. It made me sick to my stomach just thinking about it now. "I should've been there."

Forgiveness will never accept me. It will stir in me until I rot, leaving my bones to settle in the dirt, untouched by anything except for loneliness. There will never come a time when I will be set free of this, even if her ghost finds a way out.

All I can hope for is Anna's light. All I can do is believe that she will be released of this burden at the end, her soul at rest in the highest peace.

Her presence before me lingered, and I continued.

"And I'm sorry for the things I've done. All of it. With you, with them…" My voice cracked as my words fell off. "I just fucking miss you, Anna. It was supposed to be *you.*"

I forced myself to look back up at her, only to see the same blank expression as always. There was an empty ache in me, internally begging for a fraction of a smile or even a flicker of her eyes. Anything. I would take *anything*.

"It was always supposed to be you."

Up until now, I've resisted every urge to reach out to her. But now, as our time together began to tick down, I couldn't help but give it one last shot.

I stretched out my arm, palm up, extending my hand to her. All I wanted was to feel her hand in mine one final time. My fingers bent gently, waiting for her to come to me, to fill me with some sort of hope, something I could hold onto.

"Please, Anna," I begged, a silent tear slipping from my eye, falling down my face. *"Please."*

I waited, and waited, my patience for her everlasting, as long as she would come back to me at some point. At *any* point.

But with my hand growing cold in the nighttime air, I knew.

There was no hope.

Nothing.

She remained still, her eyes glued to me as I dropped my hand in defeat. With my hands at my sides, and my ghost unmoving, I broke. Again.

And I'm not sure how many more times I can break before I'm unable to pick myself back up again.

But there was one final thing I had to try, for Anna, for myself, before giving up completely.

The thing I've set out to do since the beginning. The thing I'm here for.

I needed to find Laila, and I needed to kill her.

We were ready.

There was no turning back now.

I met Emma back at the resort, and thankfully, she didn't ask any questions as we left and walked out into the quiet calmness of the conservation area. There were some nighttime activities, like restaurants and areas to mingle with other tourists. But once we were far away from those, away from the people and artificial lights and noise, all we had was nature. The wind rustled around us, making the grass dance and the trees sway. The starry sky, the same stars Anna and I watched back in Pennsylvania, acted as lights and guided me. The sound of the crickets filtered through the air as bats began flying above. The sound of silence crept between our footsteps, between our breathing and concentration. I listened to the sound of the diurnal wildlife sleeping, and the sound of nocturnal wildlife rising.

There was no word for it, besides beautiful.

And with each step, my mind and body and blood all working as one, I felt myself grow nearer.

To her.

To our fate.

To the end.

We walked onto a hidden trail, still exposed to the land and sky but miles away from the resort. We walked in silence, with Emma letting me lead the way, since we both had an unspoken understanding that I had the connection to her right now.

But as I was mid-step, my feet stopped as I felt something on my back. There was something behind Emma, something that didn't feel right. The hair on my neck stood, along with the goosebumps rolling down my arms and down my legs.

There was someone following us.

With myself planted firmly on the ground, I slowly turned and tried to see what it was, but the stars could only illuminate so much. I couldn't see anything, no matter how hard my eyes tried to adjust to the lack of light.

"What?" Emma whispered, her wide eyes searching mine.

I let the silence still around us for a minute, the feeling slowly fading over that time before I shook my head. I was still on high alert, but I wasn't going to let this stop me.

I turned and kept walking. Emma followed.

The waves of my blood grew more violent, the flow feeling like all of my veins were about to burst at once. The pressure was unbelievable, creating a deep ache in every part of my body, but I pressed on. We were getting closer.

And because we were getting closer, with the feeling intensifying, it could only mean one thing.

She wasn't moving.

She was still.

She was waiting.

The path wasn't a difficult trek, but it was long and tedious, and my body was beginning to lose its energy. And as I was rounding a curve, I looked back to check on Emma, only to see her stopped a few feet back. She was standing there, completely still and completely emotionless. I paused, cinching my eyebrows down in confusion briefly.

But then she looked past me, and I turned to see what she was looking at.

The path ended, and before me was an extensive, vast area of untouched land.

The views of the crater and the conservation area had no comparison to this.

The grass was perfectly formed and colored, there were gentle rivers flowing into the center of the land, and there were bushes and flowers and a variety of plants and trees. Everything looked to be so healthy and alive, yet it all seemed to be untouched as well.

I tore my eyes away from the sight for one second to look around. I thought we were secluded before, but this felt completely different. I felt as if I had stumbled upon a hidden territory, one that I was not meant to see but was destined to discover.

And then I looked to my left, a quick movement catching my eye.

There, leaning against a tree on the edge of the land, was a woman with long, slender legs, bright red hair, and a deep, coaxing smile on her face.

My eyes locked onto hers, and this was the moment that I've been waiting for.

That I've researched for.

That I've driven thousands of miles for.

That I've hunted for.

That I've killed for.

This was the moment I was reunited with Laila.

THOMAS

"It's beautiful, isn't it?"

Those were her first spoken words to me in *years*. Goosebumps instantly came to the surface of my skin, dotting me in a pattern hidden beneath my clothes. She could write me a hundred letters and I could live a thousand memories, but nothing will compare to her voice.

And hearing it for the first time outside of my head was sending an excessive amount of mixed emotions through my body.

Anger, pain, solemnity. Longing. *Fucking longing.* Even after all this time, I still longed for her.

It was the fact that I had one taste of her years ago, and she still managed to control me, to filter through my veins, keeping me hooked on her even though I hated her.

I still craved her.

And that raised a fury deep inside of me, one that has been dormant up until now.

She slowly pushed off the tree and began walking toward me. She swapped her heels out for black combat boots, with dark jeans and a dark grey sweater. Her hair was down in waves, the red color just as vibrant as the day I met her. Her skin was still smooth and perfect, with no blemishes or marks or inconsistencies. It was as if I just saw her yesterday, with my memory of her matching what she looked like now.

My body was frozen, my feet cramping from how hard I was keeping them to the ground. I didn't want to move, and I didn't want to think. I just wanted to wait.

She came up beside me, her arm almost brushing against mine as she turned to face the same direction as me. I quickly glanced down, hyperaware of her body next to mine, and blinked.

Focus.

Calm and calculated.

"No one really knows about this place." Her voice was soft and quiet as she tilted her shoulder toward me. "There have been a few stragglers that found it, but it never ended well for them."

My head snapped to face her, my eyes peeled wide.

"Relax. That was a couple of millennia ago. Now that the world has been saved, anyone is free to explore."

She paused.

"Well, almost anyone."

I tried to steady my shallow breathing as my mind was running in every direction. What the fuck was she talking about? Who saved the world? What is this place? And why did she lead me here?

They were all questions I had, but I couldn't form the words to spit them out.

So instead, I focused on my lungs.

Breathe in, breathe out.

In. Out.

Laila turned to look at me, in a moment that seemed to last hours, before turning and looking behind me.

"I see you brought reinforcements."

I turned and followed Laila's gaze to Emma, who was still standing in the same place I had left her, her arms folded gently across her chest. Her blonde hair was pulled back into a ponytail, the color bright under the moonlight. Her familiarity was oddly reassuring for me.

"What was your plan here, Thomas? You didn't want to meet me just to talk, did you? Did you bring her along to try to ambush me?"

I looked back to Laila, only to see her already staring at me. It was clear I didn't have to answer since she already knew why I was here, so I didn't.

"Because, from the way I see it, *you're* the one coming to *me*. You're the one following *my* direction."

She was right. I was exactly where she wanted me. I fell directly into her trap.

But I couldn't let her see me falter.

"Give me one good reason why I shouldn't kill you right this second."

She chuckled, the sound melodic to my ears. "If you wanted to, you would've tried already."

It felt like each one of my nerve endings was on fire around her. I couldn't think straight.

"First things first," Laila stepped backward to a nearby tree, leaned down, and grabbed a long, white rope.

I was too frozen to do anything but stand by and watch. Laila planned ahead for all of this. I should be surprised, but I'm not.

"Bring her here and tie her up," she commanded, nodding her chin in Emma's direction.

Making sure not to touch Laila's hand, I took the rope from her and looked at Emma. She looked worried, with maybe even a hint of fear. But in *my* eyes, once they locked with Emma's, there were messages I was trying to convey. Everything would be okay, I would handle this, and we will push through this.

I needed her to trust me.

I guided her to the tree where Laila was standing on the outside edge of the land. Emma sat down on the ground with her back against the tree, and I did my best to tie her up.

"Make it tight. Knot it correctly. Don't try anything."

I did as I was told. First, I wrapped the rope around her body, securing her upper arms and torso to the base of the tree. I could see the rope restricting her ribs, making it difficult to take in deep breaths. Once she was fully tight against it, with no wiggle room, I moved to her forearms and wrists. With her hands behind the tree, I circled them and wove the rope interchangeably, not allowing any room for twisting or turning. I tied knots against her wrists, with Laila watching to make sure there were no slip knots. I used the entirety of the rope, ensuring there was no excess for Emma to use in any way.

She was tied, and there was no way out.

I stood to my feet, giving Emma one final glance, uncertainty filling my eyes as I turned back to Laila. She had a grin on her lips, knowing that right now, it was only her and I.

This was between *us*.

"Come with me," she said gently, her voice soothing as I watched her turn and go, my steps following closely behind her. She led me down toward this mysterious spot, both of us walking cautiously through the grass, then stopping only a few feet away from it all.

Up close, I could see all the flowers and plants and vegetation. It was so vibrant and perfect, with every color complimenting each other in perfect harmony, every shape fitting together in unison. It looked like a painting. There wasn't a single petal or branch or leaf out of place.

Did I walk into a different realm? One with no mistakes, no errors, no flaws?

Since Laila stopped here and had yet to take me in farther, I squinted my eyes, trying to see deeper into the area. I could see two trees in the center, side by side, both tall and slender but healthy and strong.

"Do you know where we are, Thomas?" Laila's voice was husky in my ear as she stayed by my side.

I shook my head, still watching the magic in front of me.

And that's when she lifted her hand, placing a finger under my chin. The movement I know all too well. I turned to look at her, her touch hot on my skin as she kept her finger in place.

Her blue eyes shimmered as she peered at me through her eyelashes, with her cheeks blushing red and her lips round and full.

"This is the Garden of Eden."

Either my heart stopped, or sped up, I wasn't sure. I couldn't feel anything in my body. I had no pulse, no breath, no feeling in my hands. I looked back to the place in front of me and almost lost my shit right there. I was standing at the foot of the Garden, watching the life before me, breathing in the air it was breathing.

And it all made sense.

Where we were standing was not inside the Garden. We were just outside of it.

She couldn't go in. She was banished.

"Why did you lead me here?" I asked, finally able to muster up the strength to speak.

Laila took in a deep breath, tilting her head. "I like to come here every once in a while. Sometimes to think, sometimes just to see the one place on Earth I'm not allowed to enter. It's like a tease, you know? And sometimes I like to test it and see if it has changed at all."

I arched an eyebrow, watching her, fully aware that she didn't answer my question. "Has it?"

"No."

She has tried to enter. She still can't.

My head was spinning at the revelation. The Garden was real. I could see it with my own eyes. I could feel it in the marrow of my bones. I wanted to reach out and touch a leaf, a flower, anything. But I kept my hands at my sides, focusing on the reason why I was here.

"Where is she?" Laila asked, turning herself away from me, searching for someone.

For a second, I wasn't sure who she was looking for because I was too distracted by the Garden in front of me, but of course I remembered. I followed her search until she stopped, her gaze landing on the one thing that made my blood boil.

Anna.

"Ah, there she is," she said with a smile, looking over my shoulder to the ghost that stood about twenty feet behind me, next to a tree. Anna was just the same as before, with the shirt and the scar and the strawberry hair, just like the first night I saw her spirit. Just like the Anna that broke me about an hour ago.

"How is she? Still hanging in there?"

And that was the moment, as she lightly and sarcastically laughed, that I remembered why I hated all demons. But especially why I hated Laila. Because she took an innocent fucking soul from Earth and continued to torture her in the afterlife with no remorse.

I could feel my blood pressure rise, pushed up from anger, rage, and fury.

But through all those emotions, there was one thing that I needed to know more than anything.

"Can she see me?" I tried to ask clearly, but there was a hitch in my throat. I swallowed it down.

A hint of sympathy flashed in Laila's eyes, but it vanished quickly. "Yes. She can see everything."

God, I wanted to fucking die right then and there. For the first time since the night I burned her body, I wanted to scream. She saw all the times I tried to talk to her, all the killings, all the *sex*. All the times I looked at her while other demons were blowing me, before I slipped my cock into Emma, before coming, she could see me. When I had my hand outstretched to her, waiting for her, she could see me.

And she couldn't do a single thing about it.

"In fact, I have her sweet little soul tucked away in a small corner of Hell. She's caged up, with nowhere to go and no one to talk to, and only you to watch here on Earth. But don't worry, I give her bread and water every time you go to sleep. She has it made compared to everyone else down there."

I could feel a tear on the bottom rim of my eyelid, and I prayed for it to stay there.

"Why are you punishing her?" My jaw was fucking tight as hell as I gritted my teeth. "What did she do to deserve this, huh? Why her?" I moved in closer, my face inching closer to Laila's, but she didn't even flinch.

"It's all part of God's plan—"

"Oh, don't give me that *fucking bullshit* again, Laila. Don't you *fucking* dare."

After letting the unspoken threat linger around us for a moment, I rubbed my chin, brushing the stubble along my jaw as I stepped back, turning away from Laila. Why did she always bring out the anger in me? It was uncontrollable. I was letting it take over, and although I wanted to calm down, I couldn't find it in me.

"Was it in God's plan to make me unaware? To place me under some stupid veil of oblivion, unknowing of the fact that she was *dead* for a fucking *week* before you let me figure it out?" I came back and rushed to her, my hand reaching up and grabbing her throat, gripping tightly. "Was that God's plan?"

Laila shook her head as much as she could through my hold. "No," she admitted. "That was *my* plan."

I reveled in her admission. We were finally making progress.

"What was the reason?"

She shrugged a shoulder. "I had to get you out of the house, away from her."

I remember that night clearly. The phone call from the police, the vandalized house, the moment I found Anna on the floor.

Wait.

The vandalized house.

"You can thank *her* for that." Laila looked over in Emma's direction, who was still sitting and tied to the tree, completely silent. "Well, her and a few others. Who was it, Emma? You, Abby, Astrid?" All while she was naming these stupid fucking demons, my grip was squeezing even tighter on her neck, and my blood was churning inside me.

"Doesn't really matter. You were gone, and I stepped in. It's a good thing Anna was sweet enough to let me inside."

Hearing her name come from Laila's mouth was like a punch to the gut.

"And since you were already with the police, that meant you had an alibi. And *that* meant they would have to point the finger at someone else. It might not have been pointed at me, but I couldn't take that chance. Let me tell you, I don't do well in prison."

Her breath was beginning to thin, and her skin was turning a shade of blue as I kept my hand on her, but she continued.

"So, I made sure everything seemed normal to you. Well, as normal as it could be. So that way, when you *did* figure it out, when the veil was ripped from your eyes, you were the only one to blame."

Fuck. She was only confirming my need to plunge my knife into her.

"I wasn't expecting you to fuck her, though. That was just icing on top of the cake."

She smiled, her perfect white teeth shining at me. Teeth I wanted to knock out, one by one, until she had nothing left except for bloody, raw gums.

But instead, I let her go, dropping my hand to my side as she steadied herself. That, I could tell, was all truthful. It made sense, to keep me in the dark so she could remain in the light, with absolutely no consequences.

Laila rubbed her neck, the red marks dotting the flesh.

I narrowed my eyebrows, more questions in my head coming to the surface. "How come I'm the only one that has a ghost, Laila?"

She crossed her arms over her chest, with no answer on her lips.

"I'm sure you already know that I've met with some others. Other people who had 'The Gift' or whatever the fuck you call it. And one of them already lost the person they saved."

Flashbacks of Soren flooded my thoughts. The way the moonlight touched her skin, the way she told her story to me, allowing herself to be vulnerable. The way I promised her I would make things right.

"But after they died for the second time, they stayed gone. No lingering ghost, no spirits, no punishment. No fallout."

I could see the hesitation in Laila's face, in her eyes, in the way she leaned slightly to the side, as if her unease was casting her off balance.

"So, why me, Laila? Why the *fuck* are you so consumed by me?"

Stillness surrounded us without any answer.

"Is that why you pursued my dad? So you could stay close to me? So you could feel me through him?"

Her irises turned a deep red as she dropped her arms. She was clearly pissed off.

Good.

"I could ask you the same thing, Thomas." She closed the gap between us, raising her chin in spite. "Is that why you still call me Laila?"

I stilled, trying to keep my anger composed, but she unlocked something in me that I had never thought of. Why was it that I had a hard time calling her Lilith? Why did I refuse to? Did I want to keep that known identity pushed away, keeping my emotional draw to her justified?

Why did I feel that by calling her Laila, I was protecting myself?

Raising her arm, she rested her wrist on my shoulder as her fingers trailed the vertical scar on my neck. I watched as her eyes traced it, her lips curling up gently.

"And is that why you fucked another demon? To feel *close* to me?"

Her voice was breathy, like the thought of it was turning her on.

"Were you trying to get my attention?"

I knocked Laila's hand away, and she laughed. I glanced over to Emma, who hadn't moved at all. To be fair, I expected Laila to already have known since Emma warned me. But I wasn't expecting her to bring it up now.

Then again, nothing was off-limits here.

"Jealous?" I asked, facing her again. "Seems like you're just upset that you never got to."

Laila huffed, then lowered her voice to a dramatic whisper, narrowing her eyes. "Did you come in her, Thomas?"

Fuck. I wasn't answering that. But she already knew, I could tell. My palms began to sweat.

"Did she milk you for every last drop?" Her tongue licked her bottom lip slowly, and my eyes couldn't help but be drawn to it.

"Because," she began, her smile growing bigger. "I think she left out one very crucial detail about who she is."

My eyes darted over to Emma, who was now trying to twist her wrists out of the rope. With Laila's voice so low and us far enough away, I don't think she could hear what we were saying. But between my constant glances to her and the fact that she knew she was hiding something from me, I'm sure she was piecing it together.

"She's not just a regular demon, Thomas. She's a succubus."

I looked at Laila. *No fucking way.*

In my research, I learned all about them, but it never occurred to me that they were real.

How could I be so fucking stupid?

"A succubus. You know, a female demon that seduces and fucks men, then collects their cum to make little succu-babies." Her tone was nonchalant, as if this was an obvious thing people talked about every day.

"Shut the fuck up. I know what a succubus is."

Bile came rising up my throat at the realization, but I did my best to keep it down. I thought of everything that happened this past week and a half.

Her, fingering herself, watching me with Polly.

Us, fucking in the shower.

Me, drinking her fucking blood while my cock was buried deep in her pussy.

That's what I fucking get for not buying fucking condoms.

"And that Levi guy you offed? Yeah, he was an incubus, which is just the male version of a succubus. But he was *her* incubus."

Her, meaning Emma's. They were a pair, they were a duo, which explained why he was always following her, protecting her, trying to keep her away from me.

The look on my face must've been readable because Laila bared her teeth in a grimace.

"Looks like you can't trust the ones you think you can," she said as she placed her hands in her back pockets. "I tried to warn you. But, at the very least, I hope she was a good fuck."

I ignored the second part of her comment, letting it roll off my stiff shoulders.

But as I looked at her, with her red hair cascading down in waves past her shoulders, her posture confident, and her emotions completely in check, I found myself feeling sorry for her. I was still angry as fuck, and I still wanted to kill her, but it was clear that she wanted me to trust her over everyone else. She was giving me information I wouldn't have gotten otherwise. There was something deep inside her that needed validation, needed reassurance, even if she would never admit to it. Even if it wasn't in her demonic nature. And she needed it from me.

A small chuckle escaped me as I tilted my head, my palm rubbing against my jaw.

"I hope you know, *Lilith*, that I have never, and will never trust you. From the first night I met you, the night you kissed me without even giving me a choice in the matter, I never fully believed in your trust. At first, I thought about you constantly. You were like a fucking brainteaser that I couldn't solve. I thought about The Gift and the kiss and all the rules you gave me afterward. And then the novelty of it all died down, and I began to think about you less. Then, you began fucking my dad, which you claim had *nothing* to do with me, and somehow, you made your way back into my life again. Not only did you fuck him, but you also fucked him *over*, and that, in turn, fucked *me* over. But through all this, there was that little voice in the back of my fucking head..."

I pulled my knife out of my sweatshirt pocket and held it at my side. Lilith smiled, unfazed.

"...that said you were untrustworthy. And there was someone in my life, someone who came along fairly recently, that told me about a seventh sense. That feeling you get when you know something isn't right, or, even when it is, or when your body is telling you to be aware of something that you can't physically see or hear."

I slid the knife from its holder, bringing the shiny metal close to my face, eyeing its beauty.

"You, Lilith," I pointed the knife to her, but she kept her eyes on mine. "You have always given me that feeling. Sometimes it was masked with lust, sometimes it was masked with friendliness, but that's all it ever was. A mask. A disguise."

I pulled the left sleeve of my sweatshirt up to my elbow and let the blade rest on my skin, right below the dried cut I made before I killed Levi. I pressed down, gliding the knife along, creating an instant slice that streamed a heavy flow of blood. Lilith watched, and I could feel her eyes on the rush, knowing exactly what I was doing.

And she didn't stop me.

Instead, she stepped forward, moving in closer to me, testing me as I wiped both sides of the cool metal, coating it in my warm blood. Her eyes moved from my arm up to me, no amount of fear or hesitancy on her face.

"You better be careful, Thomas. You should know by now, there are consequences for the things you do."

I inhaled her scent, no longer letting it consume me. "You don't think I'd burn the whole world down if that meant you would go down with it?"

Lilith tilted her chin up, seduction coating her lips as she grinned, still locked on me.

She was fearless.

She was strong.

I knew that Lilith was different from the others. I knew that if I tried to swing at her, she would be expecting it. She would stop me in one way or the other. I couldn't try to stab her without something happening to me, too.

I have your blood, Thomas.

I smiled back at her.

"You're willing to kill off everyone in order to take me down?" She pursed her lips, sending herself deep into thought before coming back to me. "Okay, how about this. I'll let you kill me, right here, with that knife, if you don't say a single word while I make some sacrifices. Deal?"

She was trying to call me on my bluff. But the thing was, it wasn't a bluff.

She didn't realize how fucking ready I was to do *anything* to take her away from this world.

She took my silence as an agreement and began to walk. Her steps took her in a circle around me, like a shark in the ocean, surrounding its prey.

"Let's start with someone easy. How about, oh, what's her name? Lacey?"

Lacey? I had to think for a second, but then I remembered. Lacey Sinclair. Saved by her boyfriend, whom I met back in Ohio, John Mitchell, through a kiss given by Lilith.

I blinked but remained still.

Then, she came back to face me, her body standing tall as she looked me dead in the eye, and blinked.

A slow, long, drawn-out blink.

A moment of stillness lingered before she brushed her hair over her shoulder and smirked. "Done."

She began to circle me again, but this time, my head followed her movements. "Done? What do you mean?"

"You said you were willing to burn down the whole world, which means everyone on it. So, I'm trying to see how far you'll go with your threats."

I swallowed, my nerves beginning to heighten, my eyes starting to burn at the newfound responsibility.

"She's dead. Now shut the fuck up, and let's continue."

"How can you—"

"Who's next?"

I shut my mouth after she cut me off, hoping this wasn't true, this wasn't happening. I needed to figure out a way to make her stop.

"How about…"

She paused, stepping behind me, tapping her chin in thought.

"…your beloved little Marilyn Reeves?"

Fuck. Fuckfuckfuckfuck. I closed my eyes, trying my hardest to not say a single word.

She came to my front again, blinking the same drawn-out blink as before.

"Dead."

Fuck. I felt like such a fucking coward, not trying anything to stop her. But she needed to know I was serious, and if I tried anything, I would be dead, too. And if I was dead, I was useless.

She peered at me through narrow eyes, confused by my lack of emotion. But little did she know, I was fighting everything off on the inside.

"Alright." Her steps were growing lighter as she continued to walk her path around me. "Let's move up a level, shall we? Make things a little interesting?"

I looked over my shoulder at her as she lowered her eyes, deep in thought. She came in close to me, lifting a finger to slide along my back, my muscles tensing at her touch. Standing on her toes, she leaned up to whisper in my ear.

"This one might be a little harder for me."

Then she dropped back down onto her feet, making her way back around. My knife remained at my side as blood continued to drip down my arm and off my knuckles.

"Jackson Diesel."

My heart dropped at the name. She wanted to kill my dad? For what? To prove a point? God, my dad and I have been through fucking *hell,* and I did have a lot of hatred for him.

But that's what it was.

Hatred.

Not indifference. I still had an emotional tie to him, whether I liked it or not.

But before I could say anything, Lilith blinked slowly.

"Dead."

Dammit. I let out a long exhale as every piece of my body tried to find a way out.

"Oh, I have a good one," Lilith said through a laugh, sounding more excited than she should be. Her circling began, her hand reaching up to my shoulder, her fingers caressing the curve of my bicep.

"Soren Porter."

Soren. Another innocent bystander in Lilith's game. Someone who doesn't deserve to be muddled in this mess. Someone who I should've never approached since all Lilith liked to do was torture those who are connected to me in any sort of way.

I thought of Soren's innocence, her grief, and her strong faith in her brother. She didn't hesitate to save him, making the act heroic and bold, showing how good of a person she really is.

I gripped the knife in my hand tightly, the veins in my hands bulging with pressure.

"Don't you *fucking* dare. She has nothing to do with this," I said sharply.

Lilith stopped in her tracks, a look of shock running over her face. "Did I strike a nerve?"

I hesitated, cocking my head to the side, not wanting to feed into her gloat.

"Wow. Who would've thought…" Her voice trailed off as she stood in front of me. Her eyes raked over my body, from my feet to my face. She paused, letting her lips part, her tongue gliding along the edge of her teeth.

"Did you fuck her?"

"No."

"Do you love her?"

I pinched my eyebrows together. "I don't even know her."

She laughed a little. "But you're willing to protect her."

I froze, realizing she was right. If Lilith wasn't lying, then I let the others die, including my own father, before speaking up to save Soren. Why? Why did I feel the need to protect her? What made her so different? What made her more worthy than the others?

"That's too bad. I'll spare her, but that means you can't kill me and save the world."

She mimicked a fake pout, pushing her bottom lip out as far as it could go.

Stepping forward, I reached up and took Lilith's chin in my hand, painting spots of blood along her jawline. She looked up at me, her eyes lit by the moonlight, and I clenched my teeth together.

"Why? Why are you playing these games?"

"Because, Thomas," Lilith whispered, inching closer, eyeing the blade as she tested her fate. "It was always meant to be us, wasn't it? You and me?"

I kept my mind on my blood, the stinging pain in my arm, the sound of Emma squirming off to the side. Anything to keep my mind off of Lilith, the way she knew exactly what to say to me, and the way her voice was like silk to my insides.

I held the handle of the knife in my hand, gripping it for dear life as I remembered Emma's words from the shower, moments after we had sex.

You and me.

I forced my eyes to stay on hers, even though I wanted to look over at Emma.

"Try as you might, but we can't stay apart. We always find a way back to each other."

Dropping my hand from her face, I inhaled sharply at her truthful words. I was searching for her long before I started this. Hell, I was even looking for her before Anna came along. I was constantly looking for red hair in any crowd in our small town.

But that doesn't mean I wanted to stay with her.

"You have the first blood. We can be unstoppable, Thomas."

The first blood? What did that mean? I knew I had to kill her and all other demons with the blood of a first-born male, which I was, but her words felt different. There was a meaning I wasn't catching on to.

My fingers gripped and regripped the knife over and over, waiting for the perfect opportunity to use it.

But before I could move a muscle, I felt a presence at my side. There was someone walking, heading to the entrance of the Garden, not paying any of us any attention.

Lilith and I both snapped our heads to the side, and in an instant, every front she had up disappeared. Her features softened, her shoulders dropped, and her breathing came in staggard, harsh breaths. I looked down at the knife to see that my blood had dried during our conversation, so I used this moment to add more to the blade, coating it with fresh, wet, new blood.

"Adam?"

She spoke again, so quickly and so quietly, the name was almost inaudible.

The man turned his head, just now noticing us. He was tall and well built, with wide shoulders and large arms obvious through a long sleeve shirt, along with dark jeans and work boots. He had shaggy, dark brown hair falling down past his ears and a confused smile on his face.

"Adam?" Lilith asked again, her eyes wide and unblinking.

That's when I pieced it all together.

This was Adam.

The Adam that was Lilith's first love. The Adam that had Lilith banished from the Garden. The Adam that made Lilith one of the first demons in all of time. The Adam that somehow still had Lilith in a chokehold, even to this day.

The Adam that was being used as a distraction.

With her head turned, I scanned the area franticly. I knew this would be my only opportunity, and I only had a few seconds.

Anna was now standing behind Lilith, facing me, appearing the same as always. I looked into her eyes, knowing this would be it.

This would be the last time.

Once Lilith was gone, Anna would be too.

My heart ached at the thought of never seeing her again, ghost or no ghost.

I could hear her laugh as I picked her up and carried her over my shoulder, as she tried to kick and fight her way down.

I could taste the delicious homemade meals she always made me after work.

I could see the way she rested her chin on her fist while deep in thought, her demeanor always so elegant and tender, even when she would get mad.

I could remember all the nights we sat out on our balcony, in the calm breeze and under the stars. Her hair blowing in the wind, and her hand tucking it behind her ear.

I could remember grabbing her hand in mine as I drove the truck, with her sitting next to me as I kissed each of her knuckles, one by one.

I could feel her soft skin under my fingertips, smooth and delicate as we made love every night.

I could taste her lips on mine, even now, with the gentlest of pressure, with the lightest push of her tongue.

And with one final look, a single moment in time as I locked my soul into her eyes, I said goodbye.

Again.

My bones felt weak, my heart felt numb, my lungs felt tight.

I didn't want to let go, I *couldn't* let go.

I couldn't let her go.

I can't.

But I had to.

I sent the bloody knife deep into Lilith's neck in one swift motion, giving her a deadly wound that matched my scar. Her eyes remained on Adam as her knees gave out. I wrapped my arms around her waist, catching her, watching as her eyes went from blue, to red, to white in a matter of seconds. The knife remained in her throat as I held her, slowly moving a hand up to brush the red hair away from her face. A drip of blood fell from my nose and down my lips.

With the one thing that could distract her, pulling her attention away from me for a single second, I did it.

I fucking did it.

I killed her.

Lilith was dead.

My heart was racing beyond its limit as I held the subject of my insanity for years. She was the reason for my continued existence, as she never let me die. She was the one who brought me to the love of my life, even if it was never in the cards for us to be together forever.

I would take that single year with Anna over never being with her at all.

No doubt in my mind about it.

With Lilith limp in my arms, I lowered her to the ground and laid her down. With her red hair splayed out under her, I gently closed her eyelids. She looked oddly peaceful, considering the fact that she was the least peaceful person I've ever known. And minus the fact that she still had a knife sticking out of her neck.

I forcefully pulled the knife out of her, causing blood to spurt out all over the ground below her. Cleaning the blade on my sweatshirt, I picked my head up and looked around.

Emma was still tied to the tree, her expression happier than I'd ever seen her.

Adam was standing across from me, his feet planted right outside the garden, his hands shoved into his pockets with a blank look on his face. I had no idea what he was doing here, or if he was even real, but I appreciated him showing up here when he did.

But then I looked around, my head circling the area around me, searching for the last bit of hope I had.

With my eyes glancing up and down, high and low, far and wide, I couldn't find her.

Anna was gone.

And that made Lilith's death so fucking unsatisfying.

THOMAS

My body hovered over Lilith's corpse for a minute, but my mind was long gone. I was trapped in the final moment with Anna, our eyes locked, knowing she was watching in the depths of Hell. I hoped she knew my reasoning for doing what I did, and all I wanted was for her to find her peace.

And I hope that's where she is now. Somewhere calm, happy, peaceful.

If she's not, then none of this was worth it.

Lilith was dead, and I felt like I was too.

"Thomas!" Emma shouted over to me. I looked her way, only to see her kicking her cowboy boots in the dust of the ground, her body and arms still tied in a rope.

But she was smiling. And she was happy.

"Thomas! Oh my God!"

I put a finger to my lips, trying to quiet her. Her voice was carrying over the entire area, echoing through the valleys of Tanzania. She nodded, settling herself, but still letting a squeal of excitement sneak through.

Stepping over Lilith, I began my walk over to Emma. I motioned for Adam, or whoever the fuck he was, to stay there, and judging by the unease in his eyes, he wasn't going anywhere.

As I approached the tree Emma was tied to, I could see her eyes were lit with a thrill that couldn't be mistaken. I squatted down to her level, letting my knees hit the ground as she wiggled her elbows to me, a beaming smile plastered on her face from ear to ear.

"Thomas, we fucking did it." She lowered her voice to a whisper, but the emotion was still loud.

"Who is that?" I asked, pointing my thumb over my shoulder in the direction of Adam, trying to piece the whole thing together.

Emma glanced over at him with pride. "That's Adam. Well, not *really*. He's a demon I recruited to pose as Adam."

I cocked an eyebrow, unable to process what I was hearing. "What?"

"I met with Lucifer, and he agreed to lend me an illusion of Adam's soul. That's Bael, who agreed to help me out."

I looked back to Bael, who was no longer Adam, but a tall man with dark, shaggy hair, standing in the shadows with his hands in his pockets. He looked rough and rugged, like he couldn't give a shit about anything that was going on here.

"He followed us."

I looked closer, trying to focus my eyes on his face. He was the man on the plane. He was also the uneasy feeling I had when walking here, the one that felt like we were being followed.

"Before you tied me up and while you were talking to Lilith, I tossed him the vial that contained the mask of Adam's soul. When I knew you needed the distraction, I gave him the go-ahead and he drank it, then came out here to divert her attention."

I looked back to Emma, the situation finally making sense.

Illusion.

Deception.

Emma's specialty.

"Now untie me," she said, motioning to her tied wrists, her victory smile returning to her face.

Keeping my knees to the ground, I leaned forward and pressed my knife to the rope that was bound to her ribs, but paused before I cut through it. There was another question riddling my mind.

"She said I had first blood. What does that mean?"

"What are you talking about? You know what that means." Her smile slightly faded, confused as to what I was referring to.

"No," I shook my head, "not the blood of a first-born male. The first blood."

Emma's grin dropped completely, and I watched as her eyes turned from exhilarated to consideration. She was weighing her thoughts.

Just as I was about to move the knife away, she spoke up, her voice in a fog.

"Do you have it?" she asked, nodding to my jeans.

I looked down, my eyebrows pinched together.

"Your pocket," she added before I could ask. I reached in and pulled out my mother's ring, the one that Levi tried to steal, the one that Polly won, and the one that I stole back.

The one that, for some reason, every demon wanted.

I held it up, the silver metal and the clear diamond still shimmering, even under the muted moonlight.

"Your mother, Thomas," she said, and I looked from the ring to her, "is the last known female descendent of Eve."

I paused.

What… the fuck?

"Eve?"

Emma nodded.

"Eve. As in… Eve?" My mouth couldn't help but draw out her name, sounding it out, feeling it on my lips. Eve? Adam and Eve? I was related to them?

I tucked the ring into my palm, closing my fist around it. "Aren't we all descendants of Eve?" I asked, a legitimate question.

Emma shook her head. "Not this closely. Not like this. Your mother had a prominent bloodline in her."

I felt my eyes begin to dry. With this realization, I apparently lost the ability to blink.

"And so do you. You have the first blood."

So *that's* what Lilith was referring to. And *that's* why everyone wanted her ring. It was a symbol. It had worth.

And here it was, clutched in the palm of my hand.

My eyes moved back to Emma's face, which was covered in dirt and dust and sweat. But she was serious.

"This whole time you've been with me, you've also been with my stuff. You could've taken the ring while I slept."

She kept her eyes on me, her bound body resting against the tree. "Why didn't you?"

She did her best to lean forward, but the ropes were still holding her back. "Because I had a better goal in mind. And I needed your trust. I needed *you*."

Straightening myself, I placed the ring back into my pocket, its new significance weighing heavy in my mind. Why did our bloodline matter? What benefits did we have? It's not like my mother had any sort of superpowers or any shit like that, so what was the importance?

But then it clicked.

That's why Lilith kissed me the night of my eighteenth birthday.

That's why she dated my dad.

That's why she always kept me close.

Because I was useful to her.

Not because she loved me or needed me.

Because I had something she wanted.

I have your blood, Thomas.

God, *fuck*. How could I be so fucking stupid to think that she, the first demon in all of time, actually *loved* me? How narcissistic and naïve could I be to not even consider that I had something she wanted?

Emma picked up on my frustration because she whispered to me again.

"Hey, hey. It's fine. She's dead now. You don't have to worry about any of that."

I looked up at her with hesitation in my eyes and uncertainty in my face.

"I'm protecting you now, remember? No one will touch you."

Right.

The deal.

The promise we made to each other. I would kill Lilith, and in return, Emma would keep me out of Hell. Forever.

Her face softened, a small smile appearing as our gazes connected. She was holding up her end of the deal, as promised. I held strong, not letting my emotions crack as I squared my shoulders. I looked down at the knife in my hand, the blade clean and shiny.

And I knew what I had to do.

"You don't think I would answer for the things I've done?" I asked, small beads of sweat dripping down my forehead.

I could feel a deeply rooted pause in Emma as she felt the weight of my words. The air around us was electrified, with the power in my hands, and my hands only.

"Thomas…" she whispered, but I ignored her.

"The things I've done with Lilith, with you, to Anna," my voice cracked at the last word. I couldn't bear to think about her and the things I did to her. I've done too many things in my life that I couldn't possibly find redemption in. And even if I did, even if I had Emma's protection, I couldn't let myself take the coward's way out.

I needed to stand up and be a man. One that accepted the consequences of his actions.

"I need to take responsibility and deal with whatever is handed to me. Without you."

Emma opened her mouth to say something but then closed it. She had no words for me, no way of convincing me otherwise.

Fixing the sleeve of my sweatshirt, I pulled it back up to my elbow, exposing the two cuts along the inside. The top one was already scabbed over. The bottom one, the one I made only a few minutes ago, had already slowed its flow. It was still wet and fresh, but it wouldn't be enough.

So I pressed my blade underneath that one, creating a third line, and let the cut open a new gush of blood.

"Thomas, what are you doing?" Emma asked with panic coating her every word, and I relished in the sound.

"You lied to me, Emma," I said without looking at her, watching the heavy stream of blood fall from the new cut. At this point, both my arm and my clothes were saturated with wet, crimson blood.

Her breathing picked up, the speed increasing with the passing moments.

"You never told me you were a succubus."

She shook her head franticly. "Because I didn't think—"

"Not only did you not tell me you were a succubus," I continued, speaking over her, not interested in whatever excuse she was trying to feed me. "But you lied about something more important than that."

I wiped the sides of the blade along the fresh cut, painting the entire knife in my blood.

The First Blood.

When I was satisfied, I finally looked up to Emma, who had an intense look of anxiety on her face. Her eyes were clear and wide, her face was void of all color, and her throat moved up and down in a nervous swallow.

"You could see Anna, couldn't you?"

I placed the tip of the knife under her chin, the point pressing into her skin. She lifted her head with it, trying to alleviate the pain of the sharpness.

"This whole time," my voice was low and dark, "you could see her. Everywhere. Just like I could. And you lied to me about it."

I thought about the moment I realized her lie. When we were on the airplane, right after Emma and I had sex in the bathroom, Emma opened the door to leave. Anna was standing right in front of the doorway, and Emma stepped around her.

If she didn't know she was there, she would've walked right through her.

But instead, she avoided her by walking around her.

And that's when I knew that Lilith's letter was true. I couldn't trust her.

"I didn't want you falling off track," she spoke with a quiver in her voice. "I needed you with *me*, not focused on *her*."

"I *was* with you, Emma." I grew angry, leaning in closer to her face, keeping my bloody knife under her chin. "I killed Levi for you. I kissed you. I fucked you. I *trusted* you."

She squeezed her eyes shut as I pushed my nose against her face, speaking directly in her ear, my voice dark and ominous. My vision was layered black as my rage seeped through me, creating a deafening force that I couldn't contain.

I felt unstoppable. I made the choices, and I accepted the consequences for them.

I kept my breath hot on the side of her face.

"But now, you're nothing more than a means to an end."

"Thomas, stop. Think about this. If you kill me, Lucifer will come for you. He will find you."

I smiled, letting a small laugh slip through my lips.

"Good. I'll be waiting."

I pulled the knife from her chin and leaned away from her face. She opened her eyes to see me, with rage in my blood and fury in my eyes. No fucking mercy.

"Thomas, please."

Her plea was cut short by the swift plunge of my knife deep into her stomach, her flesh tearing and oozing around the hilt. The muscles of her torso tensed, resisting the blade before quickly loosening. I pushed it in farther, as deep as it could possibly go, then gave it a twist, all while keeping eye contact with her. Her mouth fell open, and her head dropped down to her chest. A final groan escaped from her lungs as she exhaled, without an inhale to follow.

Emma was dead.

Anna was dead.

Lilith was dead.

If Lilith was telling the truth, then Lacey, Mrs. Reeves, and my dad were all possibly dead, too.

And it was all because of me.

I pulled the knife out of her stomach, the wet squish sound ringing in my ears. I cut the rope, freeing her from the tree, and unbound her wrists. Her limp body fell to the side, away from the tree, her arms outstretched as the blood from her stomach puddled out on the land under her.

And I felt nothing.

I stood to my feet, wiping the blade for a final time before putting it back into its holder. I turned to Bael, who stood with his arms crossed, a witness to everything that just happened.

But his face remained calm, his breathing stayed steady, and his demeanor was still relaxed.

He was not a threat to me, nor I to him. He clearly did not care about Lilith or Emma, or else there would have been a completely different outcome for me.

But right now, I needed him.

"Would you?" I asked, outstretching my arms, referencing the miniature massacre that had just occurred.

With his body holding firm, he didn't move a single muscle.

I sighed. "I'm not interested in killing you. I just want this cleaned up, then you're free to go."

Bael eyed me, taking my request into consideration. I'd leave him alone as long as he would do the same, cleaning this up along the way. There was no way I could kill him, then clean it up. Therefore, he had nothing to worry about.

We had a silent understanding as he nodded slightly.

Then, he closed his eyes, his arms tight across his chest, and blinked them away.

Suddenly, the scene in front of me was gone.

The rope, the bodies, the blood, all of it was gone.

The only thing that remained was the Garden, sitting as vibrant as it was before, the gentle breeze pushing the untouched foliage around.

And I stared at it, taking in the sight, hoping that this would be the last time I ever saw it.

"Thank you," I said to Bael as he walked away, and he simply nodded in response.

And here I was with no one by my side, no one to trust, no one to go home to.

Alone.

THOMAS

A few days later, I landed back in Las Vegas to pick up my truck. It was a sight for sore eyes as I found it in the parking lot, still worn and used and loved, right where I left it. I ran my hand across the hood, feeling the hot aluminum and faded paint under my palm. We were about to have a long few days ahead as we set to embark on our drive back to Pennsylvania.

I opened the driver's door, and days' worth of Nevada heat hit me full force, instantly making me sweat as I climbed in. The leather was hot under my legs as I sat down and gripped the steering wheel, the familiar feeling washing over me like a tidal wave. I looked over to the empty passenger side.

Emma sat in this seat only days ago, with her blonde hair whipping in the wind, her elbow propped up on the rolled-down window frame, and her cowboy boots crossed at the ankle.

Anna sat in this seat only a couple of years ago, with her strawberry hair falling across her eyes, her freckles dotting the bridge of her nose, and her dark clothing sparking one of the first real conversations I ever had with her.

Reaching over, I pulled out the box of Anna's ashes that was tucked under the seat. It was exactly how I had left it- the cut of wood pristine and perfect, with the stain and gloss sealing the grain. I ran my fingers along the edge of the box, feeling its smooth ridges and chiseled corners.

When I got back to the resort in Tanzania, after killing Lilith and Emma, the first thing I did was head up to my room and shut myself in the bathroom. Locking the door behind me, I turned on the light, the sudden brightness causing my eyes to ache. But as I looked around, with no windows or hidden closets or shower curtains, I realized that I was actually alone, and I was no longer being followed.

The ghost of Anna was gone.

After everything that happened that week and a half, after using all my energy on fighting and searching and killing and trusting, there was only one thing that I hoped for.

I hoped that she was at peace.

Wherever she was, she deserved that, if nothing else.

I placed the box down on the seat and started my truck, beginning my journey back home.

After a day and a half of driving, sleeping, and driving again, I found myself back in the heart of Lawson, Missouri. I wish I could say I planned to come here, but after seeing highway signs and knowing what could be waiting for me, my hands turned the steering wheel and my foot pressed the gas, unbeknownst to my mind. It was only four in the afternoon as I let my truck idle in the parking lot, but the tavern was already open, serving a handful of guests.

A delivery truck pulled into the parking lot and drove to the back of the building, backing its doors to the kitchen exit. I watched people come and go, some with leftover boxes in their hands, and others with full stomachs and smiles of satisfaction.

It was a normal day, with normal circumstances, with no reason to hide.

But I couldn't bring myself to get out of the truck and go inside.

I wanted to, God, I wanted to. I wanted to see Soren again. I wanted to tell her about everything, from Lilith and her true identity, to my eighteenth birthday and Anna, from Tanzania, to Las Vegas and Colorado.

But then I watched her open the back door and step out of the building, helping unload boxes of food from the delivery truck with a warm, friendly smile across her lips.

A smile that I didn't want to erase.

I couldn't burden her with all of this. She didn't need to know what happened behind closed doors, especially since she was completely unaffected by it all. Her life resumed as normal as it could, and that was the best possible outcome for her.

She had Lilith in her life, and in return, she had an extra year with her brother. There was no way I could ruin that for her.

She deserved that happiness.

And she deserved to be as far away from me as possible.

I pulled my truck's shift lever into drive and drove out of the parking lot.

About halfway home, I finally turned on my cell phone. The moment the screen came on, I had a substantial number of missed calls and text messages, all starting from the moment I left for Tanzania. Pulling my truck to the side of the road, I turned it off to let the engine rest. I got out and leaned against the bed of the truck, observing the long stretch of empty road around me.

I took a deep breath, preparing myself for what I was about to read.

First, there were almost fifty missed calls, dozens of voicemails, and over one hundred texts from John Mitchell.

Lacey was dead.

They were in a movie theater, watching the previews before their showing when her neck suddenly snapped. John couldn't believe what had happened; one second, she was laughing and enjoying popcorn, and the next, she was dead on the floor. He jumped out of his seat and tried to save her, but her neck was completely broken.

Just like how she died the first time.

Police didn't end up charging him. He claimed that she had stood up and tried to make her way to the bathroom when she fell and tripped down the theater stairs, breaking her neck on the way. No one else in the theater saw what happened, but there were also no accounts of fighting or any sort of buildup that would cause people to believe he killed her.

He called me, unsure of what to think or do, and to ask if this was supposed to happen.

I didn't have a straight answer for him. I wanted to tell him that it was going to happen eventually, whether he liked it or not.

But in this time of his grief, I knew there would be nothing I could say to him that would ease his pain. I decided that I would call and check in on him in a few days when things weren't as fresh.

Next, I had a single missed call from an unknown number. Along with the missed call, there was a notification for a voicemail with it. I pressed play and listened.

It was the voice of a shaken male who hesitated before speaking. The familiarity rang a bell, and as soon as he said his name, I knew why he was calling.

It was Lucas, the son of Mrs. Reeves.

She was dead.

Apparently, a few days ago, she had taken a fall down the stairs, resulting in a ruptured spleen that wasn't treated in time. She died soon after arriving at the hospital.

Thankfully, Lucas didn't sound too upset. In the voicemail, he explained how happy she was to be with her family, her grandchildren included, and that she was happy she made the decision to move. She still talked about me sometimes, wondering how I was doing.

Fuck, that made my throat swell. I was so caught up in the mission to find Lilith that I never gave up five minutes of my time to call her.

That is something that I will always regret.

Lucas invited me to the funeral that was to take place that Saturday in Nevada.

I checked my phone, not even sure what day it was, only to realize that it was… Saturday.

The funeral was happening as I was standing here, leaning on the side of my truck, unsure of what state I was even in.

I quickly sent him a text, explaining how I'd been out of the country and how sorry I was that I didn't get to respond. I told him that I would be unable to attend the funeral, but I would call him later tonight to hear about the final portion of Mrs. Reeves' life.

Now, with those two confirmed dead, I knew what was next.

Just seeing the names on the unread texts and missed calls, all from Darrell, Jim, and others from work, told me everything I needed to know.

My dad was gone.

Instead of reading any texts or listening to any voicemails, I tapped on Darrell's name and pressed the phone to my ear.

The phone rang, and rang again, and I found myself looking around to the space around me.

Squinting one eye from the sun, I glanced at the flat, empty land around me that seemed to stretch for miles.

Wherever I was, it was nice. It was quiet, and it was calm.

It was peaceful.

Darrell picked up on the fourth ring.

"TD!" His voice boomed through the speaker, shaking my ear drum. "What the *hell?*"

"Hey, Darrell."

"Where the fuck have you been?" He sounded more concerned than anything, and that eased things up a bit.

"It's a long story."

"Fucking shit, man. Have you heard?"

I looked down to the ground, my shoes kicking up dust from the side of the road. Of course I heard. I've known this whole time.

But I silently shook my head. "Heard what?" I asked quietly.

I could hear Darrell sigh on the other side of the phone. He paused for a moment, and I hated the fact that he thought he was the one to break the news to me. It wasn't an easy job for anyone.

"He's gone, man. JD, your dad, he's gone."

I took a deep inhale as I raised my face to the sky. The sun was beaming down, warming my skin as I closed my eyes.

Everyone in my life, everyone who grew close to me, has died.

My mom, my dad, Mrs. Reeves, Lilith, Emma, Anna.

This was a new level of being alone that I had yet to experience.

"How?" I asked, my voice barely above a whisper.

"He had a heart attack on one of the job sites. He was gone before the ambulance could get there." There was a brief silence over the phone. "I'm sorry."

I pushed back any sorrow that was beginning to come to the surface. "Thanks, Darrell. I'll see you in a couple of days, okay?"

"Yeah, of course. Take as much time as you need."

I hung up and tossed my phone through the open window, watching it bounce onto the driver's seat.

Lilith wasn't bluffing. She really killed everyone to try to get to me. I should've sent that blade into her neck as soon as she began to threaten me and the others. Then, maybe, I wouldn't be so alone.

Finally, after another full day of driving, I pulled onto a familiar road in the town of Kittanning, Pennsylvania. A place that felt like home, welcoming me back with open arms. But as I drove around, my knees aching from the hours pushing the pedal, I felt lost. My mind wandered as my body took over, allowing me to drive without paying attention to where I was going. Everyone here knew me, everyone here was like some fucked up family, but never in my life have I felt on the outside more than I do now.

I found myself driving up to the edge of the Alleghany River, right under the short cliff of the yard I took Anna to. I looked up, glancing at the rock we sat on that night, just talking and looking at the stars, the town, and the river.

Hopping out of the truck, I walked around to the passenger side and opened the door. I grabbed the box of her ashes and walked to the water.

I sat down on the grass, placing the wooden box on my legs.

There were sounds of trees rustling around me, water lapping against the earth, and cars driving off in the distance. The world was still spinning, life continued on despite everything that happened in Tanzania, and despite the fact that part of me ended when Anna died. There was no big boom when I killed Lilith. There wasn't an explosion, there were no fireworks, there wasn't an earthquake. There was only the sound of her lungs deflating as I cradled her in my arms, watching as my hands stole a sliver of evil away from humankind.

There was no way I could explain this to anyone, ever. It was a secret for me to keep, to soak in, to face when the time comes. But for now, all I could do was wait and listen to the hum of my home.

"I wish you were here." My words blistered out quietly as I watched the water ripple in front of me. There was an empty, dirty water bottle stuck along the bank, and I quickly grabbed it and tossed it behind me, suddenly angry that Anna was among a place so imperfect.

She deserved better than this. But it was only me here with her now, and I was far from perfect.

I opened the box, pulled off the cap of the plastic container inside, and held her over the water.

I wanted to say something, anything, in the final moments with her. But there were no words that were good enough, nothing I could express that would come close to how I was feeling. Nothing.

So, I tilted my hand and let Anna go.

The dust of her tried to cling to the surface before slipping under the water, flowing with the downstream. My eyes followed the specks of dust that I could see as they dispersed, moving farther and farther away from me.

A big part of me hoped she would make it to Pittsburgh, a place that always held a piece of her heart, no matter how far she wanted to run from it. A place she called home.

Looking down at the empty jar, I placed the lid back on and tucked it away in the wooden box. But before I could close it, I opened the hidden compartment in the cover, my gaze falling on the sparkling silver inside.

I pulled out my mother's ring, and before I could think twice, I threw it as far as I could into the river.

ANNA

Darkness coated me like a blanket as I propped myself on my hands and knees, digging in the dirt under me. Every day, I spend hours sifting through the soil, taking out every piece of broken glass I come in contact with. There were hundreds, if not thousands, of little sharp pieces all around me, stabbing and poking me, making me bleed if I moved even slightly. I couldn't even sit on the ground without bleeding.

Darkness never ends and light never comes, so I have no idea if days are the same here as on Earth, or if they are longer, shorter, or if time doesn't exist at all. I just don't know.

It's been so long, I don't know *how long*, since the last time my ghost saw Diesel.

And when I saw him, with his hand stretched out to me, I broke.

I screamed, I cried, I grabbed the bars of my cage and shook the iron with all my might. The shards of glass under my feet left hundreds of cuts, my blood watering the dirt beneath me, but I didn't care. I didn't care how much of a scene I made, and I didn't care who heard me. All I wanted to do was grab his hand.

But I couldn't, because I was down here, locked away.

My ghost couldn't even relay a message, no matter how hard I tried. Nothing I did or said would convey correctly. All I wanted to do was talk to him, send him a message, even if it was only with my eyes. But nothing worked.

And then Lilith was gone, and everything I clung onto was gone, too.

So my cries echoed through the air, my sorrow swallowed me whole, and my hands filtered through the dirt, grabbing and tossing each piece I could find through blurry tears. It didn't help that I was always trembling, giving me excessive micro cuts on my fingers, my hands, and my knees. My blood mixed with the soil, dripping down and watering it like a garden. Sometimes a thought passed through my head, that maybe something will sprout from the ground one day, as seeds of flowers soak in my blood.

But I know better.

Because every day, the moment time starts over, the glass is back.

My hard work is erased, and I'm back to picking shards of glass out from under me, the tears never stopping.

Today, or tonight, is no different. Here I am, my fingers bent like a small rake, combing through the dark, earthy soil, trying my best to ignore the stinging sensation of the fresh cuts.

Sometimes, if I do it fast enough, I make a spot that's clear enough for me to sleep in.

That was, if Diesel slept too. Once he went to sleep, his world turned off, and I was able to close my eyes, too. But that's usually when Lilith showed up to give me food and water. And by that point, I was hungry enough to wait up for her, ditching the idea of sleep altogether. It was hard to choose between sleep and food. And it also didn't help that time is different down here. Sometimes, I had enough time for both, but it was extremely rare.

But today, there is no choice because there is no Lilith.

No one has been here to give me food or water. No one has been around to tell me what is going on. The only thing I have is the darkness, the glass and the soil, and this rusted, iron cage keeping me.

When I first got here, the need to escape was strong. The fire under me was hot. I tried digging my way out, but the glass only got larger and sharper as I dug down further. I've tried breaking the larger pieces but only ended up hurting myself instead. I've tried moving the glass, using it to dig, anything you could think of. I've tried moving the entire cage itself, but either it's too heavy, or it's literally a part of the ground.

After so long, I felt as if my options were weighed out.

I felt completely and utterly defeated.

In me, the fight was gone, and the fire was burnt out. All I could do was make myself comfortable every day.

So, I dug out the glass, sat down in the shallow hole, and rested my head against the bars.

And waited.

And waited.

But as my eyes began to grow heavy and my stomach twisted from hunger, I knew no one was going to come and feed me. I knew this was my eternity.

I watched as Diesel killed all those demons. I watched as he made love to them, too. And I even watched as he killed Lilith, despite my abandoned screams for him not to.

Because now, I was truly alone.

I'm not sure how much time has passed since the last time I ate. Days? Maybe weeks? All I knew was I couldn't find the strength to carry on anymore, even though I was being forced to. I had to endure this torture from now until the rest of time.

That is, until I heard a click of the cage door.

I picked my head up, staring at the front of the metal cage. There was no one around, at least that I could see. I didn't hear any keys or any footsteps. Only the click.

I waited for a moment, holding my breath as I listened for someone to speak or walk. Anything.

But there was only silence.

"Hello?" I asked with a quiet quiver in my voice.

There was no answer.

Standing up slowly in my soft, earthy space, I clasped my hands together and brought them up to my chest. Goosebumps lined my exposed arms and legs. All I wore, every day, was the grey shirt I used to sleep in.

Diesel's shirt.

But as much as I loved it, it didn't keep me warm.

Standing to my feet, I moved forward and eased my way to the cage's gate, stepping gingerly over the shards of glass that littered the rest of the cage. A few pieces cut through my foot and I silently winced, letting the blood leak into the ground under me.

Closing my eyes, I tried to listen for any sound, any movement around me. There was nothing, not even the *feeling* of another presence around.

"Hello?" I said, louder this time. I expected this to be a trap, for someone to grab me and throw me back to the glass, but there was nothing.

I walked over to the gate, letting my filthy, nicked-up hands grab onto the bars. The metal gave way at the motion, swinging as I let it go.

The cage was open.

I swallowed, knowing this was too easy. There's no way, after all this time, after all this trouble, that I was able to just…go.

I eyed the frame of the gate, checking for any lasers, hidden strings, or even blades that were about to drop down on the back of my neck. Anything.

But there was nothing. Just the frame of the cage.

I decided to take a chance. What's the worst that could happen, I would die again? End up back in the cage? Endure even deeper torture?

The thought had me quickly ducking back inside, where I would remain as safe as I could be.

But isn't this what I've wanted? A way out? An escape route?

My curiosity was eating away at me. I needed to figure out why I was being let go.

Swallowing my fear, I let my bloody, dirty foot slide past the metal threshold. My lungs began to tighten as my breathing turned harsh, panic setting into my core. I gripped the bars of the cage, my arms holding up my weight in case there was nothing for me to stand on.

But as my foot hit the cool, outside ground, all my cuts disappeared.

The dirt on the sole of my heel vanished.

I was clean and healed.

Glancing around again, I had a strange twist of relief and heightened anxiety. Feeling the ground below me in an area outside of this cage, free of all glass, had me wanting more. I wanted to step out and run, never looking back. But the practical side of me couldn't help but wonder what the catch was. Leaving the cage couldn't be this simple.

Could it?

Keeping my grip on the bars beside me, I brought my other foot out of the cage and placed it on the ground. The same thing happened.

No more cuts.

No more blood.

No more soil.

Just both of my feet, looking the same way they did back when I was alive. I deeply exhaled as I lifted a smile, the sensation feeling weird to me. I don't think I've smiled since I've been here.

Slowly, I loosened my grasp on the bars and let all my weight down on my feet.

Now, I was entirely outside of the cage.

I looked down at my hands, only to see they were healed as well. No evidence as to what I did every day in the cage.

Not even a single speck of dirt under my nails.

As I looked down at my hands, I noticed my clothes were also different. I was no longer wearing Diesel's shirt, but a knee-length, black, silk dress, hugged tightly to my curves with a deep, plunge neckline.

My hair was soft and fresh as it cascaded in waves past my shoulders, and my face was no longer covered in a layer of dirt, even though my scar still remained on my forehead.

My hands instinctively roamed my own body, embracing the new warmth that spread through my veins. The simple touch from my fingertips felt like a fire on my skin as I trailed down my legs, feeling the creamy flesh on the insides of my thighs. I closed my eyes, letting myself drown in this new, unknown pleasure.

I felt alive again.

With this, I knew there was more. I stretched my arms out in front of me, still lacking the ability to see in the surrounding darkness. I began to walk forward, giddy in the absence of glass under my soles. My palms hit a wall, a wall that I discovered was a plain, smooth wall as I ran my hands over it. I tried to move slightly to the right, my hands searching for any clue that could lead me to what was next. My hands eventually fell off a corner, and I spread my arms apart, feeling for anything else. My palm hit another wall, smooth surfaces now under both hands, and that's when I knew it was a hallway.

It was my way out of here.

Without looking back, I let my bare feet lead me down this path. I held my head high as my arms fell to my sides, my fingers grazing along the walls.

I walked, and walked, and walked, for what felt like miles before I could see a hint of something.

Something small, but bright. There were two of them, actually.

As I got closer, I realized what they were.

Door knockers, in the shape of lion heads, painted silver.

I approached the shimmer of silver, stopping in front of two giant, black doors.

Without a single hesitant bone in my body, I reached up and grabbed the knocker, pushing it down twice.

Tap, tap.

There was only a brief moment of silence before a voice spoke to me through the doors.

"Enter."

It was a deep, husky voice, the sound zapping me as the doors separated. The command was spoken in a language I had never heard before, but somehow, I understood it. A flicker of confusion rang through my mind, but I pushed it away as I gripped the handle to open the door. Eagerly, I stepped inside a beautiful, gothic-style room with black velvet and roses encapsulating it.

I closed my eyes and reached for a petal, the softness brushing in my smooth fingertips.

Black roses, my favorite.

I sucked in a deep breath, the heavenly smell of floral and musk mixing in my lungs, almost causing me to fall back on the doors and come right at the entrance. But I maintained my composure and straightened my spine as I looked to the desk in front of me.

There was a man, sitting in a black, leather chair, facing away from me. His knees were pointed to the fireplace, the warmth of the flames sending even more heat between my legs.

But then he spun his chair to face me. And even though it was the first time he had ever revealed himself to me, I knew exactly who he was.

Lucifer.

And, *wow*. He was beautiful.

From his dark brown hair to his smooth, shaven face, to his broad shoulders and his large frame, there wasn't a single thing that needed changing. With a white button-down shirt, unbuttoned at the neck, I could see a hint of his chest, and even that looked perfect.

He leaned forward in his chair, reaching for his drink that rested on his desk. He brought it to his lips, giving me a flash of a grin over the rim.

"Welcome Home, Anna," he said, using the same unknown language before taking a swallow, his voice filled with a roughness that I'd never heard. But I enjoyed it, and every part of my body enjoyed it, too.

And then I processed his words.

Home.

I was Home.

My heart, or lack thereof, panged in happiness, in desire, in hope. I had somewhere I belonged. I had somewhere where I was wanted.

This was always where I was going to end up.

I was no longer the soul in the cage. I was no longer the woman from Pittsburgh.

I was a completely different being.

I was a part of Lilith, and when Diesel killed her, he unintentionally made me Lucifer's first in line. I definitely wasn't complaining, but I don't think anyone could've ever guessed that Thomas Diesel is the key to unlocking Hell's future, inadvertently setting things in motion.

I gave a single nod in greeting, clasping my hands behind my back. Lucifer stood from his chair and walked around his large desk, meeting me at the front of it.

His light eyes pierced mine, the glistening, grey-colored irises sucking every bit of nervousness and anxiety out of me, the gaze feeling like a new level of intimacy that I had yet to explore. Taking a few steps forward, I moved in closer, fearlessly shortening the gap between us.

"How does it feel to be the first?" he asked, the crackle of the fireplace sounding behind him.

"The first?" I questioned, effortlessly speaking in his tongue, taking another step closer.

He nodded, leaning back against the wood of the desktop. "The first human soul to ever serve as a demon."

I could feel a surge of excitement spread throughout my being. I was the first.

The first in line.

The first to serve.

The First Blood.

There was *no one* like me.

"You are *mine*, Anna. It's you and me."

Finally reaching him, I slipped myself inside his spread knees, our first brush of contact. His hands snaked on my hips, gripping me tight as he pulled me into him.

And we kissed.

His lips tasted like bourbon, his tongue tasted like forbidden fruit, and his skin felt like euphoria as my hand grazed his neck.

Nothing about this is what I expected.

Nothing about this is what I intended.

But every bone in my body agreed with it, and every piece of me wanted more.

More.

I *fucking* loved it.

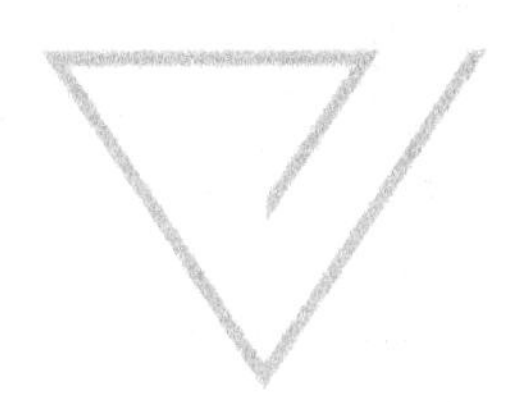

www.ingramcontent.com/pod-product-compliance
Lightning Source LLC
Chambersburg PA
CBHW020123310726

48970CB00006B/1699